THE MILAN

C000228216

Stephen Franks

Mooncat Books Ltd

Published 2021 by Mooncat Books Ltd

ISBN: 978-1-8383962-0-6

First Published in 2020 by Amazon KDP.
This edition published in 2021 by Mooncat Books Ltd,
Registered in UK 1312369313. Freeland Park, Poole,
Dorset, BH16 6EF

www.mooncatbooks.com

Printed and bound by Biddles Books Limited, King's
Lynn, Norfolk, PE32 1SF

Cover design and artwork: Richard Barker.

To Angie

FOREWORD

Polizia Di Stato (Ministry of Interior)
Serving as the state police, this national police force is part of the Public Security Department. Its responsibilities include investigative and law enforcement duties, and the security of motorway, railway, and waterway networks.

Arma Dei Carabinieri (Ministry of Defence)
A force with military status and nationwide remit for crime investigations. It also serves as the military police for the Italian armed forces and can be called upon for national defence action.

Guardia Di Finanza (Ministry of Economy and Finance)
A force with military status and nationwide remit for financial crime investigations.

(Interpol, 2020)

Sunday

Hotel Napoli, Milan, Italy

The first tram had not yet rolled out of the Messina depot and pigeons pecked and nodded between the rusty tracks along the Via degli Imbriani. The shutters on the apartments overlooking the boulevard still shielded the sleeping from the wash of pale yellow that was creeping over the flat roofs and down the plaster walls.

A black Mercedes hugged the pavement, the driver leaning forward to read the names of the buildings. Finding what he was looking for, the car accelerated briefly and swung across the tracks before sliding to a stop in front of Hotel Napoli.

His watch told him he was eight minutes early, so he called up a sports newsfeed on his mobile and flicked the release catch of his seat belt.

To the south-east, the wheels of the early Paris express train whined and creaked in protest as it was shunted into position at Milano Porta Garibaldi station. From behind the stucco-fronted apartment blocks to the north, a deep growl of laughter echoed around the walled courtyards.

The glass doors slid open and Lukas Stolz stepped out of the hotel, his eyes narrowing against the morning light. He caught a glimpse of a young girl cycling towards the city as the wheels of the express train emitted a final squeal, and the whisper of laughter faded behind the pigeons' satisfied coos.

The driver returned his smile as he rose from his seat and pirouetted neatly into position at the rear of the car. Stolz skipped down the low step, raising his bag in handover. But the driver's hand failed to meet his and Stolz turned to see what had made the young man freeze in open-mouthed shock.

A few seconds later, it was all over.

In the brief instant it took the .22 bullet to effortlessly drill a neat hole in Lukas Stolz's forehead, he relived the summer storms of his childhood. He was standing on a bridge with his parents, balls of lightning bouncing off the river and rolling towards him. His mother's lips were moving but her words were drowned out by thunderous drums so deep he could feel the wooden boards shift beneath his feet. The bridge collapsed and he was falling. His father turned away as Lukas Stolz felt himself slipping below the cold, dark water.

The second and third bullets were not necessary.

A grey-haired man viewed the scene from the hotel's second floor. His tight jaw expressed concern, and although the early Milanese sun had not yet reached his balcony, his hairline was defined by silvery beads of moisture.

Immediately below, he could see the roof of a black Mercedes saloon. The driver's door and boot were open and on the pavement, lay a cream-coloured sheet of irregular contours. Even without the rivulet of blood that had congealed before reaching the gutter, he recognised the scene of a murder; he'd been at many. But it was the presence of the Mercedes rather than the shroud-covered corpse that had unsettled him.

On the pavement next to the body, he saw a black leather attaché case and leaning against the car's rear wheel, a blue fabric bag, its white baggage label dancing in time with the gentle gusts of warm air that spat dust in spirals from between the rusting tram tracks.

An inner cordon of red and white barriers had been erected around the car and a corporal stood guard at its entrance. Two dark-suited men with narrow ties leant against the fence, sipping coffee out of paper cups whilst complaining about having to work on a Sunday. Two uniformed policemen were taking measurements on the road while a figure in white overalls crawled along the gutter looking for evidence.

The whine of a camera motor startled the man on the balcony and, instinctively, he shuffled back against the wall. He watched while a young man in jeans and ill-fitting white tee-shirt took pictures of the car and surrounding area.

Opposite the hotel, a few of the shutters had been thrown back and white-vested men smoked languidly and speculated noisily while flicking ash onto the police cars below. The sirens that had awoken the residents more than an hour ago were now silent.

A black van with a flat, round communications dish on its roof was parked opposite the hotel entrance. Trails of blue and yellow cables ran between an open flap on its side to a portable generator, which hummed gently to itself on the pavement. An irregular procession of police officers filed in and out of the van's rear door.

On the main road, a hundred metres either side of the hotel, *carabiniere* manned the barricades at the junctions with Via Antonio Carnevali to the north-west and Via Acerenza to the south-east.

A two-tone siren announced the arrival of an ambulance at the Via Acerenza roadblock and was promptly waved through. It was closely followed by a dust-streaked blue Maserati, which pulled up next to the inner cordon. A short bald man with rimless glasses eased himself from the driver's seat, and one of the dark-suited men raised a hand in recognition. He returned a cursory nod and wiped his bright pink scalp with a handkerchief before shuffling across the road. Slowly he climbed the three narrow steps running up to the van's rear door.

When he reappeared a few minutes later, he was dressed in white plastic overalls complete with hood, which he must have decided was superfluous. He was carrying a small leather bag and grey folder. The corporal offered a perfunctory salute as he passed through the gap in the fence. *'Doctor,'* concluded the grey-haired man on the balcony, edging forward to watch the new arrival.

The bald man stood over the body and retrieved a voice recorder from his bag. Awkwardly and with a pained expression, he lowered himself onto one knee and let out a curse as he jerked back the sheet to reveal the dead man's head, chest, shoulders and arms. He didn't hear the stifled gasp that came from the balcony above him.

The grey-haired man felt compelled to stare at the lifeless features of the corpse lying on the pavement a few metres below. The dark-framed glasses looked too wide for the dead man's face and the ragged brown and black hole in his forehead was in ugly contradiction to his hair, which was grey and neatly trimmed. Lean, angular, middle-aged, dressed in light-grey, woollen suit trousers, plain white double-cuffed shirt and narrow red tie. His jacket, which he must have been carrying, lay next to a lifeless hand. One arm of his shirt had turned dark red where it had soaked up blood from the pool that had formed beneath his

4

shoulder. A brown leather, bi-fold wallet lay open on the man's still and lifeless chest.

Recognition and dread arrived simultaneously.

The watcher on the balcony retreated into the bedroom, stood in front of the mirror and frowned. Sweat was creeping down from his hairline, filling an opaque teardrop on the end of his sharp-chiselled nose. He took a pair of thick-rimmed glasses from the side-table and slowly fitted them to his face. A chill started in his neck, ran down his spine and merged with the pool of perspiration that had collected between his buttocks.

Except for the ugly brown bullet hole, the corpse could have been the image of the man in the mirror.

He sat on the bed, picked up his phone and stabbed at the keypad, waited, cursed and dialled again.

"Yes?"

"It's Salt."

"Yes boss, was your hotel –"

"Fuck the hotel. What car were you sending this morning to pick me up?"

"A Mercedes. Brad hasn't left yet. Do you want to –"

"Shut up, you moron. What type of Merc were you sending?"

"E-Class. Nothing but the –"

"Colour?" barked Salt.

"Black, it's black."

"And it's still there with you, you can see it?"

"Yes boss, it hasn't moved. He was just about to leave. I'm looking at it."

"Have you got something to write on?"

"Er, yes boss…shoot!"

Salt took the phone from his ear and looked at it with loathing.

"Get hold of Giuliani. I just tried him but he ain't answering. Leo has his number." Salt spoke slowly and carefully. "Tell Giuli, there's a black Mercedes C-Class outside my hotel with a dead body lying next to it. Got that?"

"Outside your hotel, there's a stiff lying next to a Merc."

"Black Mercedes – that's important."

"Black Mercedes. I got it, don't worry."

"Don't tell me not to worry, you prick."

Silence.

"Also, tell Giuli about the plan to collect me today – have you written that down?"

"Yes boss, I got it."

"Don't forget to tell him about the car."

"OK, I'll tell Giuliani about the car."

"And tell him to go take a look at the body at the morgue when they bring it in."

"Body at the morgue, right. What's he looking for?"

"Just give him the message, he'll understand. Don't screw this up."

With that, Pete 'Salt' Salterton closed his eyes and contemplated what the hell he should do next.

Lieutenant Raphael Conza suspected the case allotted to him that morning would probably be a waste of time. State Police were at the scene of a murder and had 'reasonable belief' the killing was mob-related. In accordance with standard procedure, the attendance of a Finanza officer had been requested.

He decided to walk the forty-five-minute journey to the Hotel Napoli in the Derganino district. On the way, he grabbed a sandwich and coffee at Gina's and by the time he arrived at the Via Acerenza roadblock, he felt more disposed than usual towards his uniformed counterparts.

Conza made a note; it was 11:03 when he climbed the steps and entered the rear of the black incident control van parked outside the Hotel Napoli.

Captain Brocelli's pale, blotchy face winced as a wave of warmth accompanied his arrival.

"Shut the damned door."

The lieutenant's smile went unnoticed as Brocelli went back to typing on his laptop. Conza remained standing and looked around. The van was divided along its length between electronics and monitors to his left and a map and whiteboard to his right. Above the blank screens, the computers were silent with inactivity. In the ceiling above, an air-conditioning unit spewed metallic-smelling cold air.

In the van's narrow corridor sat Captain Brocelli; flabby chest rolling over the edge of the pull-down desk, pale blue shirt blotched by irregular dark patches around his neck and armpits. Brocelli had a widely held reputation for laziness and a general lack of care. Everyone knew he was unashamedly marking time until the day he could draw his pension.

Conza had heard the canteen gossip; how Brocelli had fallen from grace, despite once being the 'darling' of the Lombardy region. But Brocelli's fall had happened so long ago, nobody could remember why anymore.

Brocelli finally looked up and waved at a low wooden stool.

"You're Conza, I take it. They told me you were coming. What is it? Drugs, mob?"

Conza smiled. "I don't know yet. Depends on what you've got for me." He sipped lemon water from a bottle he'd bought at Gina's and waited.

Brocelli scowled. He knew Conza, knew his background. Father had been a big wheel in the foreign office. Rich. Private school. University. Fast track from civvy street, not ex-military. Never done the hard yards. A smartarse.

He held out a claret-coloured passport, which Conza had to lean forward to take from his short, stubby fingers.

"Victim's passport is in the name of Lukas Stolz. Born 1952. Address in Heidelberg, Germany. Stated occupation, maths professor. A one-year visa for Venezuela issued in Berlin, now lapsed. Plus two entry and exit stamps issued in Riga last July."

Conza flicked through the passport trying to keep up with Brocelli's narrative. He made a few shorthand notes in his pad. Brocelli clenched his jaw when Conza wrote the letters 'LV' next to 'Riga'. *'Cleverdick.'*

He passed Conza a thick sheet of paper embossed with the Hotel Napoli logo.

"Stolz checked in on Thursday, alone. He was never seen with anyone, nor seen to talk to anyone. He checked out this morning. Paid his bill by credit card."

Conza continued to write.

"Ate dinner in his room Thursday and Friday. Don't know about last night." Brocelli swiftly added, "We've asked for a trace on his bank cards."

He smirked as he watched Conza place a small tick next to 'CC – check,' in his notebook.

"No alcohol, pay-per-view or external calls, although he ordered a German newspaper on Friday."

Conza scanned the bill and identified five lines, each annotated 'SIC' – *'Servizio in Camera'* – and another line headed *'Frankfurter Allgemeine Zeitung'*.

"It seems Stolz kept himself to himself," Brocelli opined, before selecting a witness statement from the pile. His cadence quickened slightly.

"On Thursday night, he stayed in his room. On Friday and Saturday morning, he ate breakfast in the restaurant and left the hotel on foot at around eight. He returned around six-thirty both evenings. Nobody knows where he went."

Brocelli had to wait while Conza converted his narrative into neatly ordered date and time entries.

"Stolz asked the front desk to book a limo to take him to Malpensa Airport. Pick up at seven this morning."

Conza started a new page.

"The car was booked through a local agent..." Brocelli said, picking up a statement. "A to Z Limos on the Via Copernico. We've sent someone to take a statement. Chauffeur's a local kid by the name of Sami Ricci. Lives out in the sticks with his girlfriend."

"Address?"

"Chalet 2, Riva al Lago, Via Macconago," Brocelli read stiffly. Conza held up a hand until he'd finished writing.

"We've got Ricci at the station. Claims when Stolz stepped out of the hotel door, a man dressed in black, wearing a balaclava, suddenly appeared. Stolz and the killer exchanged a few words before the shooting started."

Conza didn't see Brocelli making the hand gesture of a pistol being fired.

"So, Ricci said the assailant was a man?" asked Conza.

Brocelli scanned the statement. "A figure."

"Thank you."

"Ricci dived under the car as soon as he saw the gun. He heard three shots and then a small-engined motorbike heading off towards the city. Not much else." Brocelli shrugged his shoulders in concert with his own conclusion.

Over the next twenty minutes, Conza learnt that Stolz's body had been taken to the police mortuary and he was shown photographs of the murder scene, corpse, and close-ups of the dead man's face and the injury to his forehead. There was no exit wound. He was told that one round had been recovered from the car's headrest along with three bullet cases. They'd been sent to the police lab but had already been identified as .22LRs. Brocelli believed the pathologist would find the bullet that killed him, in Stolz's skull. As for the third round, Brocelli could only confirm it hadn't yet been found.

Brocelli had to wait once again, until Conza had finished writing before tossing him a tan leather wallet.

"It's been dusted. It was lying open on the guy's chest."

"No cash," Conza muttered to himself, pulling the edges of the wallet apart.

"There's an old photograph in there – family presumably. Also, the return half of a round-trip air ticket to London leaving Malpensa 12:05 today and a ticket for a local tram. I've got a man at the depot asking about the tram ticket, but it wasn't stamped, so we've no idea when it was used."

Brocelli watched Conza turn the tram ticket over, but there was nothing unusual about it. The photograph was of a woman and two young children sitting by a fountain. *'They look happy,'* Conza thought.

"Four bank cards: two debit and one credit issued by Deutsche Bank. One debit card issued by NatWest. I think that's American or English."

"English," responded Conza casually. Brocelli ignored him.

"A couple of loyalty cards and two business cards. One in his own name and one for Hertz at Riga Airport." Brocelli added with a grin, "That's in Latvia."

Conza sighed but resisted the temptation to congratulate Brocelli on his ability to use Google.

"There's also what we guess is a security card for Skyguard Defence Industries. Ever heard of them?"

Conza didn't respond but ran his finger along the black magnetic tape running along its length, before flipping it over. The card was red, which to Conza seemed to add to its importance. The words 'Skyguard Defence Industries' were printed in white over a stylised silver shield. An arrowhead trailing thin, white streaks circled above the lettering, but the card offered no clue as to the door, zone or building it would unlock.

"Oh, and there's a piece of paper with numbers on it."

Conza found the scrap of paper in the button-down section of the wallet. On it was written 'DLR-EAC1 4D/9C/555'. Conza read it twice but, failing to discern its meaning, made another note and returned it to the wallet.

Brocelli laid a black attaché case on the table. It was black leather, expensive but well-used. Conza flicked open the locks and began searching through its contents.

"There's nothing of any value. Some scribbles in a notepad. An English magazine from last month and a newspaper, also English, printed last summer. We also found his passport, a calculator and a bunch of keys. They look like front door types."

Conza glanced at the calculator and picked up the keys. He was about to toss them back into the case but hesitated. With a deft flick, he laid them out on his palm.

The keys were joined to a plastic fob about two centimetres square sporting the Skyguard logo. Conza could see it actually comprised two squares laid on top of each other. They had been machined to form a narrow slit along the bottom edge. He tried to pull the squares apart but whilst the two halves remained fixed at their centre, they started to rotate around each other. Brocelli watched in amazement as Conza twisted the squares in opposite directions, making a slim tongue of metal appear from the slit.

"It's a USB stick," said Brocelli in amazement.

Conza exercised the fob a few times, making the blade bob in and out.

"We should let the techies see what's on it," declared Brocelli with excitement.

"We can't – unless we have sufficient grounds to believe it's connected to his murder," said Conza as he tossed the key fob back into the case. Brocelli's objection never reached his lips.

Conza started flicking through the leaves of the A4 notepad, many of which were filled with calculations in tight, neat script. On a page near the front was written 'FC-AUTO?' It was underlined and penned in a heavier hand than the rest of the characters. Conza didn't recognise the acronym 'FC' but made a note to look it up when he returned to the office.

The magazine was a well-read copy of *Jane's Defence Weekly* published a month ago. The newspaper was *The Times* dated the fifteenth of July, almost exactly a year old.

"Did he have any luggage?" Conza asked eventually.

Brocelli waved a flaccid hand towards a travel bag next to his desk.

"It's been wiped. No trace of drugs. I would have catalogued it by now if I hadn't been interrupted."

Conza ignored him.

"Did you find his mobile?"

Brocelli picked up the inventory log but was already shaking his head.

"No. I assumed the killer took it."

"You're probably right," agreed Conza to Brocelli's surprise. "But at least we can request a trace on his number."

Brocelli's expression mirrored his confusion.

"But we don't know his number."

"Try the one on his business card," Conza said, trying not to smile.

Brocelli's mouth moved, but no words formed. Conza stood up.

"What about the dead guy's next of kin?" Brocelli suddenly blurted out.

"What about them?"

"Well, if this is a Finanza matter it will be down to you to contact them to sort out a positive ID."

Conza raised his arms in mock defence.

"Oh no, I'm not getting saddled with this one yet," he affirmed with a shake of his head. "Other than the bullet to the head, this could be a botched hold-up."

"You're kidding, right? You trying to tell me this was a robbery? At seven a.m.? The junkies aren't out of their pits at that time, and the average snatcher doesn't ride around on a moped looking for victims on a Sunday morning. Seems a bit far-fetched to me." Brocelli punctuated his contempt with a snort.

"You may be right, Captain, but on the other hand, contract killers don't usually rob their victims, do they?"

The two men glared at each other in silence for a few seconds.

"Until I've finished the prelims, this remains a State Police matter. So sorry, you let the German police know one of their citizens has had his brains blown out. They'll inform his family."

Brocelli sat up and thought about arguing, but Conza was already retreating.

"Once you've bagged all this up, send a copy of the paperwork to my office. I'll write up my report and then we'll see if Finanza wants to take it off your hands."

Conza opened the van door, allowing a wave of warmth to roll in, but paused as something occurred to him.

"Is someone checking who else is staying at the hotel at the moment?"

"We do know how to run a bloody investigation you know!"

A vivid purple vein pulsed in Brocelli's pale forehead and Conza raised his hands again before pushing the door closed behind him.

Brocelli swore and grabbed the radio handset.

"Bruno, are you still with the hotel manager?"

"Yes, Captain. I'm just taking his statement."

"Have you asked him for a copy of the hotel register?"

"No. Do we need it?"

"Just get a copy and bring it to me, you bloody idiot."

4

When Amadi Abebe held his daughter a few seconds after she'd emerged into the world, she had kicked him with such force that he immediately named her Nyala; Ethiopian for 'mountain goat.' The fleeting disappointment he felt when told his wife had borne him a daughter and not a son, was no longer even a memory.

Fifteen years later, those legs, slender, dark and muscular, were rhythmically pumping at the pedals of her old bike as Nyala Abebe sped past a black Mercedes parked outside the Hotel Napoli.

Amadi had spent Saturday night working in the makeshift bakery off Via Enrico Cosenz that he rented for cash. His bread was popular, partly because it was good quality, but mostly because it was available every day of the week. On Sundays, Nyala took a few bags of bread to sell to the street cafés and mobile vendors servicing travellers passing through the railway stations, tram depot and bus terminus. This morning, as Amadi had watched his daughter set off for the city, he knew two things for certain: she wouldn't return home until all the bread had been sold; and he loved Nyala more than any other person in the world. Even more than the woman who had died in sweat and agony, just a few days after bearing her.

Nyala cherished the solitude of Sunday mornings, when the quiet, empty streets allowed her thoughts to wander. And on Sundays, when she returned from the city, she would be allowed to wear her best dress to attend church with her grandmother. Growing up in the country chosen by her father, Nyala had always preferred the comfort of running shorts or a track suit. But recently, she had started looking forward to tying her hair in tight plaits around her forehead and putting on the flower-print dress bought for her by her nana. Although she wouldn't admit it, she revelled in the reaction of the boys now they saw her as someone other than the girl who could 'run like the wind'.

As she picked her way across the junction of the main road with Via Giovita Scalvini, she heard the first curious, metallic popping sound. It reminded her of the firecrackers that she'd once heard

14

in Chinatown. She was sure the noise came from behind her, so using her foot as an anchor, she wheeled the bicycle around and stopped, raising a hand to shield her eyes.

Two more 'pops' in quick succession. She felt a cold chill ripple across her scalp and became aware of her own heartbeat. Unconsciously holding her breath, she strained to identify the cause of the noises.

The sound of the screaming motor reached her at the same moment she saw the motorcycle lurch into the road a few hundred metres away. Instinctively, she pulled her bike towards the pavement as it raced towards her.

"What is he doing?" she heard herself whisper, as the Vespa rider struggled with something attached to his head. A second later, he managed to free himself from the black balaclava and he saw her. He was only a few metres away and while she immediately recognised the face, his expression was a surprise. His eyes may have been staring wildly and jaw clenched in anguish, but there was no doubt; the Vespa rider was her friend, her boyfriend, the son of the man who rented a cellar to her father; Kadin Bennani.

Subconsciously, she started to raise an uncertain hand in greeting. But she didn't wave, she didn't smile or call out his name, because in that split second, she knew that Kadin Bennani was absolutely terrified.

Pete Salterton didn't take long to decide on a plan. His mobile told him there was a train leaving Milan for Paris at 09:10. Just thirty-one minutes to reach the station, buy a ticket and get on board. A taxi across Paris to the Gare du Nord, from where he could catch a Eurostar to London. It was going to be tight. No time to pack. He stowed his passport, wallet and mobile phone in his jacket and ran to the lift at the end of the corridor. When it arrived, he punched the button marked '0' but changed his mind and pressed '-1'.

As the lift doors opened, Salterton spotted the hotel manager talking to a policeman at the reception desk and through the glass doors, two more policemen guarding the entrance.

The lift doors closed and as he began to descend once more, Salterton puffed his cheeks out in relief.

There was no one in the dimly lit basement corridor and he scurried past a laundry room where he glimpsed the back of a short, stocky woman loading towels into a tumble dryer. She was humming along to the radio and didn't hear him as he passed by.

The fire exit was lit by a pale cream wall lamp and a sign displaying the familiar 'green running man' symbol. In silent prayer, he gently pressed the spring-loaded bar. The metal door swung open and daylight flooded the grey, concrete-lined corridor. He exhaled when no alarm sounded but held his breath when the door grated against the floor. The woman was still humming, so he stepped out into the sunshine and gently pushed the door closed behind him. He ran up the steps to street level.

He found himself at the rear of the hotel, in an unfenced yard of cracked and splintered concrete, peppered with weeds, broken bottles and discarded beer cans. To his right, a narrow alleyway ran between two apartment blocks and he could see the main road at its far end. He emerged onto a road running parallel to the front of the hotel.

Twenty-three minutes until the train abandoned him in Milan. His pace quickened. Turning right onto Via Derganino and despite his contempt for all things religious, he found himself praying.

His brother used to call him 'Lucky Pete' on account of his uncanny ability to evade the law. In his youth, if a house alarm sounded, Pete was long gone before the first police car showed up. Assault victims failed to pick him out in identity line-ups. And if his house was searched, the sniffer dogs always missed the stash of money hidden behind the bath.

His brother's nickname echoed in his memory as, passing the spot from where Nyala had watched the speeding Vespa, he flagged down a taxi that had been turned away from the police barricade.

Eighteen minutes later he was running along platform 12 at Milano Centrale to board the train to Paris via Zurich.

As he flopped into his first-class seat, he looked back along the platform. He hadn't been followed. 'Lucky, lucky Pete,' he heard a voice whisper, but the memory provided no solace.

The train moved off and Pete Salterton departed Milan along the same tracks that only a short time earlier, had carried away the person he was certain had tried to kill him.

Friday – Two Days Before the Murder

Bennani Family Apartment, Milan, Italy

Walking home from the shops, Jamila Bennani laughed quietly and shook her head, as Youssef darted behind her legs to escape being tagged by his big sister. It was becoming easier to forget that since Tuesday afternoon, Issam, her husband of seventeen years, had failed to stagger through the front door, smelling of beer, swearing and prickling for a fight.

On Tuesday evening, she'd cursed his name as she put his dinner in the refrigerator before switching off the lights in the hallway.

By Wednesday night, she'd begun to feel concern, and guilt for not being concerned enough.

It was now Friday, and she dared to contemplate life without him. The notion brought her no tears. She laughed again and tickled Youssef's neck as he giggled and squirmed away.

Seventeen years ago, she'd arrived in Italy; eighteen years-old and heavily pregnant. Her new husband had written to Jamila's father, assuring him that he'd secured well-paid work at Malpensa Airport and that he could provide a home for Jamila and their impending child. Her father had blessed the arrangement and Jamila's mother helped her pack a small, worn suitcase before tearfully kissing her goodbye at Tripoli Airport. Jamila had worn a loose-fitting long-sleeved kaftan for the journey to Milan because Issam was concerned Italian immigration would not allow a pregnant Ethiopian to enter the country.

For the first few years, married life had been bearable – even happy at times. Jamila found friendship amongst the other north-Africans who attended Sunday services in the Coptic church of San Pietro Celestino and Issam worked hard in his engineering job. Whilst their apartment was small, it was comfortable, and Issam gave her enough money to keep the family fed and clothed.

She'd also been blessed with Kadin a few weeks after arriving in Milan and when he was placed in her arms, she had discovered the true meaning of love.

And then came Issam's accident; his legs crushed when a freight pallet fell from a forklift in one of the goods hangars. For months, Jamila nursed him and comforted him when he cried with pain as he reached out to her in the night. The accident enquiry did nothing to relieve their stress, especially when the union refused to support Issam after it was discovered that he'd been drinking immediately prior to the accident. The union representative, a nationalist sympathiser, seized on the opportunity to assist in the departure from the airport, and Italy, of yet another African usurper. Issam Bennani was dismissed without notice from his job and his claim for financial compensation refused.

Four surgeries had failed to untwist Issam's shattered legs, and while Jamila knew how hard it was for a disabled immigrant to secure work, her sympathy ended when his drinking began.

Jamila took cleaning jobs as Issam's drinking bouts turned into daily events. She would often find him asleep at the kitchen table when she returned home from taking Kadin to school and their fights became a regular occurrence. Her second child, Soraya, was conceived during a short period of reconciliation – and marked the only time since the accident that Issam made an effort to quit drinking and find work. But a steady job remained elusive and so out of resignation and desperation, Issam's drinking returned. It was around that time that he began hanging around with men, who Jamila's father would have called *'jalad alqarsh'* – 'shark skins'.

And the shark skins took what was left of her husband away from her. For at least one week each month, Issam would just disappear. But Jamila soon stopped asking him where he'd been or what he'd been doing whilst away. Her questions invariably ended in a fight, and Jamila quickly discovered that she no longer cared.

Whatever it was they got him to do while he was away, Issam always returned home with money, and despite her misgivings she was relieved to be able to buy new clothes and shoes for the children. Nevertheless, as far as she could, Jamila had always tried to distance herself and the children from her husband's dealings. Eventually, she managed to convince herself that what Issam did when he left the house was not of her making. She found some comfort in the notion that her husband was not alone in providing for his family from the 'dark economy' that existed in the poorer quarters of many Italian cities.

Then, about ten years ago, Issam acquired some properties; two adjacent garages in a converted industrial unit on Vialle Vincenzo Lancetti near the city centre, and in Via Enrico Cosenz, a small cellar beneath a warehouse, which the tenant converted to a bakery. Jamila was seriously worried about the new acquisitions and for years, she wouldn't allow Kadin to accompany his father to collect the rents on a Sunday evening. But despite the reasonably steady flow of rental income, there were still nights when Jamila would lie in fraught suspense clutching her pillow if woken by a passing police car; convinced that it was only a matter of time before the front door was kicked off its hinges and scores of uniformed policemen charged through the house to take her screaming children away from her. But the police hadn't come and eventually, Jamila stopped worrying about the properties and how her husband had come to own them.

Youssef, her youngest child, was the product of one of her husband's violent and beer-fuelled assaults. Jamila never acknowledged that her beautiful, gentle boy was the product of Issam's forced penetration of her on the cold, hard kitchen floor. But the attack changed her, and while she was condemned to living with a man who had raped her, she would never allowed Issam in her bed again and fitted a heavy iron bolt to the bedroom door. Regardless, her slight frame would tremble, and her slender fingers would clench in readiness whenever she heard the apartment door slam shut.

In recent years, Jamila would call out to Kadin and he would help her wrestle Issam into the lounge or bathroom when he returned home drunk and spoiling for either a fight or sex – to Jamila there was little difference and one usually led to the other. *'Too many times,'* she thought to herself as she put the shopping bags on the kitchen floor.

On the table, she found a short note written in Kadin's lazy scrawl:

Hi Mom,

Sorry – but I forgot – I was supposed to visit the museum in Bergamo with Emil today.

Haven't seen him for ages, so will probably stay with him over the weekend.

See you on Monday – kiss Sor and Youss for me

K xxx

Jamila tutted and tried to call his mobile, but there was no answer, so she left him a voice message.

She sighed at the prospect of spending the weekend entertaining Soraya and Youssef without Kadin's help, and she mouthed a silent prayer that her husband would not return until her son was home.

San Carlo, 60 km East of Milan, Italy

It had been five days since Issam Bennani had failed to return home from one of his frequent visits to the small bar on Via Beroldo. His family hadn't missed him; Kadin, especially so. He despised his father's drinking, his shady deals and his whisky-fuelled rages. Kadin had started to believe that this time, his father had gone for good.

In the summer months, while college was closed, Kadin worked on the reception desk at the city leisure centre. He enjoyed the job, but it was Friday, and he was looking forward to a weekend off as he hurried down the dimly lit staircase to collect his Vespa from the underground carpark.

Later, he couldn't remember the explosion of pain that ran from his kidneys to his fingertips as the electrical energy stored in the cattle prod discharged into his spine. Kadin was unconscious before he hit the tarmac, and when his eyes opened, he could still feel waves of prickly heat running across his scalp and through his fingers. He lay panting in pain and confusion on the clear plastic sheet. He passed out again.

Kadin regained consciousness when he rolled against a wheel arch and banged his shoulder against the metal side of his enclosure. It took him a few seconds to work out that he was travelling in the boot of a car, although he couldn't remember how he'd got there. Desperately, he tried to search for a recent memory; he was leaving work, a colleague slapping him on the back, collecting his keys and phone from his locker, he was walking down the stairs, the door to the car park was open, there was a humming sound… and then nothing.

He felt for his mobile, but his pockets were empty. His temples throbbed and his eyes stung. Until his sight adjusted to the dark interior, he thought he'd been rendered blind by whatever had hit him. He tried banging on the boot lid but had little control over his limbs, which were still weak from being electrocuted. Panic was causing him to hyperventilate and bright dots swam through the fluid in his eyes.

The car finally stopped, and the rumble of the engine ceased. When the boot opened, a short, stocky fair-haired man beckoned to him to get out. Fearing his life was about to be brought to a sudden end, Kadin shook his head and clutched his knees to his chest. A second man appeared, much taller than the first, but just as muscular; slightly older, his dark, wiry hair pulled into a ponytail. The fingers and backs of his hands were covered in smudged, dark-blue tattoos and his teeth were streaked yellow and brown.

Kadin remained coiled and refused to move. His chest felt hollow and his legs had stiffened. He knew for certain that these men were used to violence, and believing he was about to die, he just lay still, closed his eyes and shouted for help as loud as he could. The men looked at each other and the one with fair-hair sighed. No one would hear him. They waited for Kadin to scream himself hoarse.

Still curled in a ball, Kadin sobbed and rocked against the side of the car. Urine soaked through his trousers and a small pool of yellow liquid found a crease in the plastic sheet and trickled towards the rear of the boot.

The men didn't threaten Kadin, they didn't hit him or shout. They didn't make any demands, they didn't answer his tear-filled questions, nor acknowledge his anger or hatred. They made but a single statement and delivered it without emotion, detached from the cruelty their words conveyed. They were ambivalent to his disintegration as a human being. What they said, the only words they uttered, were simple, unambiguous and not open to negotiation. If Kadin wanted to see his family alive again, he had to get out of the car. If he refused, his family would die.

It was just a statement of fact.

Sunday

Guardia di Finanza Headquarters, Milan, Italy

Some eight hours after the murder of Lukas Stolz, Raphael Conza returned to the neat, orderly office he shared with two other agents, one of whom was on holiday in Sicily, and the other in Rome attending a specialist course on money laundering. Conza was glad he had the office to himself – the quiet helped him think.

He turned on the electric fan and opened one of the wooden sash windows that overlooked the long narrow courtyard that sat between the three buildings of the Guardia di Finanza regional office.

On his computer screen he double-clicked a news icon and read a vague report on the Lukas Stolz murder. After a brief description of the murder scene, the report went on to say that *'the police were trying to identify the rider of a Vespa seen in the vicinity at the time.'*

A young, shirt-sleeved clerk knocked on the already open door.

"Lieutenant Conza?" he asked with a grin.

"Yes."

The clerk deposited a box file onto the table in the centre of the room. *'Well done, Brocelli'*, thought Conza as the clerk left without speaking further.

Across the top right-hand corner of the box file, a label read 'Copies'. In the centre of the lid was another label, 'CASE No: MIL07/20/DER/HOM101'.

Conza flicked through witness statements, photographs and other papers collected by Brocelli's team. Conza opened his notebook and selected the document labelled 'Witness Statement – Sami Ricci'.

Disappointingly, Ricci's statement only repeated what Brocelli had already told him. The chauffeur worked for a local car hire company, he was given the job the night before and didn't know nor had ever met Lukas Stolz before today. When the killer appeared, Ricci had dived for cover under the car from where he thought Stolz said "Take it," just before he was shot.

Ricci's description of the gunman was, 'medium height, slim build, wearing a balaclava and black clothes'. Ricci stated that the motorcycle then, 'headed south-east towards the city'.

Conza pulled out his mobile phone and called Police HQ front desk.

"Hi, it's Conza at Finanza. Can you put me through to Sergeant Mancini, homicide?"

While he waited, Conza reread the chauffeur's statement. He was interrupted by the light, cheerful tone of Sergeant Lorenzo Mancini.

"Hi Raffy, what can I do for you?"

"Hi Lorenzo, just a quick one…you took a statement from the chauffeur in the Hotel Napoli job?"

"That's right, Sami Ricci. Is there a problem?"

"Don't know if I'm honest. In his statement he says he only heard a small-engined motorbike?"

"That's correct. He couldn't be more specific. What's up?"

"Probably nothing, but *Milan Citynews* is reporting the killer was riding a Vespa and I wondered where they got their information from."

"They didn't get it from us. But you know what they're like, Raffy. They make up what they don't know."

Conza heard his friend chuckling.

"Thanks, Lorenzo – can you put me through to Brocelli's office please?"

"No worries. See you soon."

After a short delay, Conza heard his monotone voice, "Captain Brocelli."

"Conza here. I read on the internet that the perp left the scene this morning riding a Vespa."

"So?"

"The thing is Captain; no witness identified the make of motorbike and I was wondering why *Citynews* think it was a Vespa?"

"Well Lieutenant Conza, that's where you're wrong. A few hours ago, a witness turned up at the cordon and told one of my officers that the killer escaped on a Vespa."

Conza ignored Brocelli's antagonism. "Great. So we have a second witness."

"So it would seem."

"Where is he now, and why wasn't his statement in the box?"

"Firstly, it's a 'she' not a 'he'. And secondly, the witness is a minor and can only be interviewed in the presence of her parents."

"So, someone's been sent to speak to her?" asked Conza patiently.

"Not exactly. The address she gave was false. We're making further enquiries." He ended the sentence in a rapid whisper.

"Bloody hell. What's the name of the cordon officer?"

"Corporal Sigonella."

"Is he still on duty?"

"Only until four."

"Which roadblock?"

"Via Acerenza."

Conza took a final swipe before hanging up.

"I'll go to speak with this Corporal Sigonella, but in the meantime, you may want to find out how the information about the Vespa is already being touted by the Milan press corps."

Conza threw the witness statements back in the box, left his office and took a taxi back to the Hotel Napoli.

Garage 9, Vialle Vincenzo Lancetti, Milan, Italy

In the minutes following his brief encounter with Nyala Abebe, the vivid self-loathing and disgust at what he had just done was replaced by panic. He'd recognised Nyala immediately and there was no doubt she'd recognised him. She had even smiled.

Hurriedly, Kadin rolled the motorbike into the garage, switched off the engine and pushed the door shut. He listened. Just the tick, tick, tick of the Vespa's motor as it cooled in the still, dust-filled air. Kadin leant against the door and realised it was the first time since Friday that he wasn't being watched; he was alone. He retched, but his stomach was empty, and he spat out the acrid bile that filled his mouth and bit at his throat.

The fluorescent tube flickered and chattered before flooding the room with a blue-white glow that chased away the shadows and overpowered the weak shafts of sunlight that barely pierced the dirty, narrow skylight high above him.

Kadin had been in the garage many times, but that was before he'd become a killer. A murderer. Now, it looked different. Everything looked different; somehow sharper and more clearly defined. As if for the first time, Kadin noticed how large the garage really was. At some point, it had served as a workshop and along the left-hand wall ran a thick, sturdy workbench; scarred and scratched wood, blackened by the oil and grease of a thousand car parts being hammered or filed or bent back into shape. A tall red and rust-fringed toolbox sat in one corner, long devoid of the casters that had once made it mobile. Three shelves on the wall were filled with dusty oil bottles, petrol cans, wheel hubs and paint pots. And inexplicably, on the wall by the door, someone had hung a long case mirror and placed next to it, an elephant's foot umbrella stand.

A metre-wide strip of thick, ill-fitting planks ran down the centre of the concrete floor and the sight of it stirred in Kadin a memory.

"The inspection pit is the key to all this. You need to stay safe."

'The key is to a safe. The safe is in the pit,' Kadin remembered, praying he had interpreted the coded dialogue correctly.

Via Acerenza Roadblock, Milan, Italy

The *carabiniere* gestured for the driver to turn his cab around as it approached the roadblock. Conza told the taxi driver to stop and wait for him, then beckoned to the policeman, identity card in hand.

"Lieutenant Conza. Finanza. Are you Corporal Sigonella?"

The young policeman nodded suspiciously.

"You spoke to a young girl who witnessed the getaway this morning. Is that right?"

"Yes, but she didn't see much."

"I want you to tell me exactly what was said, Corporal. Exactly." Conza fixed the young man's rather distant gaze.

"OK, but as I said, there's not much to tell."

Conza waited.

"At about 12:45, a young black girl on a bicycle asked me if she could pass through the cordon to get home. I told her the road was closed and she would have to go around."

"Go on."

"She asked me what had happened, why the road was closed. I told her there'd been an incident up at the hotel. I asked her where she had come from and she told me she'd been delivering bread in the city."

"Did you ask where she'd been delivering?"

"Er, no. Should I have?"

"It doesn't matter. Keep going."

"I asked her if she'd been down this road earlier. She said she had."

"Good. What time?"

"At around seven this morning. I asked her whether she'd seen a motorcycle driving along this road from the direction of the hotel. She said she had, a Vespa."

"Did she get a licence plate?"

"No."

"Did you ask her for a description of the rider?" Conza asked hurriedly.

"Of course I did, Lieutenant. But she went all moody on me. Obviously didn't want to get involved. You know what these people are like."

Conza ignored the implied racial slur and pressed on.

"Description?"

"She said something vague about the rider being dressed in black. A balaclava covering his face – she said it all happened very quickly, and she didn't see anything else."

Conza raised his eyebrows in encouragement.

"I asked her about the rider's build, weight, height etc, but she just seemed to get scared, so I stopped asking her questions and radioed it in."

"What happened next?"

"I told Captain Brocelli what the girl had said, and he asked me how old she was, so I asked her. She said she was fifteen. The captain told me to take down her details and he'd arrange for someone to visit her at home to take a statement. So I asked her for her name and address, and she became really defensive. Asked me why I needed it."

"What did you tell her?"

The corporal rose to his full height. "I told her straight, I said, 'There's been a murder and you may be the only witness. We need to send someone round your house so you can make a statement in front of your parents.'"

Conza closed his eyes for a few seconds.

Confused as to why the lieutenant was shaking his head, the corporal pulled a notebook from his breast pocket.

"Nadia Touami, Flat 3, No 28 Via Ass –"

Conza raised his hand. "Didn't Brocelli tell you? The address is false. Name's probably false too."

"False?" said the corporal incredulously.

Conza didn't elaborate. He simply turned, climbed into the taxi and told the driver to take him back to the city.

The corporal watched the rear of the car until it disappeared from view.

"Asshole."

Friday – Two Days Before the Murder

San Carlo, 60 km East of Milan, Italy

The barn was silhouetted against the star-filled night sky when Kadin arrived at the depressing conclusion that no one was going to help him. He shuffled forwards on his backside and eased his feet over the edge of the boot. The fair-haired man gestured towards the door of the wooden building. Kadin rolled onto the cold concrete yard, slowly easing the stiffness in his back and stretching the cramp from his aching calves. The air was still and heavy, but a faint aroma of yeast or bread reminded him of Abebe's bakery and made him think of Nyala. In the light of the car's headlights, he saw only dried brown, mulberry hedges and rolling fields of scrub stretching out into the darkness. There were no other buildings or signs of habitation nearby, although Kadin wondered if the faint orange glow on the horizon, could be a distant town or city.

The man gestured towards the barn again. Slowly, Kadin walked forward and gingerly pressed his fingers to the cracked and split timber of the door. In that moment, in the confusion of still being alive while remaining convinced he would be killed at any second, Kadin could have imagined any number of things awaiting him in the barn. But he would have been wrong.

A bright white industrial lamp on a tripod illuminated much of the building's interior. Shielding his eyes from the glare, Kadin looked around. Two canvas seats and a picnic table had been set up in the middle of the room. Beneath the table, there was a large cardboard box and bottles of mineral water still wrapped in plastic. Against the far wall, there were two stacks of wooden pallets a couple of metres high and next to them, hanging from iron hooks, a long wooden ladder. The roof was vaulted, its apex hidden in shadow. Grey, worm-eaten timbers crisscrossed above his head and fixed to a joist by duct tape there was a metal box with a blinking red light, its lens directed at him. Another box

32

and another red light. He was being watched. *'What the hell is going on?'*

As his eyes adjusted to the contrasting light and shadow, he made out the shape of someone huddled in the far corner. He edged towards the figure and recognition came swiftly. His father, Issam Bennani, was sitting on the floor, knees slightly raised, back arched, trembling hands pawing at the top of his head in deep and consuming anguish. Issam looked up and smiled weakly. In that instant, his empty, bloodshot eyes conveyed to his son the ragged shreds of emotion that barely remained – sorrow, regret, fear and above all, hopelessness.

Kadin gasped, ran to his father and held the broken man who began weeping into the crook of one limp and lifeless arm. Kadin suppressed the compulsion to scream, to shout at his father a thousand questions, and a thousand more words of anger and rebuke. But it was pity that rose up from his stomach and caught in his throat. So he said nothing as Issam's frail body rolled onto Kadin's knees and as one, they wept together.

The sound of the BMW driving away made Kadin sit up in excitement. He dragged a sleeve across his eyes and pulled at his face.

"Quick, come on. They're going. We need to get out of here."

He wrapped his arms around his father's chest to help him stand, but Issam pushed him away and flapped weakly at his son's shoulders.

"No, stop. We cannot leave," Issam said looking up at the blinking metal boxes in the ceiling. He flopped back against the wall as Kadin released his grip.

"They're watching us. We cannot leave."

Kadin fought a rising flush of anger.

"What do you mean we can't leave? What the hell is going on, Father? What have you done? What do they want?"

Issam wiped away the last of his tears with a grubby finger.

"What I've done is no longer important. You need to listen to me. You have to listen to me."

Kadin ran to the barn door and peered through a gap in the planks. He darted back to his father and held his hand.

"Father, you need to tell me quickly. We can go. We can run across the fields to get help."

"Kadin. Shut up and listen." Issam's tone was harsh and Kadin was instantly reminded of the bursts of anger that heralded his father's return from a session at the bar. But he saw and heard something else – his father wasn't drunk or angry. He was terrified.

"Kadin, this is a mess. A huge mess and it's all my fault. I can never tell you the sorrow, the shame I feel."

Kadin waited impatiently, desperately repressing the multitude of questions that were fighting to break the surface of his fragile mind.

"We can work it out, Papa," he whispered gently.

"It will not end well Kadin. Whatever we do, they are dangerous men. Vile. They don't care about anyone. They feel nothing."

They both glanced up at the cameras.

"Kadin, there is something that we, you, have to do for them. It is a terrible thing, but you have no choice."

Kadin shuddered.

"Your mother, and Youssef and Soraya…" Issam closed his eyes as if doing so would prevent them from seeing his guilt.

"They will kill them if you don't do this thing."

Kadin's anger rose in a wave of hatred and terror, as it did when he had to rush to his mother's aid when his father started hitting her in drunken rage.

"What have you done?" he yelled, clutching at his father's sweat-stained shirt, no longer caring about the blinking red lights. Kadin shook him violently, repeating the question over and over until he suddenly saw himself as his father, pulling at his mother's clothing and shouting as she sobbed in surrender.

Kadin let him go and sank to his knees.

"We need to tell the police. Whatever you've done, I don't care. We need to get help."

"No Kadin, it's too late for that. If we don't do what they want, they'll kill us. All of us."

Kadin flopped against the wall and rubbed his pounding temples. He felt sick and utterly spent. He understood nothing about why he was in a derelict barn miles from home, next to his self-pitying father. But he knew that these men, these unspeaking monsters, would murder his sister, brother, and mother without a second's thought.

"What do they want?"

Issam closed his eyes once more.

"They want you to kill somebody."

12

Sunday

Milan, Italy

Nyala didn't look back until she was at least five hundred metres from the roadblock.

'Murder.' That's what the policeman said. *'Kadin, murder. That can't be true. Murder?'* The word kept stabbing at her. She swallowed deeply, even though her mouth was dry, and her lips dragged across her teeth. What was it that she had seen in Kadin's face, so thin and tight, his dark hair in clumped ribbons of grease? *'Was he sweating?'* Maybe it wasn't fear. Maybe he'd just been surprised to see her standing on the corner so early on a Sunday morning. Maybe he was running away because he'd witnessed the murder. *'Maybe he...'* She saw him again, wrestling to remove the balaclava. *'Kadin – Murder?'*

It was almost noon when Nyala told her father she wouldn't be attending church, claiming a headache. Amadi Abebe stirred in his slumber and smiled as his daughter emptied the money bag onto the coffee table. She looked tired and maybe a little sad. Knowingly, he nodded. *'Girl problems,'* he thought to himself as he drifted back to sleep.

Nyala changed into her shorts, vest and trainers and jogged out of the apartment block. Turning left, she headed west, following the course of the railway line until she reached Parco Franco Verga, a wide expanse of grassland, popular with dog walkers and BMXers. She sprinted the last two hundred metres to a wooden bench on the edge of a makeshift football pitch. Using the back of the seat, she stretched each of her long, dark legs whilst surveying the park. She was alone.

She sat on the graffiti-covered bench and clutched the mobile phone to her chest, closing her eyes for a few seconds. She punched in the code that made the screen light up. 'Kadin Bennani' was listed under 'Contacts'. Nyala stared at the name, rehearsing what she would say when he picked up the phone and said, "Hi Ny, how are you?" in his kind and cheerful tone. She knew so little for sure, but she knew she needed to hear his voice, to know he was all right, that he wasn't a murderer, that she had everything wrong. She wanted to hear him laugh at her for being silly and to tease her for jumping to crazy, perverse conclusions.

He was her closest friend. He had kissed her once outside of church. She'd always hoped that he wanted to kiss her again. But she could wait; he was shy and easily flustered. His courage would grow in time. She would wait.

She saw him rip the balaclava from his face.

Nyala pressed 'Call' and held her breath. *Ring, pause, ring, pause.* She fought the temptation to hang up at the end of each cycle but was released from her torment when a female voice invited her to leave a message. She hung up.

For the next two hours Nyala jogged aimlessly around the park. She bought a bottle of mineral water from a kiosk and sipped at it until its contents became warm and stale. Four times she called Kadin's number and on each occasion, her need to hear his voice grew. By the time she returned home to help her nana prepare dinner, Nyala felt she was being consumed by her desperation to know – and to understand.

She was unusually quiet during the meal and grateful that her grandmother didn't press her on why she hadn't been to church. Nyala squeezed the papery skin of her nana's hand and the old lady nodded back.

Amadi Abebe pushed his chair back in the self-satisfied way he always did after Sunday dinner.

"Hey Nyala, have you seen Kadin today?"

Nyala's mouth closed and then opened. She blinked slowly, her eyes bright white and wide in alarm.

"It's just that he didn't come round for the rent and I was wondering if you'd seen him?"

"No, I haven't seen him all day," Nyala stammered as she got up to clear the table.

In the relative sanctuary of the kitchen, as she was scraping food into the bin, she felt a gentle touch on her shoulder.

"Has something happened? Is everything OK between you and Kadin?" her grandmother whispered.

Nyala dropped a plate into the warm, soapy water and clung to the edge of the sink, arms stiff, head buried in her chest.

"Everything's fine, Nana," she said without turning.

"You know Nyala, sometimes things aren't as bad as you think."

'And sometimes, things are far worse,' she thought, fighting back the tears that were welling again.

13

Saturday – The Day Before the Murder

San Carlo, 60 km East of Milan, Italy

It had taken Issam more than an hour to calm Kadin after telling him of the plot to kill an unknown man outside the Hotel Napoli on Sunday. Kadin cried, his father cried, they both shouted; at themselves, at the cameras, and each other.

Nobody came to the barn that first night, although from the door, Kadin could see the BMW parked on a rise about two kilometres away, the hazy yellow moon picking out the bright silver metal against the brown and grey scrub.

...

As the first pale ribbons of daylight spilt onto the floor through the ragged timbers, Issam and Kadin picked at beans from a tin and drank mineral water from plastic bottles that smelt of chlorine. They ate and drank in silence.

When they had finished, Issam emptied a cardboard box onto the table. He worked slowly, avoiding his son's gaze. Four black and white photographs of a hotel entrance, two pictures of Milano Centrale station and a magazine clipping of a black Mercedes. Next to the photos he placed a slim, grey and silver padded sleeve that reminded Kadin of a bottle cooler.

"Signal suppressor for his mobile phone. Stops it being tracked. Mobile phones are like beacons, Kadin."

Finally, Issam produced the matt-grey Ruger semi-automatic pistol along with a slim, black magazine loaded with bright brass and copper-coloured bullets.

For a long time, Kadin pushed the gun away and refused to look at the pictures.

"There must be another way, Father," he implored.

Issam screamed at his son in frustration as he hobbled around the barn floor, leaving dark trails in the sand whilst cursing in Arabic. Kadin sat on a chair with his hands over his ears, tears stinging his eyes.

After each of Kadin's refusals to cooperate, Issam Bennani glanced at the cameras and placed a hand on his son's shoulder, gently whispering the names of his mother, brother and sister. He spoke of the cost of failing these men in their suits with their guns and their cameras, and their utter ambivalence towards pain, suffering and the lives of an immigrant family.

Slowly, and for only a few minutes at a time, Issam Bennani began revealing the plan that would end in a stranger's death.

Kadin watched as his father picked up the picture of the Mercédes before laying it on the table. Issam's right hand was clenched, but Kadin could see a small sliver of yellow metal between his fingers. *'A key,'* he thought, trying not to look up at the blinking red light.

Kadin shuffled forward to the edge of the table and, staring into his father's eyes, he nodded. His father smiled.

"Kadin, you need to concentrate. If you want your family to be safe, you need to listen."

Kadin picked up on the slight inflexion his father had placed on the word 'safe'. *'The key is to a safe?'* But what safe and where? What's in it? How would it help them? Kadin wanted to scream, but he sat listening, straining to pick up on further clues.

His father moved on to the photographs of the hotel and pushed a print across the table. The weight of the key dropping into his lap made Kadin flinch and he had to fight the temptation to look down. Very slowly, he slipped the key into the waistband of his jeans.

Issam took his son through the plan: from where Kadin would be dropped off to collect his Vespa, to the hotel, the killing, and then home again via the garage. But when Issam began telling him how he should escape afterwards, Kadin picked up on the stress his father was placing on certain words.

"*Don't* forget to *go* straight *home*," became, *'Don't go home.'* And there it was again; "The *key* to being *safe* is the *garage*." *'Key, safe, garage.'*

40

His father was telling him what he had to do. And what he definitely should not do.

Kadin laid a gentle hand on his father's. "Can we start again? I promise I will concentrate this time."

...

At dusk, Issam persuaded Kadin to go into the yard at the rear of the barn. Under the watchful eye of yet another camera fixed high on the wall, he patiently showed Kadin how to load, cock and fire the pistol. A sandbag was placed on top of a crate, which in turn was set on top of a steel drum. It was not lost on Kadin that the loose collection of objects was the height of a man. Kadin fired a few rounds into the sandbag from close range, but he hated the moment of anticipation as he squeezed the trigger, so he closed his eyes just before the explosion jerked his wrist upwards and sent a wave of warmth across the back of his hands.

"You need to keep your eyes open, Kadin. Aim down the sight," his father begged.

But Kadin couldn't bear to watch the twitch of the hessian as a bullet slammed into it, or the sand that spilt from the ragged hole and trickled onto the steel drum.

Eventually, Issam gave up and led Kadin back inside. He removed the magazine from the pistol and, using a wooden pallet, acted the role of the man who would step down from the hotel for Kadin to kill. Issam walked and talked and turned and walked and talked and begged. But Kadin would not raise the empty gun to his father's head and refused to pull the trigger. Suddenly, Kadin screamed in anger, threw down the pistol and collapsed into a chair. Issam dropped onto his twisted knees, imploring his son to shoot him.

Kadin glanced up at the camera when he heard the sound of an approaching car. As its headlights illuminated the open door, Kadin's hatred and anger rose up, exploding into shards of fury. He would not listen any longer. He would not kill the man at the hotel. He would not become them. He would die, but he would not die alone.

He snatched the pistol from the floor and grabbed the magazine from the table. *'At least five bullets. It was enough.'* As the headlights were switched off, he yanked his father's shoulder so that he could look into his sad and fear-ridden eyes. Issam's face was grey with dust and despair; narrow streaks of brown and silver ran to the corners of his mouth. Filled with determination and anger, Kadin spoke quickly.

"Father, I cannot do this thing. They are evil, these men, and if I kill this person I will become like them, evil and without a soul. We have to fight."

Issam's face remained frozen in hopelessness and Kadin pushed him away in disgust.

With trembling fingers, he slipped the magazine into its housing, cocked the pistol, and released the safety catch. He switched on the construction light and without looking up, positioned himself against the wall. He was breathing heavily but forced air into his lungs and held his breath long enough for a surge of energy to rise up from his stomach and out through his mouth in a long, controlled sigh. Lifting both arms, he pointed the barrel of the gun at the doorway.

The tall, ponytailed man was carrying a sports bag. He stopped, peered quizzically at the pistol and then up to the blinking red light. He let the bag drop. There was no fear, no doubt in his eyes.

"This ends right now," Kadin hissed as his finger took up first pressure on the trigger, just as Issam had taught him.

"OK," said the man, shrugging his shoulders and raising an eyebrow. "So, what's the plan?"

Kadin's arm began shaking from the strain of holding the gun with outstretched arms. The barrel slowly arced downwards.

"I kill you, and him, the other one outside in the car."

"Then what?"

"Then I take my family away. Where scum like you can't touch them."

The man looked puzzled, as if trying to imagine the scene.

"Have you ever seen a child that's been set on fire, Kadin?"

Kadin lurched forward, plunging the gun barrel into the man's face. The man didn't flinch, didn't blink, even as the gun sight ploughed a jagged trough through his cheek causing a trickle of blood to run down towards his chin.

"That man out there, the other guy. He's set light to kids before. I've seen him do it. Means nothing to him."

Kadin's hands were now shaking so much that the barrel of the pistol began drawing a red line across the man's face.

"They don't die straight away you know. They scream for a while before they go."

The sound of grinding teeth rose above the short snatches of breath escaping from Kadin's nose.

"Kill me, kill him. There's a thousand more of us that will find you and your family."

Issam whispered his son's name.

"He's right, Kadin. They will find us, all of us."

Kadin's fear, anger and rising claustrophobia exploded in a long high-pitched wail as he pointed the gun skywards and emptied the magazine in a rapid staccato of metallic explosions. Wisps of brightly lit smoke furled around their heads. The man casually wiped the blood from his cheek with the back of his hand.

"Finished?"

Kadin was on his knees, sobbing. Around his crotch, a dark patch was spreading. His father went to him.

The man picked up the sports bag and placed it on the table.

"Clothes. Put them on. We leave in an hour."

But father and son weren't listening anymore, so the man reached into his breast pocket and tossed onto the floor a black and white photograph of a grey-haired man.

"Your target," he said casually as he sauntered out of the barn. "Make sure you can recognise him."

14

Sunday

Guardia di Finanza Headquarters, Milan, Italy

After his discussion with Corporal Sigonella at the barricade, Raphael Conza asked the taxi driver to take him back to Finanza headquarters, where he read through the statements sent to him by Brocelli. He also found the pathologist's interim report. *'Subject to further examination'*, the bullet that entered Stolz's forehead was fired from a distance of around one metre. The report supported Captain Brocelli's theory that the round would be discovered in Stolz's cranium.

Conza made notes. That's what he always did. Lots of notes. In his roll-door cabinet was a cardboard box containing fifty B5 pre-lined notepads. A new box would be ordered before two months had passed.

It was while studying European history at university that Conza realised the habit he'd adopted in a childhood spent largely alone, was a blessing when it came to learning. As an eight-year-old, he'd recorded everything in writing: car numbers, train times, holidays, and visits to the house by dignitaries and politicians.

Aged twelve, he started to keep a diary, and in his bedroom closet there were sixteen volumes, each page containing at least one coded entry. Conza would occasionally read his old diaries; they helped him keep alive the memory of a father who he'd watched being carried to a mausoleum adorned with the family name. In his diary on that day, he had simply written, *'Papino se n'è andato'* – *'Daddy's gone'*.

Life after his father's passing was significantly different. His mother spent more time with him, and they both enjoyed their new-found relationship. Whilst his mother had talked of remaining in England, the country of her birth, she decided instead to take young Raphael back to Italy. So, shortly after the funeral, they moved from the Kent countryside, leaving behind the servants, the nanny and the chauffeur to set up home on the Italian coast, north of Rimini.

Whilst his father had left them enough money for a comfortable existence, they were far from rich and since she had moved to Campione d'Italia, Conza noticed that his mother was no longer surrounded by the oil paintings, silverware and porcelain that he'd helped her unpack. When Conza asked about the small Goya print that had always hung above her bed, she became irritated. It transpired that his father may have been a diplomatic *'safe pair of hands'* but had been more than a *'little free'* with the family wealth. Conza was shown a pile of worthless share certificates for companies that had long since ceased trading.

...

At twenty-two, Conza attended police college in Rome. He had a plan. It was in his diary. A timetable for his rise through the ranks. He was now twenty-nine, a lieutenant and on schedule.

He'd always known he was smart with an instinct to exploit an advantage to its fullest. He listened rather than just heard, possessed a thirst for knowledge and a strong sense of curiosity. He was resourceful and could communicate at different levels. Seniors would talk of Lieutenant Conza in terms of either, *'how far up the ladder he could climb'*, or how the force *'didn't need another clever dick'*. Lieutenant Conza was confident but was generally only liked and respected by other confident people. To everyone else, he was often perceived as being somewhat cold and patronising.

Raphael Conza was relatively fit, not tall, but with soft brown eyes and a warm smile that he'd learnt to use effectively on the girls at university. In their view, he tended towards 'attractive' rather than 'good-looking', but even so, his love life was only sporadically successful. Mainly because he'd always viewed 'intimacy' as a utilitarian rather than a romantic function – a predilection most women perceived if not on the first date, at least very soon afterwards. In his diary, the morning after his most recent girlfriend had stormed off, he'd written: 'Girlfriend – distractions – only casual from now on – three weeks maximum.' He ignored the fact that only once in his adult life, had he sustained a relationship in excess of that period.

Conza saw the word 'Skyguard' in his notepad and thought of Harry Chase, his English friend. Ex-Royal Air Force. He would know Skyguard. They hadn't spoken in a while. *'I should call him,'* Conza decided as he took a new memo pad from the carton.

He drafted a note to his boss, Colonel Scutari, explaining that he had not yet drawn a conclusion about Stolz's killing. He cited the fact that the victim was foreign as the reason for things taking longer than anticipated. But he offered reassurances that he'd be in a position to make a recommendation on jurisdiction by tomorrow. Conza read through the memo twice, making an amendment to the punctuation after the first reading, before folding it neatly into an envelope.

He reviewed the page in his notebook headed 'QUESTIONS'.

1. Motive – Contract? Robbery? Other?

2. Killer – Vespa?

3. Witness – girl – bread?

4. Mobile phone – movements?

5. Cards – spend – movements?

6. Identity?

7. Chauffeur – involvement?

8. Hotel – breakfast?

9. CCTV?

10. Notebook – FC?

11. Wallet – code?

12. USB – ???

13. Skyguard?

14. Newspaper/magazine?

He added a line at the foot of the page: '15. Call Harry!'

He tidied up the documents on the table into neat piles, locked the windows, turned off the fan and after dropping the letter at the front desk, went home to his immaculately clean but empty apartment.

15

Milan, Italy

The two-tone siren of a police car roused Kadin with a start, and he ran to the garage door to listen, but the sound faded into the distance.

He heard himself repeating his father's instructions: "Mobile, clothes, gun, station, don't go home." He pulled out the grey and silver sleeve from his jacket and placed it on the workbench along with the dead man's cash, the gun and his balaclava.

He fingered the brass key given to him by his father before running over to the inspection pit. He pulled at the first two boards allowing the acrid smell of burnt oil to drift up as he crawled forward. As light penetrated the chasm, he began to make out the floor of the pit; oil-soaked sand and old rags. He jumped down but had to push off three more planks before there was sufficient light for him to find the grey metal of the small safe, semi-recessed into the concrete. The door was no more than ten centimetres square. The key fitted snugly into the lock and the safe opened smoothly and silently.

The metal box was surprisingly deep. A green plastic A4 folder had been rolled up and pushed to the back of the recess, but there was nothing else. Kadin snatched the folder and clambered back up to ground level before emptying its contents onto the workbench; five passports, five train tickets to Genoa – valid for another two months – a thick roll of euros in an elastic band, a train timetable for Milan to Genoa, a bus timetable for a route with unfamiliar names, a nickel-coloured key attached to a brass disc on which was etched 'VN3', and certified copies of four title deeds: the Abebe bakery, the two garages and a fourth property, a building in Genoa – 'Villa Nuova'. The owner of the properties was listed as 'The J-Sky Corporation' with an address in Rome. The final object in the folder was a wristwatch. Kadin picked up each item in turn, but already knew what his father intended. *'It's a fire escape.'* A means, if it was ever needed, for the Bennani family to get out of Milan, fast. For the first time since leaving the barn, Kadin was sure of what his father intended for him to do.

"Mobile, clothes, gun, station, don't go home."

Working quickly, Kadin changed back into the grubby jeans and sweatshirt he'd been wearing when he was snatched and wriggled into a blue, lightweight anorak. He transferred the mobile sleeve and banknotes into a side pocket of his bag and flung the Ruger semi-automatic and balaclava onto the pile of discarded clothes. He threw the bundle into the pit and stowed the passports, title deeds and four of the train tickets in his bag. The other train ticket, cash and 'VN3' key, he pushed into his pocket. Finally, he strapped the watch to his wrist and threw the empty folder into the pit.

"Mobile, clothes, gun, station, don't go home," he recited for the final time before replacing the boards over the hole, pressing them down with his heel as quietly as he could.

"Thank you, Papa," he mouthed just before the sound of another siren warned him that time was running out. He snatched up the rucksack and scanned the garage before flicking off the light.

As he pushed open the garage door, Kadin caught sight of his reflection in the mirror. The skin on his face was tight and pale, his eyes red and swollen. He pushed a strand of lank, dark hair from his eyes and thought of dying. He tasted salt and the colourless image told him he was crying, but he felt nothing. Beyond his own pained and frightened face, beyond and yet inside the mirror's surface, he saw Nyala, her beautiful dark skin, her smile as it was announced by a slender ribbon of white and pink. Her hair in pleats framing her warm and kind expression. Her smooth, muscular legs that he'd glanced at guiltily as she rode away on her old bike. The girl from the bakery. His first love and the girl he'd met every Sunday since volunteering to collect rent for his father. The girl he dreamed of talking to without losing control of his words, or his cheeks. The girl who would tell the police that the vile murderer on the Vespa was him – Kadin Bennani.

Her expression suddenly changed, and she was looking at him in bewilderment; afraid and confused. Beautiful and yet vulnerable. He was on his Vespa, riding past her again, but this time he shouted out, as loudly as he could, "I'm sorry."

The vivid image of Nyala dispelled his dark thoughts of dying, and for a fleeting moment he allowed himself to believe that everything could go back to how it was if he just surrendered, handed himself in. But the sound of an ambulance ruptured his dream and he thought of his mother, brother, and sister. He'd been told what to do, and what he definitely could not do. Surrendering was not an option and no matter what happened, he wouldn't give them a reason to hurt his family.

He wiped away the tears and images of Nyala with his sleeve and breathed deeply. He locked the door and headed east towards the railway station. In his pocket, his fingers ran across the smooth matt surface of the train ticket. He'd noticed that it was a 'single'; a reminder, as if he needed one, that his return journey was neither assured nor his to determine.

He checked his watch. Eighteen minutes before the train departed. It would take him about ten minutes to walk, *'not run'* to the station. "Too tight," he muttered to himself, cursing the moments of self-pity he'd wasted in the garage.

Eight minutes later, Kadin arrived at the piazza in front of the high, columned arches fronting Milano Centrale station. The air was warm and thick, and he was sweating. He could feel drops of water tracking down his spine and between his thighs. He recognised the cycle rack from the photograph and, trying not to rush, walked towards the black bin at the far end. He dropped the mobile phone, still in its sleeve, amongst the plastic bottles, coffee cups and discarded napkins. He didn't look back.

'From now on,' Kadin thought, *'if they're watching me, they'll know that I'm not following orders.'* He glanced around, delaying his next move for as long as he dared, but when his watch told him he had just two minutes, he turned and darted up the steps to Platform 2. He thought his heart would stop when he read the screen telling him that the train had been delayed by four minutes.

Visibly shaking, he sat on the edge of a bench clutching his bag. He didn't look up, nor do anything that might attract attention. He desperately needed the toilet but suppressed the sharp stabbing pain that ran from his kidneys to his groin by rocking gently back and forth. Time passed slowly, and he tried to replace the memory of the grey-haired man who at the moment of death, had looked at Kadin with sad blue eyes.

He tried thinking of his mother but could only picture her crying, as she had so many times whilst fighting his father. He thought of his younger sister, smiling and laughing as she danced to music that he could no longer hear. He thought of his little brother, frightened and alone; calling for him, "Kadin, where are you?" he could hear Yousef screaming, but the sound morphed into a metallic squeal as the train to Genoa coasted to a halt.

Without hesitation, he scuttled aboard the nearest carriage and dived into a toilet.

As Kadin Bennani vomited into the sickly smelling metallic bowl, he acknowledged that he was about to leave Milan for what he was sure would be the last time.

16

Three Years Ago

Lugano, Switzerland

The first time Raphael Conza saw him, Harry Chase was sitting at a blackjack table. He looked bored and slightly drunk. Although it annoyed Conza that the man's chips were piled in a haphazard heap, he was also intrigued. The man knew how to play blackjack. The way he placed bets and moved around the card tables was compelling.

Seemingly, the man had three rules: he never sat at a table while the cards were being shuffled; if he suffered five losing bets, he changed tables; and winning stakes were doubled, but only ever twice. Conza soon worked out that strict adherence to these rules meant that unlike the rest of his companions, the man didn't chase his losses, but he did capitalise on his wins. It seemed to work, much to the annoyance of the other players, who not only saw their Swiss francs disappear into the croupier's money slot at an alarming rate, but they also had to put up with the fidgety Englishman who changed tables every few minutes.

And then suddenly, as if responding to an unheard call, the man stopped, threw a generous tip to the croupier and retreated to the bar. Conza heard him order a gin and tonic.

The casino was squeezed in between two hotels in the Paradiso area of Lugano. It was a relatively new construction but managed to give the impression of being somewhat 'tired'. Many of the bulbs in the faux-crystal chandeliers had blown and the rooms smelt of furniture polish, stale cigarette smoke and cheap perfume. The walls were covered in poorly painted representations of roman pillars, but the artwork was cracked and peeling, and the gold-coloured finish to the bar top had worn away to reveal grey alloy. The laminated wood floors were scuffed, and the bar stools were struggling to retain their foam padding. Conza had already decided that it was not his sort of place, but the blackjack-playing Englishman had pricked his curiosity.

"Clever system," Conza remarked as he leant against the bar.

"Sorry?"

"Your system on the tables. Very clever."

"Oh, right. But it doesn't always work. I got lucky tonight."

"I'm Raffy, do you mind if I join you?"

"Be my guest. Do you want a drink? They don't know how to make a gin and tonic, but the local wine is pretty good."

"Thank you. But let me buy you one. I'll stick to beer. Another one?"

"Thanks, I'll have a beer with you."

The men sat in awkward silence until the drinks arrived.

"You a local? Sorry, the name is Harry. Harry Chase."

"Cheers, Harry," said Conza, raising his glass. "No, my mother just moved into a house on the other side of the lake. I got bored unpacking boxes, so I took a trip across the lake to do some exploring. I live in Milan, although I was schooled in England."

"In which case, I won't feel so ashamed of myself. My Italian is an embarrassment."

They laughed.

"What are you doing in Lugano?" asked Conza, "holiday?"

"Yes, sort of. My wife is due to join me with the children in a couple of days. She insists I have a few days on my own at the start of family holidays. Apparently, I'm a bit grumpy in the transition period between work and play. Don't relax too well."

"Now that, I can sympathise with," said Conza with a grin.

It was the start of their friendship. The English barrister and the Italian policeman.

...

They agreed to meet again the following day and found themselves wandering aimlessly through the pine covered shores of the lake. They talked, ate, talked and drank. Inevitably, their conversation turned to crime and the law and unsurprisingly, their experiences crossed many similar themes.

Following a well-trodden tourist route, they took the funicular to the summit of San Salvatore and looked down at the wide, dark expense of Lake Lugano. Conza pointed out his mother's new home.

"That's Campione d'Italia over there, where the houses reach down to the shoreline,"

"And that's part of Italy?"

"Yes, it's an exclave. During World War Two, the CIA, or OSS as it was then, ran operations throughout Italy from there."

They sat on a bench outside the tiny, vaulted chapel of the Chiesa di San Salvatore.

"Don't you ever get fed up with it all, Raffy? Crime, I mean."

Conza was surprised at the question. "I guess so. But I take comfort from the fact that we're making a difference, even in a small way."

"Are we though? The criminals seem to hold all the cards these days."

"I think that sometimes. But then I remind myself that it's probably always been that way. We just know more now whether we want to or not. Crime isn't a modern phenomenon."

"I know that, but the bad guys know how to use every trick in the book. Doesn't that get to you? We aren't really solving anything are we?"

"We're doing what we can, Harry. That's all we can do."

"I used to think that. I guess I just became tired of trying to defend the indefensible. These days, I see myself as a litter picker rather than a barrister."

"Don't you ever prove that an accused is not guilty?"

"Not very often. Contrary to popular opinion, it's pretty rare for the police to prosecute the innocent."

"But surely, these people have the right to be defended; guilty or not."

"I've only been a barrister for two years. I spend my life mitigating rather than defending. It's all about trying to excuse the inexcusable. Reduced sentences, bail hearings, pleas for clemency; that sort of thing. It's all just a game."

"But you must represent the innocent on occasions. Not everyone who hires you is a criminal, surely?"

"It does happen. Just not very often. I try not to judge, but it's pretty difficult. My problem is I can't let go. I try to solve everything, take personal responsibility. But I'm powerless. Just a voice in the wilderness. I don't like my clients because of the crimes they commit, and don't like myself because I do nothing to prevent them doing it again."

Harry set down his glass and stared at the lake.

"But you're frustrated because you care, not because you don't."

Harry Chase picked up a stone and turned it over in his hand.

"You're probably right, Raffy." He suddenly roused himself. "Come on, let's go down to the casino and throw some money away."

17

Sunday

Genoa, Italy

Kadin Bennani stood beneath the pillared arches of Genoa Piazza Principe station and took a deep breath. He'd spent the journey clutching his bag and avoiding eye contact. At Voghera, where he changed trains, he bought a can of Sprite from a vending machine and sipped it until it turned warm and flat.

On the train, and despite the overwhelming exhaustion that tugged at his eyelids, he'd forced himself to stay awake. His senses had swung violently in keeping with his erratic mood. There had been painfully sharp moments of high alert, when his paranoia tried to seduce him to run away and hide, and periods of numb submission during which he'd tried to imagine the aftermath of confessing his crime to a fellow passenger, or the conductor, or to the two policemen standing in the ticket hall in Voghera. But he hadn't confessed, and he'd convinced himself that for his family's sake, he would stay strong and follow what he believed was his father's escape plan.

Kadin walked over to the map outside the station and searched for the 'Rivoli' bus stop marked in his timetable. He found it on the No. 635 bus route. Quickly, he memorised directions to the nearest stop.

"Columbus – alley – turn right at church – cross the road – 635 – Rivoli."

Kadin hitched his bag onto his shoulder and crossed the forecourt past the Christopher Columbus statue. Scanning right, he kept walking until he saw the top of a narrow cobblestone path leading steeply downwards in a direction the map had told him was towards the docks and sea beyond. Kadin began to descend until at the end of the street, he saw the blue and white of a city police car. With as much curiosity as he could muster, he stopped to read a poster outside a church extolling the virtues of repentance. He pretended to read until he saw the police car move off up the hill. Shortly after turning right, he crossed the main road and twelve minutes later, he was on the bus heading eastwards, away from the spoon-shaped basin of Genoa's main port.

The bus was almost empty, but he sat near the back, so he could maintain a clear view of the doors and other passengers. He alighted at the Rivoli bus stop and crossing back across the road, walked up a narrow incline between high-sided buildings. As he neared the crest of the hill, he spotted a three-storey, red-brick building rising above a clump of poplar trees. On a stone sign above the door were the words 'Villa Nuova'.

The entrance door wasn't locked, and it opened onto a cool, shaded hallway of white and grey marble. Ignoring the lift, he ran up the white stone steps to the third floor. The 'VN3' key unlocked the door of Apartment 3.

Not since he'd been a small boy could Kadin remember saying, "Thanks Papa", but for the second time that day, the relief and sorrow that he heard in those words, spoken aloud as he pushed the door closed behind him, made Kadin sob.

18

St Pancras Station, London, England

The maroon-coloured Jaguar sat at idle in front of St Pancras station. Its passenger stepped off the Eurostar, tired, irritable and in need of a cigarette. The driver jumped out of the car at the sight of his boss, but Pete Salterton ignored him as he stopped to light up a Marlboro and make a phone call. It was just after nine o'clock in Italy.

"Giuli – it's Pete," he said wearily, drawing smoke deep into his lungs.

"Jesus, Pete. I've just got back from the morgue. Had to wait until only the night porter was around. I couldn't believe it, nearly crapped myself when he pulled back the sheet. I really thought it was you lying on the slab."

"He was picked up by a Merc, a black Merc."

"I know, Leo told me. Shit, Pete. Do you really think the bullet was meant for you?"

"I'm not taking any chances. What have you found out?"

"The dead man was a kraut. Lukas Stolz. He's not known to us or anyone I've spoken to, but I'm still checking."

"And the shooter. What do we know?"

"Police have no leads worth a damn. They reckon the Merc driver's clean."

"Speak to him. Sometimes they don't want to get involved. He may know something that he hasn't told the cops."

"I'll get Leo to have a word."

Salt reflected on this and briefly imagined the pain that Leo's 'word' could inflict on the chauffeur.

"Tell Leo to take it easy would you?"

"I'll speak to him. Don't worry."

"Why is everyone telling me not to worry today?"

Silence.

"Cops talked to another witness. A kid. Gave a false address, I'm on to it though."

"Does he know anything?"

"It's a girl, and yes, maybe. The false name and address could mean she knows something, but kids lie to the cops all the time in the city, so it could be a dead end. On the other hand, she may be the only person who saw the shooter."

"OK, follow it up and let me know as soon as you hear anything. I'm on my way home."

Salt hung up, ground his cigarette into the pavement and without a word to the driver, climbed into the back seat of the car.

"What the fuck have you got me into, Giuliani?" he muttered to himself as he closed his eyes.

19

Apartment 3, Villa Nuova, Genoa, Italy

Kadin locked the front door and dropped his bag in the narrow hallway running the length of the apartment.

To his right he found a small kitchen with a window overlooking the sloping street he'd just climbed. In the fridge, there was milk, butter, eggs and dried meat. Kadin sniffed at a carton of milk before taking a deep draught. He looked out over the swaying masts of yachts parked in the marina a few hundred metres below. He thought once again of making a run for it.

A note was pinned to a corkboard next to the fridge. Kadin recognised his father's wiry handwriting: 'Cleaner – Tuesdays and Thursdays'.

His head throbbed as he tried to work out what day it was and for a few seconds, convinced himself it was Monday, before retracing the events of the past forty-eight hours and concluding that it was only Sunday. Still the same day he'd killed a grey-haired man in front of the Hotel Napoli.

Opposite the kitchen, Kadin found a neat, clean, windowless bathroom of white porcelain, black marble and brushed-steel. A small extractor fan spluttered into life when he turned on the light to reveal a shower cubicle with a rollback door. In a small cupboard he found an electric shaver, deodorant, cologne, and a large box of paracetamol. Kadin recognised the faint aroma of his father's aftershave and placed the milk carton on the side of the sink before dousing his face in cold water. He thought of his father, sitting on the floor of the barn, smiling weakly as Kadin was ushered out the door and into the boot of the BMW. Kadin scooped more cold water over his face but avoided looking into the mirror.

In the corridor, he found two doors that opened outwards. Behind the first was a narrow cupboard with slatted shelves on which sat an iron, neatly pressed bedsheets, a pile of clean towels and some unopened boxes of soap and other cleaning materials. A mop in an orange bucket stood in the corner. The cupboard smelt strongly of lemons and Kadin breathed in the clean aroma as if purging himself of the bitter scent of his own sweat and urine-stained clothes. A second cupboard contained a modern-looking boiler, clothes horse and washing basket.

The bedroom was further down the hall. It contained a double bed, two cupboards and a wardrobe, in which some trousers, shirts and a jacket had been hung up, still wrapped in the plastic of a commercial laundry. None of the clothes looked familiar, but the bedroom smelt of sandalwood - and his father. The growing realisation of his father's parallel existence – a secret home, the trappings of domesticity and unfamiliar belongings – aroused in Kadin a strange mixture of curiosity, disgust and grudging respect.

The wide window running the length of the bedroom's far wall was shuttered but narrow bands of sunlight spilt onto the wood-tiled floor. On the bed, the duvet had been pulled back and folded neatly in half across its width. Four clean, plump white pillows were stacked against the headboard.

Kadin shook his head in amazement, but physical and mental exhaustion drowned any further thoughts of his father's neat, ordered 'other life' and he collapsed face down on the bed, immediately falling into a deep but anguish-ridden sleep.

20

Monday

Raphael Conza's Apartment, Milan, Italy

The morning after the murder, while drinking coffee in his apartment, Lieutenant Conza received a phone call from Sergeant Georgio Moretti of the State Police incident room. Conza didn't know Moretti but listened intently as he was provided with a precise, detailed update on the murder investigation. The sergeant spoke in clear, logical sentences and Conza felt himself warming towards the softly spoken but intelligent voice at the other end of the line.

Conza took down notes as the Sergeant spoke. The chauffeur, Sami Ricci, had been reported missing by his girlfriend. Moretti sounded concerned and told Conza that a state policeman had been sent out to interview her. Conza made a new entry on the page in his notepad already headed 'SAMI RICCI'.

Conza was updated on the work being undertaken by the authorities in Berlin. Enquiries were being made and the necessary paperwork drawn up to allow access to Stolz's bank accounts and card records. The process had been delayed by the need for a positive identification of Stolz's body.

The Heidelberg address in Stolz's passport turned out to be that of his sister, Katherine Harper. She'd informed local police that her brother was unmarried and as far as she knew, she was his only next of kin. Moretti added that Stolz's sister was booked on a flight to Milan on Tuesday afternoon, from where she would be taken directly to the mortuary to confirm that the grey-haired man with a hole in his head was her brother, Lukas Albert Stolz.

Katherine Harper had confirmed that Stolz worked for Skyguard Industries at their headquarters in England and had been living in Warwick for the past two years. Conza noted down the address. Once again, the mention of England made Conza think of Harry Chase.

Conza was told that Skyguard had an office in Milan.

"Who's down to go and see them?"

"Me actually, Lieutenant," responded Moretti, "I was going to drop in this afternoon."

"I'll come with you. What time were you thinking of going?"

"Around two. The office is in the city centre, north end of Via Torino. Where do you want to meet?"

Conza pictured the long, narrow, shop-lined road.

"I'm in the city all morning, let's meet in the garden by the Piazza Duomo at quarter to. OK?"

The sergeant completed his narrative by informing Conza nothing had been discovered from the tram ticket found in Stolz's wallet, but enquiries were continuing. The search for the girl on the bicycle had stalled.

"We've given her description to the city police, but nothing so far. We weren't given much to go on."

Conza thought for a moment.

"Did Corporal Sigonella make a statement about his conversation with her?"

"Yes, I sent a copy to your office this morning."

"I haven't received it yet. Do me a favour and read it out."

A minute later, Sergeant Moretti began to narrate the somewhat awkwardly worded statement that had been given by Corporal Sigonella.

When Moretti had finished, Conza took so long debating whether to say anything, the Sergeant had to ask whether he was still there.

It had occurred to Conza that Corporal Sigonella had failed to mention the girl had been delivering bread in the city yesterday morning. The police would have no idea how to begin the task of finding her. Conza decided not to say anything for the time being.

Conza finished the call and updated his notebook. On the page headed 'QUESTIONS', he circled the words '*Witness – girl – bread*', after which he rinsed out his coffee cup, and left his apartment.

He had planned to make another visit to the hotel but that would have to wait, he had a new plan.

21

Milan City Centre, Italy

Conza walked the short distance to Porto di Mare underground station and took the metro into the city where he changed lines and climbed the stairs back into the sunshine at Monumentale. Skirting the old wall of the cemetery, he arrived in front of the central tram depot, a sprawling tear-dropped shaped building nestled between three roads on the edge of the Bullona district.

Focusing on the nearby cafés and street vendors selling snacks to the commuters and sightseers, Conza began asking the proprietors whether they usually opened on a Sunday. Only two cafés responded positively, but both confirmed they bought their bread from local bakeries. Conza recorded the details and moved on.

Next came the train stations. He began at Milano Centrale and discovered three vendors that opened on a Sunday, but the owners all denied purchasing bread for cash the previous day. Twice, Conza suspected he was not being told the truth, but despite reassuring them he was just trying to contact the bakery owner, the proprietors merely shrugged their shoulders and refused to assist him further. Conza made a note of their details before walking the short distance to Milano Porta Garibaldi station.

Conza's plan failed to uncover any further information about bread or the bakery in the first six vendors, so he sat down at a café table in the piazza in front of the station's main entrance. After asking the same questions about opening times and bread, he ordered a coffee and sfogliatella pastry from the waitress, a skinny, middle-aged woman with thin pale lips, dry, dyed-blonde hair, yellow fingers and an expression that said she probably didn't like her customers.

Conza checked his watch. *'Three more hours of doing this,'* he complained to himself with a sigh. His phone buzzed quietly. He'd missed a call from Police HQ and there was a voicemail.

He listened to Sergeant Moretti's anxious voice asking him to call back.

"You left me a message," Conza said after waiting a few minutes for the sergeant to be tracked down.

"Lieutenant Conza." Moretti hesitated before continuing. "There's a problem here."

A brief image of Captain Brocelli's sweaty frame, sitting behind his desk, floated across Conza's thoughts.

The volume of the sergeant's voice lowered to that of the confessional.

"We – someone," he corrected himself, "seems to have mislaid Stolz's belongings."

Conza tensed.

"We've still got the shell cases and bullet fragments, but everything else has gone missing."

In his mind, Conza quickly sorted through what he'd seen and heard the day before in the police van. An image of shell cases and bullets appeared on one side of the table, on the other was Stolz's briefcase, wallet, and holdall. In his hand, Conza saw the square keyring.

"I guess all hell has broken loose down there?" Conza eventually offered in sympathy, as he pictured the commissioner of police, face flushed, spitting venom at everyone in general, and anyone in particular not quick enough to move out of his way as he charged around the corridors of HQ.

"You could say that."

Conza ended the call and sat thinking about what had happened over the past twenty-four hours. He tried to pull together the fragments circling above the image of a grey-haired man with a hole in his forehead. *'The chauffeur may have just run off with a new lover or got drunk and fallen asleep on a tram. The missing evidence may have been stuffed in a locker. It wouldn't be the first time.'* But neither notion sat comfortably with him. *'Something about this case just doesn't feel right.'*

Conza subconsciously offered a quiet thank you as his coffee and cake were placed on the table.

"*Grazie,*" he repeated, meeting the pale green eyes of the dyed blonde who'd remained standing over him.

"Why do you want to know?" she asked with neither hesitation nor worry, her eyes bright with aggression.

Conza's musings about the case evaporated.

"Why do you want to know about the bread?" she repeated.

She waited patiently, her eyes not leaving his, arms folded across her narrow, tight chest. Conza knew at once that she was unafraid, and almost certainly too streetwise to believe his story about wanting to contact the bakery owner on a private matter. But he was also sure the woman knew something, something he needed. He nodded for her to join him. The woman paused, glanced over at the kitchen, and sat down, arms folded, eyes pointedly fixed on his.

She gave a casual nod when Conza showed his identity card, but he caught a flicker of recognition as she eyed the Finanza department stamp.

"I'm trying to track down the witness to a murder."

"The baker?"

"The delivery girl."

The woman considered Conza's statement for some time before responding. Conza waited.

"She's a good girl," the woman suddenly proclaimed, before adding a moment later in sad confession, "she's not like the rest of us. She could get out of here." Almost imperceptibly the woman jerked her head to her left and right to emphasise the place from where she believed the girl could escape.

"Look, I'll be honest." Conza saw an ironic smile flicker across the woman's lips. "I've got two witnesses to a murder. One's gone missing and I need to find the other one. I don't know what's going on, but if she's in danger, I need to find her. That's the truth."

"Mob?"

Conza raised his hands. "I really don't know. It may just be a botched robbery, but I don't think so. If it was a planned hit and she knows something, I need to get her off the streets – fast."

The woman unfolded her arms, leaning forward so that Conza could sense the warmth of her tobacco-and-wine-flavoured breath.

"Nyala Abebe. Father runs a bakery off Via Enrico Consenz. Don't let anyone hurt her."

The woman stood and without another word or gesture, strode off behind the counter and through the curtain of multi-coloured plastic ribbons into the kitchen.

Conza's thanks went unheard.

He quickly scribbled down the name and address, checked his watch and, throwing twenty euros on the table, hurried off to hail a taxi.

22

Abebe Bakery, Via Enrico Cosenz, Milan, Italy

Nyala spent the first few hours of Monday helping her father rearrange stores in the cellar. Together, they manhandled an old chest down the steps and Nyala helped him fill it with drums of oil and sacks of salt and flour from the pallets that were strewn across the dusty floor. But her father noticed she was unusually distracted and continually checking her mobile for messages.

"Waiting for something?" he asked as once more, she fished the phone from her pocket. Nyala shrugged and her father decided that Kadin's absence the day before, along with his daughter's low mood today, could only mean that she was experiencing 'boy trouble' for the first time.

Just after ten-thirty, Nyala was brushing the cellar stairs when the man appeared. He smiled when he said, "Good morning," but Nyala knew he was police. Nervously, she glanced back over her shoulder to see her father emptying bottles of oil into a barrel. She mounted the top three steps in a single bound and stood before the man without speaking.

Conza showed his badge.

"Nyala Abebe?"

She nodded, clasping her hands around the broom handle.

"You spoke to a policeman on the Via degli Imbriani yesterday."

She nodded again, desperately trying to dispel the image of Kadin, with his Vespa and balaclava and look of terror.

"You gave the policeman a false name and address. Why did you do that?"

She shifted her weight onto one leg and grasped the edge of the iron railing.

Conza looked past her and through the open door of the bakery.

"That's your father I take it?"

"Yes," said Nyala weakly.

"Does he know you lie to the police?"

'Too far – too quickly,' he thought to himself as he saw tears well in the girl's pale and frightened eyes.

"Look Nyala, I don't care about what you said to the policeman. I think you lied because you were frightened. Am I right?"

She nodded slowly but looked down at the stairs, turning her eyes away from his.

"What matters is what you saw. The Vespa," Conza said gently, stepping forward to place his hand on her head, tilting it back so that she had to look at him.

"I didn't see anything. It all happened so quickly. It was a Vespa. He was wearing black. That's all I know."

"So, the rider was a 'he'?"

"Yes. I think so," Nyala stammered without conviction.

"Did you recognise him, Nyala?"

Conza saw fear rising in her throat and across her lips.

"Nyala, are you frightened of him?"

"No. Of course not!"

"So, you did recognise him. Do you know him well?"

A man's voice rose from the cellar.

"Nyala, come down here and help me, would you?"

She clasped her hands together in prayer.

"Please go, please. I don't know anything else. Please."

Conza heard the blonde woman say, *'she's a good girl'.*

He stepped back and lifted her chin gently so that she could see his face. He took a small white card from his jacket and placed it between her long trembling fingers.

"You need to talk to me, Nyala. He's in more trouble than maybe even you realise. He's done a terrible thing, but right now, he's the one whose life could be in danger. And because of what you know, maybe your life too."

Her eyes closed tightly shut.

"My number is on the card. You need to call me. This isn't going to go away. If you care for him, you need to believe that you and I may be his only hope."

Conza turned and stepped across the road just as Amadi Abebe climbed the steps.

"Who was that? What did he want?"

"He was looking for someone." Nyala whispered sadly, as pangs of relief and fear washed over her. She wiped her face in the crook of her sleeve and squeezed the white business card into her back pocket.

"He looked worried. I hope he finds him."

23

Apartment 3, Villa Nuova, Genoa, Italy

Kadin woke in darkness and for a fleeting moment, imagined he was home. But an early morning ferry sounding its departure from Genoa harbour shattered the illusion. He sat on the edge of the bed, the sickly-sweet smell of dried urine filling his nostrils, and fought the urge to retch. His head throbbed and sleep still hung heavy around his shoulders and through his thighs. His kidneys ached and he wanted to go back to sleep, but he dragged himself to the bathroom.

The warmth of the shower ran across his face, down his chest and over his crotch. The physical evidence of the past few days disappeared in a whirlpool of pale froth and grey bubbles. He took two paracetamol from the cabinet, washing them down with cold water.

In the bedroom, he found a pair of jogging trousers in a drawer and put on a clean white shirt from the wardrobe, folding the cuffs back along his forearms. He felt empty, hollowed out and totally alone. Every sound offended him, and his thoughts whirled in uncontrollable spirals. He considered whether he was any longer sane. *'I killed a man.'*

He wasn't hungry and still felt sick but forced a couple of slices of prosciutto into his mouth. The meat tasted bitter and clammy, so he returned to the bathroom, cleaned his teeth and rinsed with mouthwash. He finished the meat with a slice of bread before wandering back down the corridor to the door he had not yet opened.

The room contained a sofa, coffee table, four chairs and a long four-door cabinet on which sat a television. In the corner, an office chair had been placed in front of a workbench that was covered by a green cutting mat. On the bench there was a lamp, soldering iron, plastic box of pull-out compartments and a rotating storage unit full of tools. He ran a finger over the well-maintained screwdrivers, pliers and wire snips. In the box, he found clips, screws and various electrical connections that he didn't recognise. Kadin knew his father had once worked as a communications technician, but he had no memories of that time and had never seen his father work on anything more complicated than changing a light bulb. He wondered if he'd ever really known him.

Once more, questions cascaded through his tired mind. *'Had father been working from here? What did he make? For whom?'* Kadin thought of the two thugs in the barn and shuddered. Next to the table, two large stackable bins were filled with batteries, electrical wire, switches, and components of what Kadin thought could be cameras, microphones, and light sensors.

Too many questions. He slumped onto the sofa.

Using the remote control, Kadin flicked through TV channels aimlessly. He avoided lingering on news programmes, afraid that at any second, his photograph would appear and a reporter standing outside the Hotel Napoli would relate details of the vile murder and the search for a youth on a Vespa. He selected a movie, turned down the volume and drifted back to sleep.

When he awoke, his back was damp and cold with sweat. The television was showing an old black and white Western.

Kadin had been dreaming of his father, sitting on the barn floor, smiling, as Kadin raised the gun to shoot him in the face. Kadin panicked, desperately trying to separate dream from reality. The grey-haired man's eyes flashed across his memory and Kadin buried his face in his hands.

His thoughts turned to Nyala, but her image couldn't dispel his depression. He went to the bathroom and emptied the pockets of his filthy clothes before stuffing them into the washing basket.

In the kitchen, he removed the elastic band from the roll of notes he'd found in the garage and bent them backwards until they lay flat. To the pile, he added the dead man's money which comprised euros and English pounds. As he separated the notes into currencies, a passport-sized photograph fell onto the table. It was a picture of an Alsatian dog, ears pricked, eyes bright, lips slightly parted in anticipation. *'Looks friendly,'* he thought, causing another stab of guilt to pierce his chest.

He tossed the photograph to one side and resumed counting; 14,940 euros and £160 sterling. He had never held such an amount of money before and for a moment, considered fleeing the apartment and catching a flight to somewhere remote; a place without cameras and guns. Then he thought of his mother, brother and sister, and knew that he could never run, never leave them.

He picked up the photograph of the dog again. *'It must have been between the notes in his wallet.'* On the back of the picture was written, 'Fideccio'. Using a drawing pin, Kadin stuck the picture onto the corkboard.

'Who the hell calls their dog Fideccio?' he wondered.

24

Skyguard's Regional Office, Milan, Italy

Sergeant Moretti didn't look at all as Conza had imagined. He was of medium height, round and balding with a permanent look of cheerful surprise in his eyes and on his rounded cheeks. Conza estimated his age to be early thirties. When they shook hands, Moretti grasped his arm with his free hand and grinned, his clear, sharp eyes holding Conza's until they'd finished making their introductions.

The pair set off to walk the short distance to the Skyguard offices, chatting about the missing evidence along the way. Moretti's hands moved in rapid animation whenever he spoke, and Conza found himself smiling as Moretti described the inquisition the commissioner had already begun. As head of the investigation, Captain Brocelli had been subjected to a tirade of accusation, insult and abuse. Conza was glad he had not yet been called upon to provide an account of the brief moments he'd spent in the company of Stolz's missing belongings.

Suddenly, Moretti stopped and grasped Conza's arm, his eyes narrowing with concern.

"Something stinks, Lieutenant. This isn't a case of someone leaving Stolz's stuff in the wrong place. It's really gone, and it didn't walk out of the evidence room on its own."

Almost as soon as he'd finished speaking, the warmth returned to the sergeant's eyes and he smiled.

"We're here," he said nodding to a glazed aluminium door, recessed between two shop windows.

In the first-floor reception area, Conza recognised an enlarged version of the Skyguard logo from Stolz's security card. The walls were covered with photographs of missiles; on launchers against cloudless blue skies or at the moment of launch – streaks of orange flame and white smoke signalling their imminent departure. High up in the corner, a CCTV camera silently watched over them.

They were met and signed in by a tall, slim man with immaculate hair and manicured nails; the head of operations, Lanfranco Pisani. He confirmed Lukas Stolz had worked for Skyguard Industries before taking them through a heavy reinforced door which he unlocked by swiping a red security card across a slim, black box.

They were shown into his glass-walled office but declined refreshments. The meeting lasted around two hours and was of some use. Sergeant Moretti led the questioning in polite, friendly and encouraging tones and much to Conza's satisfaction, made detailed notes and followed up with quick, relevant questions when something new or interesting was disclosed.

Moretti began by asking about the company. *'Good start – get him talking,'* thought Conza, as Pisani launched into an enthusiastic précis of the work undertaken by his employers. He explained that Skyguard Industries was a tri-national enterprise involving Britain, Italy and Germany. The company undertook national and NATO procurement projects, primarily as providers of battlefield defence systems. The policemen were shown a slick and no doubt expensively made film on a giant screen that took up most of one wall. There were images of sleek grey and white missiles on the backs of specially adapted vehicles being dragged into position and firing at unseen targets, and short, grainy clips of recent conflicts in Afghanistan, Iran and Syria. The film also contained graphics depicting the 'Skyguard II Defence System' as a stylised umbrella over a fictional battlefield. The narrative was delivered in English. The deep, dramatic voice spoke in short, powerful phrases littered with technical and military jargon, unfamiliar to the policemen.

When it was over, Sergeant Moretti modestly admitted that much of the film was, "interesting, but quite technical". The manager smiled and nodded sympathetically.

"So, what's your role in all this, Mr Pisani? I mean, where does this office fit in to all that?" Conza asked.

Pisani crossed his arms.

"Much of the Skyguard system is highly sensitive, top secret, as I'm sure you'll understand. But as you've seen, we design and manufacture battlefield and point defence systems."

"You shoot down hostile aircraft?" Moretti offered.

"Yes, and other threats. Missiles and RPVs for instance. Skyguard II acts as a shield against anything that may strike whatever it is we've been asked to protect."

"Hence the umbrella," said Moretti, deciding to pass on an explanation of 'RPVs'.

"Exactly. Skyguard Industries is divided into several offices, manufacturing plants and assembly facilities. The Milan office is primarily responsible for event analysis and logistic support."

"Event analysis?" Conza asked.

Pisani smiled again.

"Each missile firing is called an event, it's our job to analyse the technical data recorded by the system before, during and after each event."

"And logistic support?"

"That's simpler to explain. We manage the contract for all printed materials used by Skyguard II operators." Pisani swept his hand towards a twin-shelved wooden bookcase running half the length of his office.

Pisani told them Lukas Stolz had visited the Milan office last Friday. Stolz's job was essentially technical, and Pisani couldn't elaborate on the reason for his visit, other than to say he'd spent time reviewing the operator manuals. Stolz had hardly spoken to other staff and declined to join them for drinks after work on Friday evening. When asked if Stolz had visited the office on Saturday, Pisani punched a few characters on his keyboard and leaned over his desk to retrieve a print-out.

"Yes, he was in the office, alone, between 07:42 and 15:11 on Saturday."

Pisani didn't think this was an unusual occurrence, so Conza made a note and gestured for Moretti to move on.

The head of operations confirmed that Stolz was a bachelor living in England, but he confessed to knowing very little about the German who'd only visited the Milan office once before and who'd never engaged in more than the briefest of conversations with the office staff, of which there were only three. Moretti took down the employees' contact details but assured Pisani it wouldn't be necessary to talk to them today.

Conza showed Pisani his notebook and the characters 'DLR-EAC1 4D/9C/555'.

"Mean anything to you?"

"No – sorry."

"Do you recognise the term 'FC-Auto'?"

Pisani's face lit up.

"Yes, of course. That's one of the settings for the Skyguard II system." He crossed quickly to the wooden bookcase to retrieve a manual comprising punched, plastic-coated cards bound together with black zip ties.

Pisani turned a page towards them. In English, under the heading '*Fire Control Settings*' was a series of bulleted instructions. The final entry was headed '*FC-Auto*'. Pisani provided an explanation.

"The fire control, 'FC', of the Skyguard II system has various modes, the setting of which depends on the prevailing environment."

Conza looked at Moretti but he shrugged, and Pisani continued.

"Most of this is highly classified and off-limits I'm afraid. Suffice to say that '*FC-Auto*' is one of the modes that the missile system can be set to. Where did you hear the term?"

"It was written in Stolz's notepad."

"How odd," was all that Pisani offered, but didn't seem too concerned.

"Was that where you came across the other characters, Lieutenant?"

"Yes, Mr Pisani – why would you ask that?"

"Curious mind, Lieutenant – that's all."

"Stolz also had a Skyguard key fob that doubled as a USB stick. It's small, square and has the Skyguard logo on it."

Pisani smiled as he pulled out of his pocket a set of keys attached to a key fob identical to that discovered in Stolz's attaché case.

"We call them 'gimmes'," Pisani explained, "marketing trinkets. We've all got one."

Conza took Pisani's keys and twisted the fob so that the USB bayonet protruded.

"Is it likely that Stolz's fob would have anything secret or confidential saved on it?" Conza asked.

Pisani's back stiffened as he snatched his keys back.

"Absolutely not, Lieutenant. Skyguard is practically anal about security. Our computers aren't fitted with USB ports, so it would be impossible to use this to download anything sensitive. In any event, Herr Stolz would never compromise security."

Moretti brought the meeting to a close, and after responding to Pisani's questions about the murder, they thanked him, and were shown out.

They walked in silence until they were back at the piazza. Moretti was first to speak.

"What do you think, Lieutenant?"

Conza gestured towards a bench.

"Truthfully, Georgio, I was pretty certain it was a contract killing, but there are too many inconsistencies."

"The cash and mobile being taken, you mean?"

"Exactly. That doesn't fit the pattern of a hit. Also, Stolz doesn't have the background for a mob contract."

"I must admit, that bothered me too. Why would anyone want to bump off a maths professor?"

"Stolz worked for a government-backed agency. If he had access to state secrets, he would have been vetted, which presumably means he's clean and not likely to get mixed up with criminals or piss them off enough to get taken out."

"Unless there's something that we don't yet know."

"Perhaps. We need to talk to the sister – she's arriving tomorrow I hear," Conza said, flicking through his notes until he found the page headed 'Lukas Stolz'.

"What about his job? He had access to high-grade military data. Is that relevant?"

"I thought about that as soon as I heard he worked for Skyguard. They've been in the press quite a lot over the past two years. But it's all a bit 'James Bond' isn't it? I know someone in England who may be able to help. I keep meaning to call him."

The two policemen sat in the gardens as chattering shoppers and tired-looking office workers strolled by. They didn't speak for a while, but once again, Moretti was the first to fill the void.

"Maybe it was just a really unusual, screwed-up robbery. Maybe we're looking for something that isn't there. His cash and mobile were taken, but not his credit cards. That smacks of an opportunist theft, despite the hole in his head."

"But why leave his briefcase?" asked Conza, staring into the distance. "Men like Stolz usually carry iPads and other valuables in their briefcases. No, it's all wrong."

"And the chauffeur going missing," said Moretti, picking up on Conza's doubts. "His disappearance is another anomaly, but not as concerning as the evidence being stolen."

"I agree."

"So where do we go from here?"

"Well, the first thing you need to know is that I've found the other witness; the girl."

Moretti raised his eyebrows in surprise.

Conza told him about his visit to the bakery and brief encounter with Nyala Abebe. Moretti wrote her name and the address of the warehouse in his notebook.

"How did you know it was a bakery?"

"She more or less told the idiot on the cordon," Conza responded with a grimace, "he just forgot to mention it in his report. I'm fairly sure she knows the Vespa rider. She's terrified but I think she'll talk. I'll go see her again tomorrow. She's a good kid."

Moretti briefly wondered at Conza's final statement but decided to leave it.

"Do you want me to file a report on the girl?"

"No thanks, Georgio, I'll come back to the station and file it myself. But I'd be grateful if you could get yourself on the detail to meet Stolz's sister. We need more on his background. In the meantime, I'll call my friend."

"If you're coming back to the station, you may want to stay out of the commissioner's way," warned Moretti with a grin.

25

Apartment 3, Villa Nuova, Genoa, Italy

Kadin spent most of Monday pacing the apartment and watching television. At lunchtime, while forcing himself to eat the last of the meat from the fridge, he flicked onto a channel reporting on the Hotel Napoli killing. A picture of the front of the hotel appeared, and a female voice in serious tones stated the police had yet to confirm the identity of the victim, but were appealing for witnesses, in particular anyone who saw a man on a motorbike leaving the crime scene. An inner-city map was displayed showing the location of the Hotel Napoli and the route of the fleeing Vespa. Kadin felt sick.

'She hasn't told them' he suddenly realised. The notion produced a strange mix of emotions and he wasn't sure he welcomed the realisation that Nyala had failed to name him as the murderer. It scared him and, for a second, made him wonder whether he'd known her at all. He paced the lounge. *'Maybe she didn't recognise me?'* But he gained no comfort from the idea. He knew it wasn't possible.

'OK, when she saw me, she didn't know there'd been a murder. She was going into town to deliver bread. It's what she always does on a Sunday. Why didn't I remember that before?' he chided himself bitterly.

'It doesn't matter now, focus. When would she have found out about the murder? Probably not until the evening, from the television maybe, or the internet?' Kadin knew Nyala didn't usually follow the news. *'Surely, she would come across it somewhere. Someone would have mentioned it to her. Her father? Her grandmother maybe? Or maybe she still doesn't know – is that possible?'*

Kadin almost laughed, but then it struck him. *'I didn't turn up to collect the rent yesterday and she would have been calling my mobile ever since. Even if she doesn't know about the murder, she knows something's wrong, but she can't get hold of me to find out what. My absence is going to make her ask around. Talk to my family maybe? At some point, she's going to find out the man on the Vespa killed someone and then she's bound to tell the police who that man was.'*

Kadin had reached another dead end, another reason to hate and to cry.

He sat at the lounge window and watched container ships sailing in and out of the port. He paced around the apartment. He thought of his father and cried. He thought of his mother, Soraya and Youssef, and he cried. He thought about Nyala and chewed at the skin around his fingernails until they bled. He tried to see beyond the next hour but couldn't. He had no plan, no ideas, no hope.

He heard himself promising his father that he would, *'stay out of sight, contact nobody and watch the television'*. Instructions he'd been made to repeat, over and over again. *'But what am I waiting for? I will need to buy food. I've got money, but it won't last for ever. Did father pay rent? Bills will start to arrive, surely? There must be an end to all this, but what had father seen as that end? Me, living the rest of my life alone in Genoa? Or eventually being arrested? Or returning home having evaded the police? Does he really believe I could go back to a normal life after what I've done?'*

His father didn't seem to have a plan at all, and constantly Kadin was haunted by the threat hanging over his mother, brother and sister. Would they be burned alive in their beds if Kadin made a wrong decision? Or if he failed to interpret correctly what his father had been trying to tell him.

As far as Kadin knew, the thugs in the barn would still believe he'd followed the instructions given to him.

"When you've finished at the garage, go home and wait to be contacted," that's what they heard Issam say.

'Do they already know that I've disobeyed them? Do they know that I'm not at home? Would it be important to them? Now I have done as asked and the grey-haired man is dead, will they leave my family alone?'

'And my father – what will they do to him? Will they let him live? And why the hell did father think it important that I watch

the damned television – what am I looking for? News of the murder maybe?'

'*None of this makes sense,'* Kadin thought as he fell into his father's bed just after midnight.

Central Police Headquarters, Milan, Italy

Conza and Moretti arrived back at the Central Police Station. Moretti withdrew to a quiet back office to write up the Skyguard interview and Conza found an empty desk in the incident room to type a report on his encounter with Nyala. He printed off a copy and placed it in a new folder that he labelled 'Nyala Abebe'. He left it on the desk in Captain Brocelli's office.

While he was at the police station, he decided to catch up with the active case file.

Europol had conducted a search by name and passport number. Lukas Stolz was 'clean' across Europe and North America. Conza wasn't surprised.

An A3-sized road map of Milan had been produced, on which thin black lines were drawn between dots annotated with times and dates. Conza recognised the triangulated positions of Stolz's mobile phone signal as he'd moved around the city. Stolz's locations correlated with Conza's notes. He'd been tracked moving between the airport, Hotel Napoli and Skyguard's office between Thursday and Sunday of last week. The mobile trace ceased at around the time of the murder. *'The killer wasn't stupid,'* Conza thought.

The murder weapon hadn't been recovered, but the cartridge cases were confirmed as '.22LR Rimfires', a bullet used in a thousand different gun makes around the world.

Frustratingly, Stolz's bank was still refusing to grant authority to trace his bank cards until a formal identification had been made. Stolz's sister was due to arrive tomorrow afternoon at 14:10 on a flight from Stuttgart. Sergeant Moretti had already volunteered to pick her up from the airport and escort her to the mortuary.

CCTV footage taken from the front of the hotel was of little help. Conza flicked through the black and white stills. Evidently, the camera was fixed to the ceiling in reception, just inside the main doors, pointing towards the street. The first picture showed the empty road and pavement immediately outside the front doors. In the upper right quadrant of the second photograph, Conza could see the radiator grill of a Mercedes. The third picture was an image of the back of a tall, slender man carrying luggage as he stepped through the doors. The final photograph was taken a couple of seconds later. The man had moved to the right edge of frame, his jacket and bag still in his left hand, briefcase in his right. There was a note on file that told him CCTV taken from buildings adjacent to the hotel and along the Vespa's escape route were being analysed. Conza smiled. *'Perhaps Brocelli wasn't so lazy after all.'*

As for identification of the Vespa rider, Conza read that little progress had been made, although the Department of Transport had been asked to provide a list of all Vespas registered to owners living in the Milan area.

"Good luck with that," he said out loud, thinking of the thousands of Vespas that littered the city's streets.

Finally, Conza read the statement taken at the home of the missing chauffeur; Sami Ricci. His girlfriend had seemed genuinely distraught; Ricci had never gone missing before and it was out of character for him to go a day without contacting her. A passport photograph of the young man had been clipped to her statement, along with a note saying Ricci's friends and family were scheduled for interview over the next few days.

Satisfied that he was up to date, Conza left for home where he ate reheated pasta and drank a cold beer.

Before going to bed, in his 'QUESTIONS' list, he underlined the words 'Hotel – breakfast?'

At least that was one anomaly he would resolve in the morning.

27

Tuesday

Parco Ticino, Italy

The old pontoon bridge, with its bleached planks and battered barges straddling the Ticino River, is the unmarked entrance to the park of the same name, a narrow strip of forest and scrub hugging the river running south-west of Milan and north-west of Parva.

On summer days, Ticino Park is popular with ramblers and nature lovers. On Friday and Saturday nights, adolescent couples would drive their parents' car down one of the narrow tracks cutting across the wooded floodplain, and in the shadows of pine trees, make promises that wouldn't be kept.

It was Tuesday morning, and on Tuesdays, Gabriele cycled across the bridge on his way to the convenience store where he filled shelves, counted stock and readied the recycling bins for collection.

Gabriele had yet another new love in his life, and today he was grinning to himself as the bike's front wheels met the first of the uneven boards.

The barges' hulls were hollow, which made the dull and heavy knocking sound rise above the rush of the petulant river as it frothed and bubbled in frustration at being divided by the pontoons. He stopped his bike, curious as to the cause of the thumping sound, which was at its loudest just past the centre section of the bridge. Laying his bike on its side, he leant over the grey-painted fence and peered into the dark, foam-speckled water. The thin steel cable that would normally have moored the middle barge to the framework had snapped and was hanging from its cleat into the river. The trailing wire had snagged on a passing tree branch and grey-green twigs scratched spitefully at the prow of the barge in their effort to escape. A thick section of the branch drummed slowly on the hull to the rhythm of the surging water. He tutted and began to turn away, but the flash of pale white bobbing up between a tangle of twigs made him stop. Narrowing his eyes, he stared at the flotsam just a few metres below.

At first, he thought it was just a plastic bag, but leant further over the railing to gain a better view. It was then that he made out the mottled, bloated and ghostly-pale face lying just below the water's surface, the nose and forehead bobbing up into the air as if trying to snatch a breath before sinking gently back below the waves. Each time the face rose to the surface the branch of the tree thumped against the barge.

Clutching the rail in excitement and disbelief, he quickly shifted left to confirm what he'd begun to suspect. In the tangle of cable and branches he could see a pale white ribbon which ended in fingers, gnarled and broken, their tips black and stunted.

Gabriele snatched up his bike and ran alongside it until he'd gained sufficient speed, before leaping onto the saddle. The bridge rattled and bobbed as he sprinted back home, from where he would report that he'd found a lifeless and broken body snagged against the barge bridge in Ticino Park.

A body that the corpse's grief-stricken girlfriend would soon identify as Sami Ricci.

28

Hotel Napoli, Milan, Italy

Conza dropped by his office in Finanza before heading off to the hotel. He wanted to update the colonel on his findings and to advise him that despite his misgivings, he believed the killing of Lukas Stolz should remain a State Police matter. As it happened, the colonel wasn't in, so Conza began drafting a memo, but changed his mind and left a message with the colonel's secretary instead. He asked her to tell his boss that, '*Lieutenant Conza hasn't yet reached a conclusion on the Hotel Napoli murder.*'

...

Conza took the tram and on the way, sorted through the hotel staff's witness statements. He reread them and made a few notes.

The street outside the hotel had been cleaned. Only a dark patch of tarmac bore witness to the violent event committed two days previously. The police cars, vans and ambulances were gone, the cordons dismantled. A sign appealing for witnesses had been fixed to a lamppost.

On the internet, Hotel Napoli was described as '*boutique*' and the prices were set to dissuade the casual traveller. It had a reputation for discreet service and was the venue of choice for city professionals, the well-heeled, and those seeking a quiet venue to further their extra-marital affairs. The rooms were individually styled and offered comfort as well as understated decadence. In each room, the glass-fronted refrigerator contained French champagne and hand-made Swiss chocolates. There was no charge for these *en suite* luxuries; it wasn't necessary. The Napoli didn't encourage the sort of guests that would abuse its generosity.

The foyer was brightly lit by suspended teardrops of steel and frosted glass. The panelling, which extended even into the lift, was teak, inlaid irregularly with brightly coloured ceramic tiles.

The carpet felt like a deep sponge and the reception desk was a wall of red and gold glass cubes, topped with yet more teak.

As he stepped through the sliding glass doors, Conza caught the scent of roasted almonds, which together with the lights, made him think of Christmas and his father. He would have approved of the Hotel Napoli.

Conza was invited into the manager's office and commenced the meeting by asking about Stolz's bill.

"Mr Romano, it says here that Mr Stolz was charged for breakfast in his room on Friday and Saturday morning. Am I understanding that correctly?" he asked, pushing a copy of Stolz's invoice across the desk.

The manager glanced at the dated entries with a stern expression.

"That is correct, Lieutenant – Mr Stolz had room service for breakfast on both those days."

"Then perhaps you could explain why one of your staff swears they saw Stolz eating breakfast in the restaurant on Friday and Saturday?" Conza placed a witness statement in front of the manager.

"May I?" Romano asked with an embarrassed smile as he picked up the document. Conza watched him read it before tapping at his keyboard. He shook his head in dissatisfaction.

"One moment please, Lieutenant," he said, picking up the phone.

"Ask Lucia to come into my office for a moment please."

A short, bespectacled, middle-aged woman knocked before entering. She smiled weakly at Conza and, almost curtseying, stood in front of Romano's desk, hands behind her back, head bowed.

"Lucia, there's nothing to worry about. This is Lieutenant Conza. He has some questions about the poor man who was killed here on Sunday."

Lucia bobbed awkwardly and began to whimper.

Conza smiled. "Lucia, in the statement you gave to the police, you said Mr Stolz had breakfast in the restaurant on Friday and Saturday. Is that correct?"

She wiped her eyes with a well-used tissue.

"It's true sir, Mr Stolz was in for breakfast twice last week. I served him myself."

The manager considered her assertion for a second before rising and pulling at a drawer in a metal filing cabinet.

He handed a sheet of paper to the waitress.

"Lucia, the man you served at breakfast on Friday, what room number did he give you?"

Lucia scanned the entries and pointed.

"Room 29. That's it there. He told me Room 29." She had started to cry again and with a sympathetic pat on her shoulder, the manager ushered her out of the office.

"I think I can explain what has happened," Romano said, once again rifling through the filing cabinet.

He placed in front of Conza a photocopy of an English passport in the name of 'Salterton'. The man in the photograph looked vaguely familiar.

"Mr Salterton stayed in Room 29. I believe it was he who was served breakfast in the restaurant by Lucia."

"Why do you think that?"

The manager placed on the desk a similar image, this time of Stolz's passport.

"Quite a likeness don't you think?"

Conza picked up the two photographs and held them side by side. Salterton was heavier around the chin, and Stolz looked a little older, but the manager was right. There were similarities.

"It's the glasses that make the real difference. One cannot wear them in passport photographs," he stated, picking up a pen from the desk. Conza watched as he drew thick-rimmed glasses on each portrait.

"That's amazing!" said Conza, holding the pictures up. "They could almost be twins."

"Quite. It struck me the day Herr Stolz was killed. Strange isn't it? The other odd thing is that on the same day as the murder, Mr Salterton not only failed to check out, but he left all his belongings behind in his room. It would appear that he left in quite a hurry."

"When?"

"We can't say for certain, but his room was empty when the maid went to clean it at one o'clock on Sunday afternoon."

"Just a few hours after the murder," Conza concluded. "I know this may seem like a stupid question, but are you sure that there were two different people staying with you; Stolz and Salterton?"

The manager laughed.

"In the circumstances Lieutenant, not a stupid question at all, and I would have asked the same had I not seen Mr Salterton at around eight-fifteen on Sunday morning, not long after Mr Stolz had been shot."

"Where?"

"He was in the lift."

Conza held the photographs side by side. Romano was right, it was the glasses.

...

The manager took Conza up to the first floor. Room 41 was sealed off by yellow and black police tape which Conza ducked under before quickly inspecting Stolz's room, which was as he'd left it. A breakfast tray with a half-eaten croissant, empty coffee pot, and some untouched fruit sat on the cabinet under the mirror. The wardrobe and cupboards were empty, and the bed slept in.

"Will we get the room back soon?" asked the manager politely.

"I don't see why not. I will check with the station."

Conza made a note.

Room 29 had been cleaned but remained unoccupied. It smelt of lavender even though the shutters had been thrown back and the balcony doors were wide open. Conza checked the bathroom and opened a drawer in the bedroom before stepping onto the balcony. Three discarded Marlboro stubs had blown against the flaking white posts of the balustrade. The manager tutted, but Conza didn't seem to notice as he leant over the fence. Immediately below, he could see a dark patch of tarmac.

Conza went back inside and paused in front of the mirror.

"Have you got CCTV of Mr Salterton leaving the hotel?"

Romano shook his head in disappointment.

"I asked the duty manager to check yesterday, and the answer is no, I'm afraid. Your colleagues prevented anyone leaving by the main door on Sunday, so he must have left via the basement. There's a fire exit down there, which leads to the rear of the hotel. And that ties in with seeing him."

"Why is that?"

"Well, when I saw Mr Salterton, he was already in the lift when the doors opened. Which means that he must have entered it either on an upper floor or the basement. He didn't get out, and at the time, I merely presumed that having seen the commotion in reception, he decided to return to his room. But of course, he could actually have been on his way down."

Conza considered the manager's hypothesis and nodded in agreement.

"I reckon you've got that spot on. You're in the wrong job."

The two men smirked at each other.

"I don't suppose the rear door has CCTV?"

"Sorry, no. The back-door camera stopped working two weeks ago and hasn't been repaired yet."

They went back downstairs to the left luggage room and Conza picked through Salterton's belongings. He turned over a baggage label and made a note.

"What would you normally do with these in the circumstances?" he asked, pointing at the bags.

"It's happened before. We contact the guest and ship them back to whatever address they give us."

"Have you made contact with Salterton yet?"

"Actually, no. It was the next job on my list."

"Don't. We'll do it. I'll send someone over to collect his things. In the meantime, can I get a copy of Salterton's registration card, passport, invoice and credit card."

"After hearing what Lucia had to say, I asked for all Mr Salterton's documents to be put in an envelope ready for you."

Conza shook his head. "You really are in the wrong job."

When he left the hotel, Conza checked his watch and decided to walk to the Abebe bakery. On the way he called Sergeant Moretti and asked him to carry out a background check on a Peter James Salterton. Conza listened as Moretti repeated the name, address and passport number.

"And Georgio, he came in on British Airways. Check the flights out of Malpensa to the UK on Sunday for a reservation in the same name."

29

Café Roma, Milan, Italy

The policeman sipped nervously at his lukewarm cup of coffee and checked his phone for the fourth time in as many minutes. He was glad lunchtime trade was slow and only two other tables were occupied, but the heat was making his scalp itch and he desperately needed a beer. A crowd of tourists had gathered outside the Ambrosian Library just a few metres from his table, but he ignored their chattering and excited laughter. *'I'll give him one more minute,'*, he promised himself without conviction.

For ten minutes, Giuliani Zeffirelli had been observing him from the corner of a building about a hundred metres away. Satisfied, he strode across the cobbled street and sat down.

"Where the hell have you been? You're late!" exclaimed the ageing policeman in a hissed whisper.

"Relax. I'm here now," Zeffirelli stated with upturned palms before waving the approaching waiter away.

"How's the investigation going?" Zeffirelli asked casually, loud enough to make the policeman wince and look around.

"Keep your voice down…please."

Zeffirelli waited, his gold and platinum-covered fingers clasped together.

The policeman leaned forward.

"The chauffeur's gone missing. Nothing to do with you, I take it?"

"Probably run off with his mistress. You know what a mistress is don't you?"

The policeman briefly visualised the young man he would return home to that evening. He considered getting up and walking away from this vicious bastard but knew that that was an option he'd forsaken a long time ago.

"We've found the girl," he whispered so quietly that Zeffirelli had to roll forward to hear him. The policeman pushed a scrap of paper under the sugar bowl.

"It's the address of the bakery where she works. Her father works there too."

Zeffirelli looked at it for a second before snatching it up. He mouthed the name and address.

"Does she know anything?"

"Lieutenant from Finanza filed a report last night. He's convinced she knows the killer. He's going back out to interview her this afternoon."

"Time?"

"How the fuck would I know!"

Zeffirelli shrugged and took a small blue envelope from his jacket and placed it on the table. The policeman's hand darted out, but Zeffirelli was quicker and pulled it out of his reach.

"Who's the Finanza guy?"

"Conza… Lieutenant Conza." His eyes remained fixed on the envelope.

Giuliani Zeffirelli nodded, stood up, tossed the envelope onto the table and walked away.

"Give my love to your boyfriend," he shouted over his shoulder, loud enough to make those in the queue cease their chatter and stare at the man in uniform.

30

Apartment 3, Villa Nuova, Genoa, Italy

Kadin was already awake when the sun rose above the lush, green foothills of Monte Fasce to the east. His sleep had been fitful, and he'd dreamt of the grey-haired man, guns, BMWs and cameras. But he was surprised his most vivid dream was of his father repeating the instruction, "Stay out of sight, contact nobody and watch television." *'Watch television?'*

Kadin suddenly saw himself sitting on the barn floor. It was early on Sunday morning, and he was pointing at the blinking red light of a camera.

"Do they ever switch those off? Do they ever sleep?"

Surprisingly, his father had laughed but answered him, *"Quis custodiet ipsos custodes?"*

At any other moment in his life, Kadin would have been shocked to learn that his father knew any phrase in Latin, but at the time, nothing could have penetrated the dread that had formed in his frightened mind. His father had translated the phrase for him.

"But who watches the watchers?"

Kadin's eyes widened and he sprinted up the hallway to the lounge. He flicked through the TV channels. An advert for breakfast cereal, news, a cartoon, a weather channel. He stopped pressing the remote and tried to think.

The television was sitting on a long Spanish oak cabinet. Kadin rushed forward, fell to his knees and tore back the double doors. Two shelves, filled with humming black boxes, cables running between them and LEDs shining like small green eyes. At the rear of the cabinet, three of the cables disappeared through a hole, presumably joining the boxes to the television.

The boxes were plain, dimpled black metal, devoid of manufacturers' logos or other markings. Kadin was sure they weren't just satellite receivers or DVD players, and there were so many of them.

He shuffled back to the sofa and scanned the buttons on the remote. He selected 'Source'. On the screen, a menu appeared, giving him the option to select inputs to the television. Three icons: 'Satellite', 'HDMI 1' and 'HDMI 2'. There was a tick next to the satellite icon. He used the down arrow to select 'HDMI 1' and held his breath in anticipation. The screen flickered for a few moments before four black and white images appeared, each in its own bordered quadrant. In the top left square, he recognised the empty forecourt. Top right, the table, chair and tripod lamp. Bottom left, the pallets and ladder hanging on the wall. And in the bottom right square, the steel drum, crate, and sandbag, its frayed top twitching in the breeze.

Kadin slumped back onto the sofa and gasped.

"But who watches the watchers?" he heard his father say again.

31

Milan, Italy

Zeffirelli left the café and darted down a narrow alley before using his mobile.

"Leo, grab Paolo and a police ID and start driving out to Via Enrico Cosenz. It's in Bovisa. Call me when you're on the road."

A few minutes later, his phone buzzed into life.

"You on the way, Leo? Good, yes. Enrico Cosenz. There's no number. You're looking for a bakery."

…

"Now listen carefully. You're going to talk to a Nyala Abebe, write that down. N Y A L A A B E B E, that's right."

…

"She witnessed the Hotel Napoli shooter leaving the hit."

…

"She's young and scared already, so you won't need to get heavy. I don't want this ending up with another body in the river. Have you got that? Keep things simple and don't start throwing your weight around."

…

"She's already been interviewed by a dick called Lieutenant Conza. C O N Z A, yeah. He's convinced the girl knows the shooter. You need to find out a name."

…

"No, she'll talk. Her father might be there, so use him for leverage if you need to. Now listen, this Conza guy is due back there again this afternoon, so you need to get in and out pretty sharpish. OK?"

…

"No, I don't have a fucking time, just don't hang around."

…

"Good, that sounds like a plan. Remember, no unnecessary rough stuff. Salt's getting twitchy and he'll have my dick in a sling if we bring heat on the family."

...

"No, that's fine. Call me when you're done and watch out for that Conza guy turning up."

...

"Yes, OK. And Leo, don't leave there without a name and address."

32

'The Junction' Café, Milan, Italy

Conza reckoned it would take him around fifteen minutes to walk from Hotel Napoli to the bakery but decided to stop on the way for coffee and a sandwich at a café just off the Piazza Giovanni Bausan. He placed his order and sat at a pavement table in the sunshine.

He called Sergeant Moretti, but before he could bring him up to date with developments at the hotel, Moretti's voice rattled in excitement.

"I'm glad you called. The ID check on Salterton, it lit up the system like a Christmas tree. The guy has done time for everything from handling stolen goods to GBH, with a lot of other things in between. Nasty piece of work. He's well known to the Brits. I've put in for a call to the Greater Manchester Police. I also saw his name on the guest list at the Hotel Napoli, but I'm guessing that's no coincidence."

"No coincidence, Georgio."

Moretti whistled when he heard Conza's account of how a man looking like Stolz had fled the hotel shortly after the murder.

"Wow, Raffy, now that is interesting."

"I'm going to take a wild guess that Salterton wasn't in Milan sightseeing. Georgio, find out who he deals with over here, there may be something on his Europol file. If not, ask the Manchester Police, they may have some names."

"OK, I'll get on with it."

Conza was about to hang up when the sergeant suddenly exclaimed.

"Lieutenant, wait…"

"Sorry, Georgio, I'm still here – go on."

"Shit, I almost forgot to tell you. They've found a body snagged up under the Ponte delle Barche in Ticino. From the description it looks like Stolz's chauffeur, Sami Ricci. I think he was tortured to death… Lieutenant… Lieutenant?"

But Conza was already running.

But Conza was already running.

33

Abebe Bakery, Via Enrico Cosenz, Milan, Italy

Nyala had slept with the phone next to her pillow. She'd left twelve messages on Kadin's mobile and had made up her mind that if she hadn't heard anything by morning, she would call Lieutenant Conza. Nyala knew she had no choice and the memory of the policeman's words echoed as she awoke. "He's the one whose life could be in danger and because of what you know, maybe your life too."

She lay in bed and listened to her grandmother preparing breakfast. *'I'll give him until lunchtime,'* she decided as she tapped out another text message.

"I'll have breakfast when I get back," she shouted to her nana as she darted out of the apartment.

It took her just over twenty minutes to jog to the running track in Parco Sempione, where she timed herself over five thousand metres. She was slow. Her legs felt heavy and she found it difficult to control her breathing. She sat on top of the steep grass bank and tried to call Kadin again. Still no answer.

On the way back home, her phone rang twice, and she felt herself panicking in case it was him. But on both occasions, the name on the screen wasn't Kadin's, just clients trying to place bread orders. She let the phone ring until it switched to voicemail.

It was after eleven by the time she reached home to receive a ticking off from her nana for missing breakfast. Nyala could only mutter some excuse about not being hungry, as she retreated to the bathroom to shower and change. While she was getting dressed, she received another call from a customer, but there was still nothing from Kadin.

She picked at a cheese salad her grandmother insisted she eat, but as soon as she could, Nyala slipped out of the apartment and walked round to the bakery to give her father the phone messages.

As she turned the corner into Via Enrico Consenz, Nyala spotted the maroon-coloured Alfa Romeo parked next to the bakery's steep narrow stairs. She stopped and swallowed deeply. It was the police, and she knew that the time had come. She recalled the image of Kadin on the Vespa, ripping the balaclava from his head. She couldn't put this off any longer. *'He's the one whose life is in danger.'*

As she reached the top of the cellar steps, she heard a man's voice, deep and forceful. She was sure it didn't belong to the policeman who had visited her the day before; this voice sounded harsh and almost angry. A sudden chill ran down her neck and she felt her scalp tense. Keeping close to the wall, Nyala tiptoed down towards the half-open door.

"As I've already explained, Mr Abebe, Lieutenant Conza is a colleague. He was going to talk to your daughter today, but got held up, so he asked us to speak to her instead."

"And as I've already explained, my daughter isn't here, and I want to know what this is all about."

"We just want to talk to her that's all." A different voice, struggling to remain calm.

"What about?"

The first man again trying to remain reasonable but assertive: "I'm not your enemy, Mr Abebe. Nyala's in a lot of trouble, she's lied to the police and she's trying to protect a murderer. We need to talk to her. Just to put things straight. Get her story, that's all."

"What murderer? Nyala would never get involved with such a person."

"Does she have a friend, or know anyone who rides a Vespa?" The second voice again.

"Kadin? Kadin Bennani?"

Nyala stepped around the corner of the doorway.

"It's me you need to speak to."

But the tall, thin one with the tattooed neck was not quick enough and she saw his hand closing around the hilt of the knife. She looked away as if she hadn't noticed.

"What do you want to know?" Nyala asked with as much confidence as she could muster.

"Are you Nyala Abebe?"

"What's all this about, Nyala?" her father asked.

She ignored him, but Amadi Abebe knew something was very wrong. His daughter was trembling, and her eyes kept flicking towards – *'What? The bread paddle?'*

"I heard that Lieutenant Conza sent you?" she said, her voice cracking.

Amadi slowly reached out a hand and wrapped his fingers around the heavy oak handle.

"That's right," said the tall one. "Conza asked us to speak to you. Now, where can we find this Kadin Bennani?"

"What department does Lieutenant Conza work for?" Nyala asked, stubbornly ignoring his question.

"What?" Nyala saw his fingers fiddling with the end of the knife.

"It's not a difficult question. You say he's a colleague of yours. So you must know which department Lieutenant Conza works for."

Amadi Abebe's hand slowly raised, drawing the shovel level with his shoulder; neither man noticed, their gaze remaining fixed on Nyala.

"We don't need this shit, Leo," the tall man said angrily, taking a step towards her, his hand opening so that the knife dropped into his palm.

"They're not police!" yelled Nyala suddenly.

The tall man with the knife made to grab her, but Amadi Abebe was poised and the man's head rocked sideways as the oak paddle crashed against his skull with a sickening crack. The man's legs buckled, and he groaned as he landed on his knees, blood pouring into his eyes and onto the stone slabs.

Nyala screamed.

As Amadi had brought the shovel down, the other man had instinctively ducked. Now it was coming back towards him from the other direction and he was caught in a crouched position. Just before the blow struck, he raised his hands in defence and took the full force of the strike on his right forearm, the bones shattering instantly. He screamed in agony. In launching his attack, Amadi had swung himself off his feet, stumbling backwards onto a stack of flour bags.

"Run, Nyala – run!" he boomed so loud that it made Nyala jump.

She yelped, but couldn't run, she couldn't move.

The man on the floor started to rise, pulling himself to his feet using a table leg. Nyala could see the knife in his hand. Amadi regained his balance and raised the shovel in readiness for the next assault, just as the one-armed man reached into his jacket to pull something out. Amadi's face froze in horror, but he managed to shout one last time.

"Run, Nyala!"

The man with the knife lunged at her as she leapt towards the open door. She reached the steps in two bounds, but the explosion of the gun made her stumble forward and she tripped.

Crying and screaming, Nyala Abebe began sprinting up the steps, just as she felt fingers wrap around her ankle.

34

As Conza sprinted into Via Enrico Cosenz he caught sight of a red Alfa Romeo turning right at the far end of the road. He slowed to a walk when he reached the top of the stairs and as he descended, he saw two small pools of blood near the cellar door and specks of red sprayed on the wall near the bottom step. Stopping to listen, he pulled out his service revolver.

"*Polizia*. I'm coming in."

He peered quickly around the door frame. No movement.

"*Polizia*," he shouted again, training his gun on the cellar's interior. Edging forward, he spotted the body lying face-down in front of the open oven. He put his gun back in its holster and ran towards the motionless figure.

The man's sleeves were rolled up to his elbows, the flour on his forearms contrasting with his dark olive skin. Conza knew immediately the man was close to death; his breathing was shallow and Conza's trembling fingers could only find a weak pulse in his neck. He'd also lost a lot of blood; it framed his shoulders and chest in a red shiny pool.

Conza rolled him over and ripped away the blood-soaked shirt. By wiping the man's chest with the side of his hand, Conza found the single bullet hole, below and to the right of the man's sternum. Blood was bubbling out of the wound and the man's breathing began to sound wet and erratic. Conza pulled out a handkerchief and pressed it over the hole.

On his mobile, he thumbed the number for dispatch.

"Lieutenant Conza, badge number 751092, I need an ambulance and police back up at the following address, a man's been shot."

Conza read out the address and checked the man's breathing. He could hear gurgling in his throat and his pulse was weak and slow.

His mobile rang. He put it on speaker.

"You OK?" Sergeant Moretti asked with concern.

"No not really, Georgio. I'm at the bakery. The girl has gone, and the father's been shot. I'm doing my best to keep him alive right now."

"Shit, Raffy. Is help on the way?"

"They should be here soon. Not sure the old man will make it though. He's bleeding pretty badly."

"Did you see who did it?"

"I saw a maroon Alfa leaving the scene in a hurry. Too far away to get a number."

"Do they have the girl?

"I don't know. God, I hope not."

"Maybe she wasn't there, or she managed to get away."

Conza looked back over his shoulder at the open door.

"You could be right, there's blood splatter on the stairs. I don't think it's the old man's and if it's not hers, then maybe she escaped. There's been quite a scrap down here," he added, noticing a clump of black hair matted with blood on the blade of a large oak paddle.

"Did she live there – at the bakery?"

"No, it's just an old warehouse, I never got her home address, but I'm guessing she doesn't live far away."

"I'll contact social security and see if the family's registered. She must go to school. Education may be able to help."

Moretti rang off.

"Shit, shit, shit," shouted Conza, as he pushed his index finger into the wound.

35

Apartment 3, Villa Nuova, Genoa, Italy

K adin stared at the images of the barn. His father had made this happen. He'd somehow wired the system so that the cameras would send their pictures to the black boxes humming quietly in a cupboard in Genoa.

Kadin pushed the rewind button, but the pictures remained static. He got up and looked again at the black boxes. No controls. *'One of these boxes must be a recorder,'* he concluded.

Kadin called up the 'Source' menu again and selected 'HDMI 2'. The screen flickered and suddenly a grainy, close-up image of his father's face appeared in the top right quadrant. The remainder of the screen was black. Seeing his father again made Kadin's chest tighten and he realised he was trembling. He pressed the play button on the remote, but nothing happened.

Kadin found the second remote controller in the drawer of his father's worktable. He pushed the play button and for a few seconds the image became distorted behind a black and white band that flickered and danced across the screen. At the bottom of the image, a date and time box appeared. He was watching a recording of the day his father had failed to return home from the bar – last Tuesday. The screen cleared and his father's face withdrew as he stepped down from the ladder. One by one, the four mini screens came to life as Issam Bennani connected them to the system.

Kadin twitched when he heard the car pull up outside. He ran to the window and saw a middle-aged woman in a blue smock dress slowly pulling herself out from behind the wheel of a battered Fiat.

"Shit – cleaner," he said as he ran to the kitchen.

Snatching up two 100 euro notes and a red felt-tip pen from the corkboard, he scribbled on one of them, *'No cleaning for next 2 weeks – sorry, Issam.'* He pulled out a drawing pin and sprinted to the front door.

Kadin pushed the door gently shut and laid his head against its frame. He heard the lift whine into life followed by the sound of the gates opening and closing on the ground floor. He held his breath. The lift doors opened and closed, much nearer now. A key sliding into the lock. He braced himself. The scratching of fingernails against wood. The metallic rasp of the key being withdrawn, followed by a thin chuckle. The lift doors opening and closing again. The electrical whir of the lift as it descended.

Kadin ran back into the lounge and, crouching low, carefully eased the window closed. The car started and moved away towards the docks. He sat on the floor, his cheeks filling before blowing out in relief.

...

For the next two hours, Kadin watched his father fixing cables into the barn ceiling under the ambivalent gaze of the two men. Occasionally, his father would answer a question or make a comment, but generally, he worked in silence, painfully hauling himself up and down the ladder, his arms straining to compensate for his deformed and strengthless legs.

When Issam Bennani climbed down the ladder for the final time, Kadin watched him explaining how the cameras worked. The short, fair-haired man was called Max. Issam gave Max a tablet-sized monitor and showed him how to turn the cameras on and off. Max pressed the screen, looked up, pressed it again and walked to the next camera to repeat the process. He seemed satisfied.

Kadin laughed out loud and clasped his hands above his head. All the time, these idiots thought the cameras were under their control, whereas his father had wired them so that only the red lights and the corresponding images on their monitor turned on and off. In reality the cameras were always working.

"The watchers are being watched," Kadin said aloud in amazement at his father's ingenuity.

Issam and the two men left the barn and with the film set to fast-forward, Kadin watched shadows dancing across the screen as day turned into night. Grainy images of a fox sniffing the air as it paused on the forecourt, peering at the camera for a few seconds before following the scent of something unseen. Daylight brought crows to peck at the sandbag, but inside the barn, nothing stirred but the odd mouse as it flitted across the dirt-covered floor.

When the recording reached Thursday morning, a car pulled up outside the barn, but the occupants didn't get out. Kadin switched the recording to play in normal time. A few minutes later, the silver BMW pulled into the yard and Kadin sat up. Five men got out of the two cars: Max and the tall, pony-tailed thug, a bald man in a suit, a slender man also in a suit, and a very tall, older man with wide shoulders, an enormous head and long arms. He was wearing slacks and an open-necked shirt.

The large man and bald man embraced before walking towards the barn. *'They know each other,'* Kadin thought. The three others remained in the courtyard and the slender man offered the other two a cigarette, which they accepted.

On the second camera, a shadow filled the bright oblong of the doorway as the large man stopped and held up a shovel-sized hand. Kadin turned up the volume.

"What's with the cameras, Marco?" *'The bald man's called Marco.'*

Marco squeezed past him and picked up the tablet from the table.

"Relax, Alex, they're off – don't worry." Marco showed him the screen. *'The big ugly one's Alex.'*

Alex's giant hand fell away, but he remained staring into the camera.

"What they for?"

"You tell me this job is important, my friend. I take that seriously. I'm guessing this will be your last job, so I want to personally oversee preparations. From a distance," he added with a faint grin.

Alex thought for a few seconds before turning away to drag a chair towards him.

"I hate fucking cameras. And why do you think this will be my last job?"

"Come on, Alex. You've been talking about it long enough. You're ready to retire. We both are. I've always said, when you stop, I will too."

The men sat down opposite each other, and Kadin could now see them quite clearly. Alex's face was pockmarked, his nose pitted and bulbous. He had bushy grey eyebrows that almost met above his nose and he spoke Italian in short, clipped sentences. *'East European?'*

Marco wasn't short, but his rounded waist made him look squat against the bulk of his partner. He fidgeted with his cuffs and pulled at the lapels of his jacket whenever he spoke. He talked in long, thoughtful phrases and cocked his head to one side whenever he asked a question.

"Do we have a target?" Marco asked, feeling the need to change the subject.

"We do. You'll get photographs tomorrow. We don't have much time, he's due to check out of his hotel on Sunday morning. He needs to be taken down before he leaves Milan and don't forget, we need his phone."

"Which hotel is he staying in?"

"The Napoli. It's out in the suburbs. Quiet at the weekends but you set your own agenda. The timing is your call. I'm trusting this to you, Marco."

"And I have no intention of letting you down, Alex."

Alex glanced up at the cameras again and scowled. Marco continued.

"Hotel Napoli, yes, I know it. Very good." His head was still leaning to one side. "Did he bring a car?"

"No, flew into Malpensa. He has a return flight booked on Sunday. I'll send you the details. He'll be collected in a black Mercedes sometime after six-thirty. We don't have an exact time."

Alex sat back in his chair. "Who will you use?"

"Yes, well I've been thinking about that. I've discounted our usual friends. You asked for someone '*disposable*'," he said with relish.

"That's right. I want this one buried once it's over. No traces. Can't you use a druggie? Someone high and in need of a few euros?"

Marco laughed, sure of himself.

"No good I'm afraid. If he's high on crack, he'd never hit the target. If he's been dried out, he's probably…" Marco searched for the words as he fingered his lapel, "too emotional, and more likely to shoot himself than the mark."

Alex was irritated by the bald man's procrastination.

"So who will you use?"

"You've met my techie?"

"The cripple?" Alex stated in disbelief.

"Yes, but not him. His son. He's perfect. Complete unknown, no criminal record and no direct link back to us."

"Will he do it? Can he be relied on?"

"Oh yes. There'll be no problem there, the father is a washed-up alcoholic, and the son loves his family. Sees himself as their protector. No, there'll be no problem there."

"And after. How will you tidy up?"

"Simple; a few days after the hit, the police will receive a tip-off on the murder weapon. It will be discovered along with the boy's blood-stained clothes and they'll trace him back to his low-life, petty criminal father and put two and two together."

"And what will you do with the boy?"

Marco brushed imaginary fluff from his sleeve.

"Oh, I expect the police will find coke under his bed and the whole thing will just go down as one more drug-crazed African kid robbing the rich to feed his habit."

"They won't buy it. It doesn't even smell like a robbery. They're not that stupid."

"Maybe not, but they are desperate. They *will* buy it because it suits them. They won't care. They'll have the killer, the weapon and enough evidence to point at drugs as a motive. After that, they'll stop asking questions. They need to solve murders. We're going to help them." Marco smiled at his own joke.

"Won't the father be a problem – when his son gets wiped out?"

"No Alex, don't worry about the father. If he stays sober long enough to even notice his son has gone, he'll assume his eldest died in tragic circumstances, racked with guilt, topped himself in his bedroom. In any case, I intend sending him the same way as his son. Shame really, despite his drinking, he's been a good technician, but all things must come to an end."

Alex nodded slowly and rose from his chair, his bulk overshadowing Marco, who suddenly looked very small again.

"OK, you seem to have a plan. But don't fuck this up. You know who's paying for this. He plays serious and plays rough. He doesn't ask me questions, but he does expect results."

"I understand Alex, don't worry. This will go like clockwork."

Kadin paused the film and stared at the screen. He'd just witnessed two people reducing the value of his life and that of his father, to a few casual phrases. No doubts, no regrets. *'Are they human?'* he thought. *'Do they really feel nothing?'*

He got up and went over to the window. A small dinghy was sailing out to sea from the marina. Two people on the deck laughed, then kissed. Kadin thought of Nyala and found himself feeling sorry for the men in the barn, but his pity only made him angry.

He fast-forwarded the recording until his father reappeared. It was Friday morning. Marco and Alex had gone, leaving the two thugs to tell his father of the plan. Kadin watched as Issam begged them not to involve his eldest child in the murder of a man he didn't know. They weren't listening and eventually, after being told what would happen to his wife and children if he failed to cooperate, his father sobbed his acceptance and agreed to prepare his son to commit murder.

Issam Bennani's surrender was complete, and Max threw a bottle of whisky onto the floor, from which Issam drank in long, breathless draughts.

But his father hadn't surrendered. It was an act. In reality, he'd fought them with the last shreds of resistance that alcohol and despair had failed to erase. He'd set them up. Kadin knew his father had watched Marco and Alex plot the death not only of some stranger, but also of his eldest child. How had his father felt when he saw and heard them scheming, without remorse, without emotion, except for the bloated arrogance and pride in their ability to arrange the deaths of others?

Kadin was crying. He was exhausted. For a while, the screen remained frozen on the image of his father holding a bottle to his lips, but Kadin couldn't look away, because now for the first time, he thought he understood.

Eventually, he ran the film forward to Sunday morning, the early sunlight lying in thin bands across the barn floor. He saw himself and his father sleeping. They were holding hands. His father stirred and slowly leant over to kiss the crown of his son's head. As Kadin watched this extraordinary moment of tenderness, he knew without the slightest doubt that his father loved him, but he also knew that his father was saying goodbye.

The two men entered the barn shortly after and Kadin watched himself hugging his father before being led away. For a long time after his departure, Issam remained sitting against the wall. Every few minutes, he checked his watch and Kadin guessed he was waiting for the time of the murder to pass.

When the clock on the recording read 08:30, his father rose slowly, his image swapping to the camera at the rear of the barn. He heaved the ladder from the wall and leant it against the beam directly in front of the lens. He went behind the pallets and returned holding a thin nylon rope.

The panic that gripped Kadin's stomach was excruciating. He wanted to switch off the recording, wanted to run back to the barn and save him. Stop him doing what he'd always planned to do but could never tell his son. Kadin bit into a cushion and sobbed as his father slowly climbed the steps, his face suddenly filling the screen. He was smiling. With trembling fingers, Kadin reached out to touch the screen. Issam looked at him and spoke. Gone was his fear, and Kadin knew he was trying to tell him that he'd finally found peace.

"You will not use me anymore and I will never be able to betray my family again. I'm not worthy of them, and I'm sorry that it has taken me so long to feel the love of a father. All of my life, I've been searching for something, if only I'd known that I'd already found it. Please forgive me, Kadin."

113

His son's hurt, anger, love and despair erupted in a long and painful wail.

The bottom left quadrant of the screen turned black as Issam disconnected the feed, and a few seconds later, in the top right image, Kadin watched a shadow rolling backwards and forwards across the floor of the barn.

Guardia di Finanza Headquarters, Milan, Italy

Conza needed to do something to reduce the adrenaline-fuelled anxiety induced by his attempt to keep Amadi Abebe alive. He also had to do something to prevent his thoughts from being overwhelmed by the distinct possibility that the dying man's daughter had been kidnapped, and like Sami Ricci, may end up floating in a river somewhere. *'She's a good girl',* had become a perpetual echo.

He made a fresh pot of coffee and tried to focus on the recently delivered case notes. He needed to find something to repel the dread.

There was a memo confirming Katherine Harper had positively identified her brother's corpse. Another memo told him the tortured body pulled out from the Ticino river was indeed Sami Ricci. There was also a grainy photograph taken on Sunday, by a security camera in Milano Centrale station. Peter Salterton had left Milan by train.

Sergeant Moretti was on his way over as Conza fought to make sense of the past three days. He took up his notebook and walked over to the whiteboard. Using a thick black marker, he drew four columns, labelling them, 'Lukas Stolz', 'Nyala Abebe', '????' and 'Peter Salterton'. Using magnetic strips, he hung the photocopied passports of Stolz and Salterton next to their names. In the Stolz column he added the words 'Contract killing?', 'Robbery?' and 'Skyguard?'. He also added 'Chauffeur', 'Sami Ricci' and 'Tortured to death?'.

In the 'Nyala Abebe' column he wrote 'Knew killer?' and drew an arrow between Nyala's name and the four question marks. He wasn't yet ready to write 'Kidnapped'.

In the '????' column he added the word 'Vespa'.

Under Salterton's name, he wrote 'Known criminal' and 'Stolz's double'. Underneath he added the question 'Milan Associates?'.

"I can help you with that one," chirped Sergeant Moretti, as he knocked on the open door of the office.

"What have you got, Georgio?"

"Before I answer that, how are you?" he asked, nodding at the bloodstains on Conza's shirtsleeve.

"I'm OK. Nyala's father is touch and go, however. He lost a lot of blood and the medics took ages to stabilise him, but they managed to get him back to hospital alive. I've sent a couple of uniforms to watch over him."

"Forensics gone in yet?"

"Yes, they're there now. They'll have no trouble finding evidence. I think one of them got a whack round the head. Every policeman in Milan is on the lookout for the Alfa Romeo. Maybe we'll get lucky."

"Funny you mention luck. I've got some news about Salterton and his associates." Moretti took over writing on the board as he talked.

"Better than associate, actually. Salterton's brother-in-law is one Giuliani Zeffirelli aged forty-three, born in the city, married Salterton's sister Margaret, in the nineties. Been in and out of jail since he was a kid. Assault, GBH, fraud, gun running. He even did time for passing off horsemeat as beef and selling it to the British Army."

"Really?"

"Hey, don't knock it, the scam may have been worth more than four million euros, although the prosecution could only secure evidence for less than one mill."

Conza tutted.

"Anyway, word on the street is that he's still involved in cross-border rackets. Only difference is that this time it's humans instead of horses."

"What? People smuggling?"

"Looks like it, although no one seems to know too much. My contact heard that Zeffirelli recently started arranging transport for fee-paying men, women and children from North Africa through Italy and France to England and maybe Scotland. It's big money too. Poor sods are asked to pay up to twenty thousand each."

"Is Salterton involved?"

"My contact has never heard of him. But maybe he runs the English end of the operation. Manchester Police know all about Peter Salterton, however. He's been under their surveillance twice in the past three years, but they've never been able to dig up enough evidence to make anything stick. He's always managed to stay one step ahead of them. Apparently, he's known as 'Lucky Pete' to his family, and he's been living up to his name."

"Well, I think last Sunday, 'Lucky Pete' had the fright of his life. Either he recognised Stolz and was somehow tied up with him – which seems unlikely. Or he saw Stolz getting gunned down and assumed he must have been the intended target. I have to admit, they do look very similar and he was due to check out the same day. I reckon he got spooked and ran."

"Maybe, and it would explain the torture of Sami Ricci."

"It would. If the target was meant to be Stolz, why murder Ricci? They could have killed him at the hotel. No, Ricci was killed because someone thought he knew something. I think they were trying to find out who carried out the hit. The only alternative is that someone associated with Stolz thought Ricci was involved and took revenge. But, given Stolz's background, that's a little far-fetched. My guess is Ricci had his fingers broken to see what he knew. Stolz's murderer is not the same person who tortured and killed Ricci."

"OK, so someone is trying to find out who killed Stolz before we do. Which would explain why the guys turned up at the bakery. Either Stolz's friends are trying to find out who killed him, or Salterton is doing the same because he thinks the bullet was meant for him."

"I think we can rule out Stolz's friends being behind this, given his background. I think it was Zeffirelli's men who tortured Sami Ricci to see if he knew who ordered the hit they thought was meant for Salterton."

"Exactly. The same guys turned up at the bakery looking for Nyala. The father wouldn't cooperate, he gets shot and they take the girl," said Conza flatly.

Moretti's face tightened and he looked puzzled. He walked over to the board and drew a line under the word 'Robbery'.

"So, you think Salterton believes the bullet was meant for him. If that's true, he must have known it was a planned hit rather than some random robbery."

"We don't believe it was a robbery, Georgio. Neither would he. But go on."

"OK, let's say Salterton was on his balcony and saw Stolz take a bullet to his brain; it spooks him that they look alike. But he's got to take a pretty big leap of imagination to go from there, to believing he was the intended target."

"I see your point but just look at their photographs. Salterton couldn't miss the resemblance and maybe he's paranoid. Maybe he's in Italy for the first time and watched *The Godfather* once too often. He sees a killing outside his window, recognises himself in the dead man's face and panics. Or maybe he's nervous because he's just started working outside of his home patch. Who knows?"

"In that case, if it was a contract killing, why go to the effort of trying to make it look like a robbery? It doesn't make sense. Contract killers don't rob their victims. They wouldn't bother asking for the guy's cash and mobile. They want the world to know that the victim was killed to order. It sends out a message."

Conza was irritated, but knew Moretti had a point.

"Look, I can't see the whole picture yet. I know there are holes. Regardless, I am pretty certain that this wasn't a random robbery, and someone is hell-bent on finding Stolz's killer. My money's on Salterton and therefore Zeffirelli."

"I grant you; it looks that way, albeit with some unanswered questions. But there's something else bothering me. Why try to get to the girl? She told Corporal Sigonella she hadn't seen the killer's face. Why go after her? As far as everyone knew, she didn't know anything."

Conza leant back on the desk and shook his head.

"You're asking the wrong questions, Georgio. First, you should be asking how the thugs knew the names and addresses of the only two witnesses when their details hadn't been released. Second, Sami Ricci made a statement saying he couldn't identify the killer, but it didn't stop them breaking his fingers to see if he'd told us the truth. And third, I wrote a report last night, in which I stated my belief that Nyala Abebe almost certainly knew the identity of Stolz's killer. Less than twenty-four hours later, at least two thugs pitch up looking for her at an address that I'd only just discovered."

"Yes, but Raffy, witness details, their statements and your reports are filed and stored in a restricted-access incident room, in a secure office, inside the most heavily guarded police station in the country."

Moretti's expression suddenly shifted. "Shit, Raffy, you don't think someone at work..."

"Why do you think I asked you to come over here, Georgio?"

37

Abebe Family Apartment, Milan, Italy

When Nyala felt the fingers clutch at her ankle she instinctively kicked out. She immediately knew that her foot had struck bony flesh and she'd heard the man yell as his nose erupted across his face.

She had stopped screaming by the time she reached the end of the road and turned to look back in wide-eyed panic. The man was not chasing her. She wheeled around twice, not knowing whether to go back to her father or to continue running away from the men with their knives, their guns, and their hatred. She'd decided they weren't policemen as soon as she saw the knife, but who were they? What did they want? Whatever it was, it was to do with Kadin and the murder outside the Hotel Napoli. They were trying to find him. The image of Kadin's face swept across her thoughts and she screamed again. The Alfa Romeo was still parked outside the bakery, but she turned away, pulling out her mobile as she ran.

"Police…please send police – they have my father. Two men are there. They have guns and knives. Please hurry."

Nyala tried to respond to the operator's questions, but her mind was imploding, and she could only talk in short breathless bursts between gasps of mucus-filled sobs. She ran up the steps of the apartment block and burst into the kitchen. Her grandmother stared at her in shock.

"Nana, we need to go now," she shouted.

"Nyala, whatever is the…"

"Nana, *now*," yelled Nyala as she rifled through the kitchen drawer and snatched at the blue zip-bag in which her father kept some cash and all their important documents. Her grandmother had never seen Nyala like this but recognised abject fear. Something terrible had happened, her questions would have to wait. She shuffled quickly into the hall and grabbed her winter coat.

"Do we have time to…" she began to say, but Nyala's anguish-ridden eyes stopped her in mid-sentence.

Supporting her under one arm, Nyala steered her grandmother out of the block's rear door and across the narrow strip of grass that ran beside the main rail track. Helping her to climb, Nyala led the way over the embankment, across the rails and down the other side. They followed the line of the railway in the lee of the grass mound and Nyala kept looking back to see if they were being pursued. Her grandmother, pale-faced and breathless, clung to her but didn't protest and didn't ask any questions.

Nyala looked back one last time as they reached the bridge across the Via Bovisasca. They clambered down and followed the road north until they found a café just past the main postal sorting depot.

Apartment 3, Villa Nuova, Genoa, Italy

It was late afternoon by the time Kadin stopped staring at the image of his father's shadow. Something deep within him had changed and he no longer feared them. He may die fighting, he told himself, but he would not allow his father's sacrifice to have been in vain. Kadin knew his father had died so that they could never find out from him where his son was hiding. In ending his life, Issam had also ended the possibility of betraying Kadin again. He had saved his son's life.

Kadin rose from the sofa and went to the bathroom to shower. He needed to wash away the pain, cleanse himself of their hatred. His anger had transformed into fierce resolve and, like his father, he would surrender no longer.

He dried and brushed his hair back with damp fingers.

"Now we fight Papa, together," said Kadin to his reflection. "We are not like them. We are capable of love and we won't let hate win."

Kadin grabbed the pile of euros from the kitchen table and sprinted down the stairs.

He headed towards town. He had a plan, but he needed to buy a mobile phone.

The 'Postbox Café', Milan, Italy

They sat down at a table at the rear of the café and ordered coffees. Nyala's face was puffy, her eyes bloodshot and she was still shaking. Her grandmother grasped Nyala's fingers and waited in silence.

Nyala needed to speak; to confess, to unburden. She couldn't shake off the dread when she pictured her father and she was terrified of telling her grandmother that she'd abandoned her son, her only son, to men with knives and guns. But Nyala knew she could no longer face any of this alone.

So, slowly, in whispers, she began to tell her grandmother everything that had happened since she stood on the Via degli Imbriani, watching a Vespa speed past. Her grandmother listened without comment, glassy eyes fixed on her granddaughter's face. Even when Nyala began to cry in anticipation of telling her about her son and the two men in the bakery, she tried to comfort her with a supportive smile.

But before Nyala could confess, her phone rang, and she snatched it from her pocket. The number was from an 'Unknown Caller', and for a second, Nyala wanted to hang up, but somehow not answering it seemed infinitely worse, so she pressed the green telephone icon and listened without speaking.

"Nyala. Is that you?" she heard Kadin ask gently.

September 1989

Leipzig, East Germany

The university in Leipzig hadn't reopened in September and Lukas Stolz, the third youngest faculty head in its five-hundred-year history, found himself without a class to teach.

As a child, Stolz's tutors had been astonished at his ability to solve complex mathematical puzzles. When the other children played with their toy cars or kicked a football around the park, young Lukas would play with prime numbers and quadratic equations. He had grown up with numbers, lived with numbers and had learned to love them.

But now he'd been thrust into the midst of a rebellion and he would never again hear the claps and cheers of his students as he solved the Rubik's cube puzzle in a matter of seconds. He'd always lived life in discernible and wholly predictable patterns. Now, nothing was predictable.

He recognised the faces of his students amongst those holding banners or lighting candles to friends who had fallen in their attempt to win the 'freedom' that had been so obviously absent in their lives. At first, he'd remonstrated with them, but it was clear that he'd suddenly become the personification of everything they had come to detest.

One night he found himself surrounded by baying students in Wilhelm-Külz-Park and some of the demonstrators recognised him. An argument resulted in him being been punched so hard, that he blacked out for a few seconds. When he came round, he was being dragged out of the park by two young female students who'd seen fit to save him from a further beating. His nose was bleeding profusely and when he tried to thank them, they hadn't hidden their scorn.

"You're running out of allies, Professor – your time is over. Soon there'll be nobody left to save you."

He went back to his college rooms and washed his face. His nose was broken. The blue-red swelling had already spread around his eyes and along the top of his cheeks.

'They don't know how lucky they are – they never will.'

Spoiled as children by a state that had provided them with a first-class education and intent on spurning the opportunity to make their country better, stronger, smarter. They didn't feel compelled to give back, they had no loyalty, no conscience. Like the Americans they were desperate to emulate, they just wanted to take, to gorge, to waste, to value nothing.

From his kitchen window, he watched the light of a thousand candles as they bobbed along Neumarkt and he knew they were right, at least about one thing. His time was very nearly over. He was twenty-nine years old and his ordered life was being dismantled. It depressed him.

The following morning, with small wads of gauze pushed into his nostrils, he left Leipzig, returning to his father's home in Potsdam to prepare for the end of the world.

41

The 'Postbox Café', Milan, Italy

Nyala ran out of the café with the phone still squeezed tightly against her ear. "Wait Kadin, I need to go outside."

She darted around the back of the building, out of sight of the road.

"Kadin, where the hell are you?"

"I had to run away Nyala, but I've stopped running now, I'm so sorry."

Nyala sobbed pitifully, but a burning anger rose up through her chest.

"Sorry Kadin? Sorry means nothing right now. What the hell have you got me into? I'm standing in the back yard of a café, terrified. Dad's been shot and I've had to grab Nana and run. It's me who's in hiding, Kadin. What have you done?"

"Nyala, stop, I don't understand. Who shot your dad? Is he OK? Why are you running?"

Nyala told Kadin all that had happened since she'd seen him on his Vespa on Sunday morning. When she recounted the tale of the men in the bakery and her father screaming for her to run, she heard a faint whimper. Her grandmother had been standing behind her the whole time.

"Kadin, I have to go. Nana is with me. I need to find somewhere to hide and I have to find out if my father is alright."

Her grandmother was pale with shock and Nyala thought she may faint.

"No, wait Nyala. My family's in danger too. But I need your help. I can't do this without you."

"Do what, Kadin?" Nyala asked as she clung to her grandmother's hand. "I still don't know what you've done."

Kadin was dreading this moment but knew it was the first step to some kind of redemption.

"I killed a man, Nyala. They made me. I can't explain everything now, but you must trust me, please, I need you to trust me."

Nyala looked down at her nana who had started to cry, but she nodded at her granddaughter.

"All right, Kadin, what do we need to do?"

42

Apartment 3, Villa Nuova, Genoa, Italy

Kadin sat in the apartment and stared at the mobile phone, wishing he could still hear her voice. The news about her father being shot and Nyala being on the run, left him feeling confused and powerless.

But he'd forced himself to think clearly and eventually, Nyala had agreed to go along with his plan. She trusted him and her faith had helped to restore some semblance of self-belief. But he only had until one o'clock tomorrow to get things ready, and there was much he needed to do.

Rewinding the film back to the beginning, he began noting down the times and dates of all the key events. He needed to be able to take the police through the film in a planned and logical way. He worked quickly and after an hour, had reached his father's suicide. He let the recording run on at high-speed, and after the clock had moved forward a couple of hours, the two thugs and Marco reappeared. Kadin pressed play.

"Find a shovel and bury him out back. It appears Mr Bennani was more emotional than I'd realised. Shame, he was good with a camera."

The men disappeared and Kadin saw the man with the pony-tail fetch a shovel from a wooden lean-to at the side of the building. They took turns to dig.

Kadin watched as they lifted his father's corpse and half carry, half drag it to the pit.

'He can't feel anything anymore, they can no longer hurt him.'

"Can you believe it? He left a suicide message," said Marco laughing. "Quite moving it was, I watched it live. Shame his family will never get to see it. Very touching," he added, as the men kicked dirt over the body.

In the darkest corner of his mind, Kadin imagined shooting Marco between the eyes. The image was brief but made Kadin angry with himself.

When the three men went back into the barn, Marco turned to them.

"OK Max, how did it go?"

"All fine, killed him with the first shot." Max pointed to the centre of his forehead. "He got the mobile."

"Did he get away all right?"

"As far as I know. We couldn't follow. He was driving like a maniac and it would have drawn too much attention to keep up with him."

"No, that's fine – he'll be at home by now. Did you pick up the phone?"

Max pulled out the grey and silver sleeve.

"When you've dropped me off, take this over to Alex's contact, he's waiting for it." Marco pressed a piece of paper into Max's hand. "Address is on there."

"Did you see him at the station?" Marco asked as they were walking towards the door.

"I thought so, but I lost him when I went to get the phone out the bin."

The men stopped in the forecourt.

"Excellent, so now we wait until Wednesday. That should be enough time to make them desperate. We tip off the cops about the garage. It shouldn't take them long to work out the owner is Bennani. On Wednesday morning, wait until the boy's mother takes the kids out and then go in and put him to sleep. Make it look like suicide. Like father, like son. And Max, don't forget to leave a bag of something in the boy's bedroom."

'Nice and simple,' said Marco to himself with a grin as he pulled open the car door. *'Alex will be pleased.'*

43

'Benito's', Via Mercato, Milan, Italy

In the dimly lit bar off Via Mercato, Sergeant Moretti ordered beers and turned to Conza.

"The problem is, we don't have enough on Zeffirelli to arrest him. All we've got at the moment is a theory."

Conza agreed. "Forensics will have a field day at the bakery. Let's hope he was there. I forgot to ask you; how did you get on with Stolz's sister?"

"Katherine Harper. She's a nice lady. Educated, rich, married an English guy, moved back out to Germany when she became a widow, a couple of years ago. Told me she'd only been reunited with her brother since last Autumn. They'd been separated as kids. Sad story."

"Tell me, I need cheering up."

"No, really. Her mother worked in the East Berlin underground, helping families escape to the west over the wall. Brave woman by all accounts."

"Sounds it."

"She was shot by an East German patrol one night. Katherine was with her. Apparently, a woman with a child was less likely to be stopped by patrols. They managed to get to a hospital in West Berlin, but she died a few days later."

"Shit, that really is sad, Georgio. Sorry. How old was Katherine?"

"Ten. From what she told me; she was lucky to get out alive. When her mother died, she was taken in by the family they'd helped escape. They took her to England in '69. She wasn't allowed to return to Potsdam. Too dangerous."

"So she lost contact with the rest of her family?"

"There was just her father and brother. She used to get the odd message from her father, via escapees."

"So how old was Lukas when his mom died?"

"He would have been sixteen. She said her father never told Lukas how his mother died."

"That's strange. Why not?"

"She said her father was trying to protect him. The less Lukas knew, the less danger he was in. Apparently, he told him his mother and sister had been killed in a car accident."

"You would think he would have been told the truth when he grew up though, wouldn't you?"

"I asked her that. She was a bit vague. I got the impression that there'd been a rift of some sort, between Lukas and his father."

"But she knew she had a brother. Why didn't she contact him after the wall fell?"

"She did, kind of. Well, she met her father Dieter Stolz in Berlin in 1990, just before he died."

"Lukas wasn't with him?"

"No, just Dieter. They hadn't seen each other for more than twenty years. Very tearful reunion by all accounts. They visited Mrs Stolz's grave together and laid flowers. But something happened in Berlin that day, I'm certain of it."

"Why do you say that?"

"Because her brother wasn't there. When I questioned her about it, she became really defensive. Kept saying it was a family matter."

"But she must have asked why Lukas wasn't there to see her. Father and daughter reunited after God knows how long, surely she would have asked where her brother was."

"I'm pretty sure she did, but whatever the old man told her, it was enough to keep brother and sister apart for another twenty-eight years."

"That's terrible. What do you think happened?"

"I've no idea. She just refused to talk about it. I didn't press her. She was still in shock over Lukas's death and it sounded like a family matter."

"But eventually they were reunited. How did that come about?"

"She wrote to him. Tracked him down via Skyguard."

"When?"

"Last summer."

"It must have been a hell of a shock for Lukas to find out his father had lied to him all that time."

"Must have been. She said the story of how his mom died hit him pretty hard too."

"I bet it did."

"It would have broken me, I think," said Moretti earnestly. "All those lies."

The two men sipped their beers in silence for a few minutes.

Conza had been thinking.

"Why last year? Why did she contact him after all that time? What had changed?"

"I asked her that. All she kept saying was that it was 'the right time'."

"That's odd."

Conza took out his notebook.

"So, her brother was brought up in East Germany. Did she tell you anything else about him?"

"Not much. They only met once. As adults, anyway."

"And she couldn't think of a reason why anyone would want to kill him?"

"It's funny, but when I asked her that, she took a long time to answer. She did say he was a gentle man. Abhorred violence. But she never did answer the question."

"When's she going back to Germany?"

"Tomorrow evening. His body can't be released yet, so there's no point in her hanging around."

"I'll talk to her. Where's she staying?"

"The Castello."

"Expensive tastes. I'll drop in on her in the morning."

Conza ordered another beer while Moretti went outside to take a phone call.

132

44

9th November 1989

Stolz Family Home, Potsdam, East Germany

Lukas Stolz hurried past the excited crowd congregating on the steps of St Nicholas Church in the old market area of Potsdam. A hundred candlelit faces singing about a new world, a new life, a new Germany. Their collective voice depressed him, and he avoided looking up as he shuffled across the road.

The Berlin Wall was about to fall.

For weeks, at the library, in shops and in cafés, he'd heard them whisper about their secret meetings, their ambitions, their plans. Then they'd stopped whispering and they started talking; openly. And they no longer went silent when he entered a room. Then they stopped talking and they started shouting – and singing.

East German society as he'd always known it was being vandalised. By the talkers, the shouters and the singers.

Throughout autumn, civil unrest spread through towns and cities like a virus. By mid-October, Potsdam's military curfew collapsed. People congregated without fear, unopposed by the soldiers sent to suppress and disperse them. Trepidation had been replaced by resolve and there was no one willing to stop them. There were simply too many dissenters and too few soldiers. '*Freedom*' and '*liberty*' were on the lips of every East German. *'Self-determination'* was the returning Messiah. Lukas Stolz didn't understand.

"As far as I can see, freedom," Lukas preached to his father, "is the right to act as criminals. To destroy the fabric of society. To sow disorder and dissent. To bite the hand that feeds."

His father didn't respond, he'd been in the congregation of too many of his son's sermons. Dieter Stolz was dying. But by will alone if necessary, he was determined to drag his tumour-ridden body on one final journey before it succumbed. He would make that journey soon.

But tonight, along with the rest of East Germany, Stolz and his father were fixed to the television news. The unusually awkward presenter was close to tears as she announced that the government would, with immediate effect, permit all citizens to cross the border into the west.

Lukas Stolz clenched his fists in fury. East Germany had been betrayed, exposed and thrown to the EEC and the Americans. He scowled as the cheers of his neighbours rolled down Schlaatzstrasse.

He didn't notice that his father was smiling or that his eyes had filled with tears of joyful relief.

45

'Benito's', Via Mercato, Milan, Italy

Conza had ordered their fourth beer by the time Moretti returned, still holding his mobile.

"That was my wife. I've only known you a couple of days and she hates you already."

Conza looked at his watch.

"Sorry Georgio, but between you and me, your wife's in good company. I seem to have that effect on most women."

Moretti grunted as he retook his stool at the bar.

"She knew I was a policeman when we married. She'll be all right."

He emptied his glass.

"This case, Raffy, so many holes. The evidence going missing for a start. I've been thinking."

"I'm all ears."

"We're presuming Salterton ordered Zeffirelli to dig around for the killer. But Zeffirelli doesn't have the clout to remove evidence from a police station, and even if he did, it wouldn't help him."

"I know. So why was Stolz's stuff taken?" Conza agreed, as the beers arrived.

They sat in silence for a few minutes, thinking and drinking.

Conza suddenly set down his glass.

"Let's start from the beginning. Just forget Salterton for a second. A visiting maths professor is shot. It looks like a planned hit, but oddly, his cash and mobile are taken. In the absence of a reasonable motive, we would have to conclude that it was a botched, albeit pretty odd, robbery. Do you agree?"

Moretti fingered the top of his glass and nodded.

"Subsequently, the victim's luggage goes missing – so what? There must be two hundred pieces of evidence passing through the station every day. If whoever killed him needed Stolz's belongings, they would have taken them when he was shot. That would still apply even if the wrong man had been murdered. If it was a robbery, what was left behind is hardly relevant. Either way, they're just the personal possessions of a murder victim. If other things hadn't happened, we wouldn't spend a second wondering who took them. We would conclude that they'd been misfiled or put on the wrong shelf. It happens all the time. The widow, or sister in this case, would receive a letter of apology from the commissioner, blaming budgetary cutbacks for the loss of her brother's washbag and a few shirts."

"OK," said Moretti, "so the missing evidence is just a distraction, an unfortunate coincidence?"

Conza waved at the barman and pointed at his glass.

"That's what I think. Forget the missing luggage. Stolz was just in the wrong place at the wrong time. We need to find out who wanted Salterton dead. We also need to find Zeffirelli."

"Maybe."

On the bar, Conza's mobile vibrated. He looked at his watch, sighed and answered the call.

"Lieutenant Conza."

"Is my father dead?"

Conza clutched Moretti's arm. "Nyala. Where the hell are you? Are you all right?"

"We're going where they can't find us. Is my father dead?"

Conza held the phone from his ear so that Moretti could listen in.

"He's been seriously injured. I'm so sorry. He's got a collapsed lung and there's a lot of damage to his spleen. He lost a lot of blood. They've put him in an induced coma, but he's under police protection. He's safe for now."

"Will he live?"

"Doctors say it's not looking so good, Nyala. I'm so sorry."

The phone went quiet and Conza could hear her trying to draw breath.

"Nyala, were you at the bakery when the men came today?"

"Yes, I was there, but I had to run. My father was screaming at me and they started shooting." Conza could hear regret in her voice.

"Nyala, did you recognise the men? Had you seen or met them before?"

"No, I didn't know them and nor did my father. They said they were policemen. Colleagues of yours. They wanted to know about the Vespa rider."

"Colleagues? Did they mention me by name?"

"Yes, they said Lieutenant Conza was due to visit me, but you'd been held up and had asked them to come instead."

Moretti closed his eyes and shook his head in despair.

"They were trying to find the man on the Vespa. To kill him, I suppose?"

"Yes, that's exactly what I think they intended. They came to the bakery because they think you're the only person who knows who he is and where he is."

"I do know who he is. The man on the Vespa. I've spoken to him, but I don't know where he is. That's the truth."

Conza didn't speak. He needed her to fill the void, break the silence, help him to save her life.

"He wants to speak to you."

Conza could hardly believe what he'd just heard. Moretti punched the air.

"OK, does he want me to phone him or meet him somewhere?"

"No, he'll call you. He has your number, but there are three conditions."

Conza took out his notepad.

"Go on."

"One, you must promise that as soon as this call's over, you place his family under some sort of protection. Two, when he calls you, you must give me your word that you won't try to find him until you've investigated what he has to say. Three, you must swear you won't try to find me or my grandmother."

Moretti mouthed, 'We can't.'

Conza ignored him.

"OK Nyala, I promise you I won't ask where you are, or where you're going, but you must promise me something."

"What?"

"You must promise to call me when you get to wherever you are going. I won't trace your call and I won't contact you unless I believe your life's in danger, but we need to stay connected."

Conza heard her hand cover the phone mouthpiece and he guessed that his demand was being discussed with whoever she was with. *'Is Stolz's killer with her?'*

"OK. I agree, but what about the other two conditions?"

"That's fine. I agree, Nyala, but I need to tell you I'm not happy about it, his life's in grave danger."

"Lieutenant, please don't talk to me about what makes you happy. I really couldn't care less. My father may die, and I'm running for my life. Your happiness doesn't come into it."

"I'm truly sorry, Nyala. I arrived at the bakery just after your father was shot."

He could hear her crying.

"Don't let him die, Lieutenant, please."

"From what I can make out, your father fought off those guys so you could escape. He's strong. You both are."

"Thank you, I don't feel very strong right now, so I hope you're right."

Conza listened and took detailed notes as Nyala described the men who'd shot her father at the bakery. Moretti was listening and suddenly waved a beer mat at Conza; on it he'd written a name 'Leo Calpresi'.

Just before the call ended, Conza heard a tannoy announcement in the background. He made a symbol of an aeroplane. Moretti gave him the thumbs up.

"OK, I have to go now," said Nyala. "I hope to God I can trust you, Lieutenant Conza."

She paused to take a final deep breath.

"The man you are looking for is Kadin Bennani."

46

'The Manor House', Hatchmere, Cheshire, England

Salterton was adjusting the security cameras on the console when his mobile rang.

"Talk to me, Giuli, what did you find out?"

"We got a name. Kadin Bennani."

"Do you know him?"

"Maybe. I know an Issam Bennani. Could be related. I'm having it checked out."

"What's Issam Bennani's background?"

"Libyan immigrant. He's a technician. Bugging, wiretaps, surveillance stuff. Pretty good at it by all accounts. In recent years, he's done work for a guy called Marco Fanucci."

"Fanucci. What's his story?"

"Runs covert stuff. Blackmail, extortion, bringing down security, that sort of thing."

"So, do you think this Fanucci wants me dead?"

"We're on it Salt, believe me. I'm working every hour on this. I'm trying to track down Fanucci through a mutual contact."

"If this fuck wants me dead, I want to know why, Giuli. And if it turns out it's down to your new operation, I swear..."

"Come on Salt, give me a break. I'm not behind this and neither is the operation. I'm as pissed off about this as you are. If they want you dead, I'll be next on their list."

"OK, so remember that when you speak to this Fanucci. Now, where did the girl say this Kadin Bennani was hiding?"

"The boys didn't get that far. They were pretty badly beaten up."

"Which boys? Leo?" Salterton asked in amazement. "Beaten up by a girl?"

"It was the father. Leo has a broken arm and Paolo's got a cracked skull. They're in bad shape."

"Where are they? Not in hospital? Please don't tell me they're in a hospital."

"I might be crazy, but I'm not stupid Salt. I sent them up north. They've got a private doctor. He's on the payroll."

"Where's the girl now?"

"She made a run for it. She knows the shooter, which is why she ran, but she won't get far. I've got people asking her friends where she might go. Her flat's empty, but we're on it. My guess is when we find her, we'll find Bennani."

"Any other leads?"

"No, but neither have the police. The shooter's disappeared."

"For Christ's sake, Giuli, my wife's gone to stay with her sister, the floodlights are on all night and I'm paying three ex-marines nearly five thousand a week to play hide and seek in the flower beds. When are you going to find out what the fuck is going on?"

"Salt, I swear I don't know what's happening. I've got people asking around about Issam Bennani and once I confirm he's related to the shooter; I will find him."

"Well, you'd better find him – and quick. In the meantime, we should stop trading."

"No, no, we don't need to do that Salt, I'm sure this is just some misunderstanding. I'll sort it out. I am sorting it out."

The phone slammed down and Zeffirelli knew it was just a matter of time before his wife's explosive brother started taking matters into his own hands.

47

Central Police Headquarters, Milan, Italy

As soon as Nyala's call ended, they hurried the short distance to Police HQ, from where Sergeant Moretti, with the blessing of the duty captain, organised the collection of the Bennani family.

Moretti chose two officers who were known to him but hadn't previously been involved in the Stolz case. He told them they were being deployed under the instructions of Lieutenant Conza, and that Captain Brocelli would be informed. They were ordered to take the family to a small chalet in Cambiago, a village between Milan and Bergamo; a Finanza-funded safe house. Nobody was allowed to write the address down.

Conza stopped the guards as they were rushing out of the station.

"Just to be clear, no one enters that house unless you see me or Sergeant Moretti standing next to them."

The two young policemen nodded and ran off to collect an unmarked SUV from the garage. Conza and Moretti sat in an interview room to decide what to do next.

"I need to call Captain Brocelli," said Moretti anxiously.

"I know," we've just got to work out what to tell him. This station leaks like a sieve, and we have to assume everything we tell Brocelli will get back to Zeffirelli."

"I know you made promises to the girl, Raffy, but we can't keep this to ourselves. If the girl's story turns out to be a pile of crap, we're guilty of assisting a self-confessed murderer. The commissioner would have our guts."

"She's not lying. Why would she? She's just seen her father get shot and she's running scared."

"We only have her word for who put a bullet in her father. What if it was Bennani who shot him, and she's trying to buy time for him to escape?"

"But you recognised Calpresi from her description."

"True, but what's to say that Bennani wasn't with him?"

"That's stretching it a bit far, Georgio."

"All right, I accept it's unlikely, but we're still taking a big risk by basing everything on the word of a runaway with a track record of lying to the police."

"I was there, Georgio. I saw with my own eyes the aftermath of a fairly big fight. I think the father landed some blows on whoever it was who attacked him and at least one of them has a bent skull. There was blood on the stairs. All of it matches Nyala's story of how she escaped."

"And I agree that she may be telling us the truth, but we can't take everything she says as gospel."

"So, Georgio, answer me this, why burden yourself with the grandmother? If Nyala was trying to escape and buy time for Bennani, why would she take an old lady with her?"

"That's just a neat solution to a practical problem. She's a minor and wouldn't be able to get through border control on her own."

Moretti showed Conza his notebook.

"These are the flights that left Malpensa within two hours of the phone call."

Conza read the page. Nine flights: Munich, Ibiza, Bari, Paris, Vienna, Düsseldorf, Birmingham, Abu Dhabi, and Palermo.

"I've asked for a check on all of them," Moretti said without making eye contact.

"OK Georgio, I agree we have a duty to find out where she's headed. But trust me, I'm not going to try too hard."

Moretti shrugged.

"And as for Kadin Bennani, he hasn't confessed yet, at least not to us. He's calling us tomorrow and even if we do nothing until then, we won't be losing anything. We have no idea where he is and the only person who could tell us, is already halfway to Dubai or Spain. Let's face it, Bennani's just a suspect who has been brought to our attention. We'll follow it up tomorrow and if he doesn't call, I'll be the first to tell Brocelli. But until then, Nyala's phone call stays with you and me. Agreed?"

Reluctantly, Moretti nodded.

"In any case, we'll soon have Bennani's family in a safe house, so that has to count for something when it comes to persuading him to give himself up."

"What about the safe house?" asked Moretti.

"It's been cleared by the colonel, and he agrees that in the circumstances, Brocelli doesn't have to know the address. He said he'd call the commissioner to tell him what's going on and get retrospective authority for sending two guys up there as protection."

"In that case," said Moretti standing up, "all we can do is wait for Bennani to call."

"Georgio, do me a favour, go out to the safe house in the morning, talk to the family. See if the parents can shed any light on things."

"Will do Raffy," Moretti said, sighing as he checked his watch. "I'll be able to make an early start, I'm in the spare room again tonight."

48

Malpensa Airport, Milan, Italy

Mazaa and Nyala Abebe sat in the sprawling airport concourse and devised a plan of their own. Nyala was genuinely shocked at her nana's conspiratorial attitude, and how quickly she'd embraced the necessity of putting distance between Nyala and her son's attackers. She'd gained strength from her grandmother's resolve and although they'd wept together, they seemed to enter into an unspoken pact; a mutual understanding that grieving for Amadi would have to wait.

They counted the money in the zip-bag and checked their passports. They soon realised that they didn't have enough cash for a flight and accommodation for more than a couple of nights.

Mazaa looked up at the departures board and read aloud the names of the destinations as they clicked and whirred into view.

"Birming – ham," she said suddenly, pronouncing it as two words.

"Birmingham," she repeated as if remembering the name whilst grabbing Nyala's arm.

"Your Uncle Ephrem. He lives in Birmingham. We took you there once, don't you remember?"

Nyala knew she had an uncle living in England but had no recollection of visiting him.

"Are you sure, Nana? I've never been to England."

"Yes, you have. We all went, just after the funeral."

"Whose funeral?"

"Your mother's," she announced, suddenly realising her mistake.

"Of course, Nyala, you were just a baby, you wouldn't remember."

Nyala could see her grandmother's eyes start to fill again as the memory of yet another family tragedy came flooding back.

"It's fine, Nana, don't worry. I don't remember, but it's not important. Do you know if Uncle Ephrem still lives in Birmingham?"

"Your father's phone. Ephrem's number may be saved in it."

"Shit," Nyala gasped, her hands clasped to her mouth. "Wait here," she shouted as she ran off down the concourse.

She returned a few minutes later, the phone in her hand.

"Kadin told me to get rid of it after we talked to the policeman, so I turned it off and threw it in a bin."

They looked at each other and spontaneously erupted into a laugh so loud that other travellers turned to look at them.

Nyala grinned when she found her uncle's number and for a few seconds, Nyala and Mazaa Abebe hugged each other and laughed again.

49

3rd January 1990

Berlin, Germany

Lukas Stolz's life in Germany after the wall fell seemed surreal. He couldn't ignore the widespread sense of optimism, nor fail to hear the talk of '*hope*' and '*opportunity*'. They were all deluded, of course. The people had surrendered. Confessed their collective failure. They need only prostrate themselves before the altar of the holy trinity: '*money, choice and liberty*'. Absolution was the gift of the west. And the west's sanctimony in pardoning them of their sins was unfettered.

Everything he'd once held important was suddenly '*prehistoric*' or '*prohibitive*'. Achievement, invention, progress, imagination; if it emanated from an ex-Soviet state, its importance was reduced to nought. Stolz knew that history was written by the victor, but these victors were tearing out entire chapters. 'East Germany' had been reduced to a footnote. No one listened to him anymore. His was a whisper amidst a cacophony of betrayal.

But faced with the overwhelming optimism of his countrymen, he was forced to admit the battle had been lost. He was compelled to come to terms with the reality of a unified Germany.

In early January, and despite persistent snow showers, Dieter Stolz asked his son to drive him to Berlin so he could visit an old friend. Lukas knew his father was dying; that he was starting to say his goodbyes. But they didn't speak of such things. For much of Lukas's life, they had rarely spoken about anything.

Stolz dropped his frail and jaundiced father near the Brandenburg Gate and parked his Trabant on Französichestrasse. It was snowing again, and the red bands of the Fernsehturm tower were obscured by a dense white curtain. The buildings took on a dull, grey hue in the half-light and people shuffled along the grit-strewn streets, heads down, collars raised. His shoes were leaking at the seams, and his toes ached. He rubbed his nose with the back of his hand. It still hurt whenever the weather turned cold.

At the end of the road, he turned right and gingerly picked his way down Niederkirchnerstrasse, which was bordered on one side by the now broken, graffiti-covered wall. The ragged gaps in the concrete and steel offended him, and he imagined rivers of corruption flowing through the holes and settling in septic pools across the east.

He found the house near the U-Bahn station in Spittelmarkt. Like his father, he also wanted to visit an old friend.

...

Four hours later, Lukas Stolz sat in a tourist café on the Unter den Linden and thought about the conversation he'd just had with the retired Stasi major. It seems that not everyone in East Berlin had rejoiced when the wall was breached.

He was not alone after all.

50

Wednesday

Milan, Italy

In the early hours of Wednesday morning, Conza took a call from the safe house. Mother, brother and sister of Kadin Bennani were safely ensconced in the chalet.

"No father?" asked Conza sleepily.

"No. Apparently, he's been missing for a week. The wife flagged it up at the same time she reported her son's disappearance."

"OK thanks," said Conza as he turned over in bed.

"Is there anyone in this case that hasn't gone missing?" he asked himself before drifting back to sleep.

...

He was showered and dressed before seven. He grabbed a coffee on the way to the office and went straight in to report to Colonel Scutari, a short, blond-haired man in his late fifties who Conza thought looked more Scandinavian than Mediterranean.

The colonel was shrewd, smart and spoke only when necessary. He had a reputation for not abiding laziness or stupidity, but he did encourage initiative provided it did not extend to ill-discipline. Nevertheless, he was a ferocious advocate for justice and believed it was best served by following procedure. In the two years Conza had worked for him, he was thankful that he'd never been on the receiving end of one of the colonel's infamous admonishments. Conza worked hard to keep it that way.

The colonel fixed him with his bright, green eyes as Conza apprised him of the events of the past seventy-two hours. Conza had already decided to tell the colonel about Kadin Bennani, but when he repeated what Nyala had told him, the colonel raised his hand.

"Does Captain Brocelli know all of this?"

"Most of it. I filed a report last night, all except the part where Nyala Abebe named Kadin Bennani as the killer. I also haven't disclosed the address of the safe house."

The colonel seemed satisfied.

"Good, carry on."

Conza completed his report with how the Bennanis had been taken to the safe house and the list of flights that Nyala may have taken the previous evening. The colonel sat back in his large, red leather armchair which, Conza thought, made him look smaller. He thought for a few seconds, one index finger pressed to his thin, tight lips.

"So you believe Stolz was mistaken for Salterton and was shot in a pre-arranged assassination?"

"I do, sir."

"Odd that they tried to make it look like a robbery though, don't you think?"

"I admit that it is strange, and I can't explain it yet."

"I wouldn't worry about it too much. Criminals don't always act in ways we expect. But tell me, Lieutenant, do you think you will ever hear from her, or him again?"

"Absolutely, Colonel. I believe they're just two young people who have somehow managed to get themselves mixed up in a whole pile of trouble."

The colonel's eyes didn't leave Conza's.

"But according to the Abebe girl, this Kadin Bennani lad has admitted killing Stolz."

For the first time during the meeting, Conza felt less sure of himself – and his instincts.

"Of course you're right, sir. But until I've heard what he has to say, I'm not prepared to throw him to the wolves."

For one dreadful moment, Conza feared he'd spoken too forcefully, so was relieved when a smile touched the colonel's lips.

"I agree. Thank you, Lieutenant. Keep me informed."

The colonel turned to a folder on his desk and Conza was left in no doubt that the meeting had ended. He stood up and had to resist the urge to tiptoe out of the office. Conza saluted and gently pulled the door closed behind him.

He went back to his office and debated whether to bother re-interviewing Katherine Harper. It seemed pointless now and the Stolz family rift was almost certainly irrelevant. But Moretti's story about Lukas Stolz and his sister had pricked his curiosity and even though he was desperate to hear the voice of Kadin Bennani, that call was still five hours away; if he called at all. Time would drag if he just hung around the office. He had to keep himself moving.

He left the office and waved down a taxi.

Hotel Castello, Milan, Italy

He'd called ahead, so it wasn't long before Katherine Harper appeared in reception.

The lobby was bare oak, black slate and smoked glass. Vivaldi's 'Spring' trickled through unseen speakers. The air was tinged with fragrant rosemary and expensive perfume. Two early morning tennis players sauntered by; tanned legs, bright white skirts and gold wristbands. They gave him a playful smile as they passed by. *'Perfect teeth,'* thought Conza.

Two uniformed concierges eyed him with interest. They'd heard him say "Lieutenant" to the receptionist. Policemen, at least low-ranking policemen, were not commonly seen at the Castello.

Conza's mother would have opined that Katherine Harper *'had looked after herself'*. She was slim, bright-eyed and dressed in a calf-length black dress. A small tear drop of pink and blue diamonds hung on a slender chain around her neck. Her hair was grey, but the wrinkles were light and only around her eyes. She was with another woman, younger, not quite pretty, but attractive all the same.

"Lieutenant Conza, this is my private secretary, Georgina."

Georgina smiled but did not offer her hand.

"Thank you for agreeing to meet me, Mrs Harper. Please accept my condolences."

Her eyebrows rose for a moment.

"You speak English very well, Lieutenant."

"My mother was English. In many ways, it was my first language. At least when I was young."

"You are still young, Lieutenant."

He felt his face warm. Georgina smirked.

"I asked the hotel to provide us with a room so that you and Katherine can talk," Georgina said as she turned away to lead them along a glass-walled corridor. She ushered them into a small oak-panelled anteroom set back from the main foyer. On the other side of the window, the tennis players were warming up.

"I will bring drinks. Coffee for you, Lieutenant?"

"Thank you, yes."

Conza turned to Katherine Harper who was watching the two young women on the court outside.

"Thank you again for seeing me. I only have a few questions. Just following up on your discussion with Sergeant Moretti."

Conza took out a notepad.

She turned her back on the window and paused before answering, her eyes warm, the hint of a wry smile.

"I have to say, I'm not surprised. I don't think your sergeant was wholly satisfied with some of the answers I gave him."

Conza knew better than to respond. She would fill the silence.

"The story behind my family is somewhat complicated. I'm not sure how much of it is relevant to the murder of my brother, but I have arrived at the conclusion that if I leave Italy without telling you the truth, I will always wonder. Which is why I agreed to this meeting."

Conza smiled encouragingly.

"All I can ask is that if you discover what I'm about to tell you is as irrelevant as I suspect, you give me your word that it will remain between us. There has been too much pain in my family for too long, I really don't want to add to that misery."

"Mrs Harper, you have my word that if you tell me something that is unconnected to the death of your brother, I will never tell a soul."

"Very well. I will take you at your word. But we need to start again. And, if I'm to expose my family's dirty laundry, I need to do it with someone I can at least call by their first name."

"Raphael. My name is Raphael; with a 'ph' on the insistence of my English mother. Or Raffy if you prefer."

"Thank you, Raffy. Please call me Katherine."

Conza placed his notepad on the coffee table. She acknowledged the gesture with a thin smile.

"Secrets. My family has always had secrets. Now, where to begin?"

She moved over to the sofa and sat down, feet together, hands clasped on her knees.

"The first thing to tell you is that Stolz isn't actually our family name. My father was born Dieter Reisman. He was Jewish. In 1936, he worked as a junior clerk in the Interior Ministry in Berlin. He saw what was coming. He was a very clever man. He moved his parents to France and took the name of a dead dock worker from Bremerhaven."

"The authorities never found out?"

"No, he had a meticulous mind. Lukas inherited many of his traits. Not that my brother would credit him, of course. My father left Berlin, extinguished all traces of the Reisman name and moved to Potsdam."

"Why didn't he go to France with his parents?"

"Because he was a patriot, Lieutenant. Germany was his weakness."

She shuffled in her chair but quickly composed herself.

"The labour camps opened up after *Kristallnacht* in 1938, and my father took a job as a postal worker. I don't think he was very good at it, but the work gave him access to the names and addresses of those he was trying to help."

"Jews?"

"And others, especially in the early days. Many of his communist friends were among those he helped get out of Germany."

"He was a communist?"

"Very much so. Communism was his real faith, far more than Judaism. Indeed, he despised religion."

"It must have been very dangerous work, infiltrating the Nazi regime."

"I'm sure it was. But I believe it was in his blood, helping others escape tyranny. I think he saw it as a war, his own private insurrection."

"Sort of anti-authoritarian?"

"You're beginning to understand, Raffy. My father was a revolutionary."

The door opened. Katherine stood up and looked out of the window as Georgina set down a tray of drinks and pastries. When they were alone again, she returned to the sofa.

"He met my mother in 1949. They were married a year later. She was fifteen years younger than him. Quite common in those days."

She poured coffee into two Meissen porcelain cups.

"Germany was in a sorry mess after the war ended and it only got worse after the wall was built. East Germany became isolated. My father said that from then on, he'd always thought of himself as an exile."

"But as a communist, didn't he welcome East Germany's move towards the Soviet Union?"

She placed her cup down and dabbed the corner of her mouth with a fine damask napkin.

"When I was ten, my father showed me an empty factory building in Mitte. There were holes in the floor where the machinery used to be bolted down. The Russians had all the best machines in East Germany shipped back to Moscow."

She was staring into the distance now.

"He said, 'The uniforms may not be the same colour, but they're no different to the Nazis. Stalin, Hitler, Brezhnev. They're all cut from the same cloth.' I think he quite liked Khrushchev, but he didn't last long. Germany had been ripped apart. He had a new revolution to fight."

"And your mother?"

"Oh, she agreed. Even before they met, she'd been helping people escape, over the border, and inside Berlin, across the wall."

"And she was shot trying to help a family escape?"

"Yes."

Katherine Stolz was staring into her past. Seeing her mother again. Blood running down her leg from the hole in her back, beseeching little Katherine to run. The searchlights. Dogs barking. A siren.

"I was with her that night because a mother and child were rarely stopped by the patrols. She was a nurse at the hospital in Friedrichshain. She taught me how to feign sickness. When we were stopped, she would tell them I was ill and she was taking me to the doctors, or hospital."

"You must have been very scared."

"I don't remember feeling frightened. It was all a game, I suppose." She smiled, but Conza could see sadness in her eyes.

"Who was the family? The ones trying to escape that night?"

She sat upright, as if the question had startled her.

"Felix and Eva Schuman, and their son. You may have heard of him. Josef Schuman."

"You mean Josef Schuman, the ex-German vice-chancellor?"

"The very same."

"Yes, my father met him once."

"Really? Was your father in politics?"

"No. Well, sort of. He was a diplomat. He died when I was quite young, but I remember him talking about Josef Schuman."

She wasn't smiling and Conza suddenly felt very self-conscious.

"What did he think of him?" It was a demand more than a question.

Conza could see the entry in his diary, 'Papa said Herr Schuman was a horrible beast.'

"Truthfully, I don't think he liked him very much. I'm sorry, I don't mean to be disrespectful. His family took you in after all."

"Please don't concern yourself. Your father was right. He's not a very nice man."

Conza felt as if he had passed a test. She suddenly relaxed.

"Anyway, it wasn't Josef who gave me a home, it was his parents. I don't think he would have done the same if given the choice."

"Why did the Schumans need to get out of East Berlin?"

"Felix Schuman was about to be arrested for treason. He had a job in the Defence Ministry and was passing confidential information to the British. He would've been shot, Eva and Josef sent off for re-education, if they were lucky. My mother overheard two Stasi officers talking about it at the hospital. The Schumans owe their lives to her."

"What happened? What went wrong?"

She closed her eyes.

"There's a bridge over the River Spree in Berlin called the Michaelbrücke. It used to mark the border between East and West Berlin. On the eastern shore, the bridge passes under the U-Bahn viaduct. Below are warehouses that open onto the water; built to service river barges, presumably. My father noticed that patrols in the area were sporadic and a narrow stretch of river near the bridge was not covered by floodlights."

"And that's where they crossed?"

"We all did. The Schumans, mother and me. In a small rowing boat, yes. We had to go with them, so we could take the boat back. So others could use it to escape."

"But you were spotted?"

She stopped looking at Conza. She was in the boat. The oars knocking against the gunwale. Her mother pleading for Josef to lower his voice. The river lapping gently against the prow as they edged forward. The hollow rasp of wood on concrete as the keel scraped along the shoreline.

She looked up.

"We had reached the western side of the river but were still in no man's land. The Schumans managed to scramble up the embankment and get away, but I think the noise of the boat alerted the guards."

Conza could see tears gathering in her pale eyes.

"I remember everything turning white, hearing the gunshot and my mother falling to her knees. Blood, I remember the blood."

"She was very brave, Katherine. She was wounded but managed to get you to safety."

"It's nice of you to say that. But she died doing what she wanted to do, for other people."

'But not for you,' Conza thought.

"So, you shared a house with Josef Schuman in England, I understand?"

"Yes, for two years. Until he was old enough to return to Germany. I haven't seen him since. Never wanted to."

"You didn't get on?"

"Raffy, I'm not the sort of person who speaks ill of others. We're all products of our childhoods, I'm painfully aware of that. And we don't get to choose our parents. I have always tried not to judge."

Conza pretended to write.

"And God knows, young Josef had his fair share of troubles as a young man. Imagine what it was like for him, being ripped away from home, school, friends. Escaping a regime that he knew would have almost certainly executed his father."

"It's bound to have an effect," Conza agreed.

"I'm sure it did. But even without the trauma, Josef Schuman was not a nice person."

"In what way?"

"He was devious, manipulative. He could be charming when it suited him, thoughtful, kind even. But he possessed a dark side, a cruel side."

Kathrine Harper leant forwards.

"It may sound stupid, but he used to hurt my dog. Pinch her, make her cry. I think he got some sort of kick from inflicting pain. Or maybe he just enjoyed exerting power over the weak. Lulu, my poor dog."

"Did his parents ever challenge him?"

"His father did. Actually, he was quite intolerant of Josef, perhaps even disappointed. I think Felix knew how nasty and underhand his son could be. Josef's mother idolised him, however. She would never allow a bad word to be spoken about her son."

"You were ten when you escaped, how old was Josef?"

"He's almost six years older than me. A year younger than Lukas. He went to university in Germany when I was thirteen. It was like a shadow had lifted. I was comparatively happy for a while."

Conza wrote a couple of dates in his notepad.

"I left when I was eighteen. I was grateful to the Schumans, especially Felix. He was a caring and generous man, Raffy, and I will never forget his kindness. He protected me."

"From Josef?"

"Yes, I think he did. There were always rows and I was often at the centre of them. I didn't recognise it at the time, but I now believe Felix stood up to Josef because of the way he treated me."

"And how did he treat you?"

"Oh, you know; crueller than teasing, but short of anything criminal. My toys would go missing, or I would find them broken or burnt. That sort of thing. Sounds trivial now, but at the time, it was very painful."

"No really, it doesn't sound trivial. You'd been taken from your family. You must have felt very lonely."

She didn't respond.

"Georgio, Sergeant Moretti, told me you managed to stay in touch with your father?"

"On the odd occasion. Sometimes an escapee would deliver a coded note. Secrets, Raffy, always secrets."

"I expect you missed him and your brother, of course."

She glanced at him and shook her head gently.

"I will get there, Lieutenant, be patient. This is the first time I've discussed my family with a stranger. I will get there."

Conza looked down at his shoes.

"My father sent me a message after the Berlin Wall fell. We arranged to meet in Berlin."

"In January 1990?"

"That is correct. We visited my mother's grave together. It was the most difficult day of my life."

"But your brother…"

"Wasn't there. That is also correct." She stood again, staring out of the window.

"Can you tell me why, Katherine? What did your father say to you?"

She turned, the tears picking out the soft down on her cheeks and chin. She suddenly looked old.

"He told me what Lukas had done. My father was dying and needed me to know."

She folded her arms, angry palms slapping against her biceps. Conza didn't blink. And then it came; bubbling and angry, like water from a burst main.

"My father told me the truth. It was Lukas who had informed on Felix Schuman. Lukas who told the Stasi what Josef had confided to him about his father's secret radio. Lukas who started the chain of events that put my mother and me on the embankment that night. He may not have pulled the trigger, but it was Lukas who killed my mother."

Garage 8, Vialle Vincenzo Lancetti, Milan, Italy

The tip-off came early on Wednesday morning in the form of an anonymous call to what had been dubbed the '*Hotel Napoli incident room*'.

The garage and surrounding area were cordoned off and the padlock on the door removed with a bolt cutter. Two plastic-suited forensics experts started to catalogue and search the property for the gun and clothes that had been used in the murder of Lukas Stolz.

After three hours, the cordon was packed away, and a letter, sealed in a plastic bag, was taped to the door. The letter apologised for any inconvenience caused by the 'legitimate police operation' and invited *'Whoever it may concern'* to contact the Ministry of Justice to file a claim in compensation for the broken lock.

In the garage next door, a blue Vespa continued to gather dust.

Hotel Castello, Milan, Italy

Conza had heard enough. He needed to take notes. Katherine Harper was seated once more, long elegant fingers clutching at her upper arms.

"Did Josef Schuman know that Lukas had informed on his father?"

"He didn't know before my father died, I'm certain of that."

"How can you be so sure?"

"Because I spoke to Josef in 1990. He called me."

"What did he say?"

"He told me he'd received a letter from my father's solicitors. The letter told Josef the whole story about what my brother had done."

"But how had your father found out? How did he know his son was an informer?"

"That, Raffy, is the saddest part. My father had always known."

"Always? Since when?"

"Since Lukas started working for the secret police in Potsdam. When we met in Berlin, my father showed me original Stasi documents proving Lukas had worked for the Stasi since he was fourteen. There was an entire folder of accusations made by my brother concerning treason, treachery and dissent on behalf of his teachers, friends and even the local baker's daughter. She was arrested because Lukas told the Stasi she'd complained about food shortages. And of course, there was also his statement about Felix Schuman acting as a spy for the British. There was no doubt. I saw the file with my own eyes."

"But your father never confronted his son about it? Why ever not?"

"Because while Lukas was passing information to the secret police, my father could carry on helping families escape."

Conza stopped writing.

"Don't you see? Lukas was his cover. The family home was above suspicion. It was never raided because Lukas Stolz the informer lived there. My father was never suspected of acting against the state because he was the guardian of one of their best young sources. It was perfect."

"That's incredible."

"You begin to understand. We were both extras in our parents' drama. Lukas and I were merely bit-part actors."

"I can't imagine what it must have been like for Lukas and Dieter, living together after your mother died. Father and son on opposite sides of the political divide."

"Secrets, Raffy. Always secrets. I try not to think about it. It's too painful."

"But Lukas never knew about your parents' involvement in the escapes?"

"No, not at all. I didn't know until the night my mother was shot. I'd been with her many times; meeting people, taking them to drop-off points, passing messages, that sort of thing. But I had no idea what she was doing. She always gave me plausible explanations, and I was a child. I believed what she told me. It was only afterwards, years later, that I pieced it all together. My father made sure that Lukas never knew a thing."

"When your father died, did you attend his funeral?"

"No. When we met in Berlin, he told me he only had a few weeks, maybe days to live. It felt so cruel. He was being taken away from me once more."

She was at her mother's graveside. Snow was falling. The petals of the roses were already crystallising. She was holding her father's hand. His fingers were without strength, and he felt devoid of weight, of substance. She had to hold his arm as he leaned forward to stroke the cold granite.

"He made me promise not to attend his funeral. He told me he'd asked to be cremated. We said goodbye that day."

She dabbed at her eyes with the napkin. Conza waited.

"So you never got in touch with Lukas because of what your father told you."

"How could I? What he did resulted in my mother being shot and me losing what was left of my family. I even blamed him for my father's death, which was stupid, I know. But every tragedy in my life seemed to involve my brother. I despised him."

"But you did end up meeting. How did you and Lukas get back in contact?"

"He found me. Found out I was still alive."

"How?"

"He discovered my mother's grave."

"And your name wasn't on the headstone. He knew you hadn't been killed."

"They opened a museum at Checkpoint Charlie in Berlin. They created a list of everyone who'd escaped from the east, and everyone who had died trying. The names were in all the papers. My name appeared alongside the Schuman family as an escapee. He must have seen it. After that, I imagine it was quite easy to track me down."

"So he made contact?"

"In 1994. He wrote to me. I didn't respond."

"And then?"

"And then last year, I was diagnosed with cancer. I was suddenly faced with my own mortality. It turned out to be a false alarm, but in the intervening period, I found myself questioning everything I had once believed. Especially my inability to forgive. I was not kind on myself."

"So you decided to get in touch?"

"Not initially, but I did open his letters. There were dozens of them. I have never cried so much, or for so long. I went from anger to utter shame in the same day. I wrote to him and we arranged to meet in Berlin last year, in May."

"It must have been a difficult reunion."

"Actually, it wasn't. I'd convinced myself that my brother was the devil incarnate. The truth was far more painful. He was gentle, kind and painfully shy. Not what I was expecting at all. Clearly, he struggled with people, not just me, everyone. He was just made like that. It shocked me how vulnerable he'd become. Or maybe he always had been."

"There's something I don't understand. When Dieter told Lukas that you and your mother had been killed in a car accident, didn't he wonder why there was no funeral? He must have asked."

She sat forwards, leaning her elbows on the arm of the sofa.

"I'd never thought of that. I don't know, I'm afraid, but that is a good question."

Conza made a note and Katherine looked at him quizzically.

"You know, Raffy, other than when I was very young, I only met my brother once, but I think he would have believed anything my father told him. When I said he was vulnerable, that's not quite right. There was more to it than that. Lukas was actually quite naïve. There was something very childlike about him. I think he would have believed anything if it met his idea of logic – and that was certainly not founded on his understanding of how human beings behave. Does that make sense?"

"I think so. He was emotionally unaware."

"Yes, that's right. I imagine many people would see him as being cold and defensive. But I don't think he was really like that. He just had no idea how to express himself."

"Did you talk about his work for the Stasi?"

"Not at first. We were both so happy to have found each other. But I knew it couldn't be avoided, it had to come out. When I told him how our mother had died, I also told him that I knew he had betrayed Felix Schuman."

"What did he say?"

"Nothing. I think it came as a terrible shock. I'd just told him he was responsible for the murder of his mother. He just stared at me."

"And said nothing?"

"Eventually he did. He was crying. Despite everything I'd once felt, I actually felt guilty. He just kept saying sorry and that he was young and impressionable at the time."

"It must have been terrible for both of you."

"It was a truly miserable day, Raffy. It broke him, I think. After my disclosure, he withdrew into his shell. I couldn't get through to him. I found and lost my brother in the space of a single day."

The incongruous sound of laughter trickled in from outside.

"Tell me about the conversation with Josef Schuman after he received your father's letter in 1990."

Her back stiffened. The time had come.

"Well, that is why we're here, I suppose. Why I needed you to understand our background. I'm sure Josef didn't mean it. It was just anger and it was so long ago."

Conza watched her face contort in memory of a past wound.

"What was?"

"Josef Schuman told me he was going to kill Lukas."

15th January 1990

Michaelbrücke, Berlin, Germany

Dieter Stolz died less than a week after meeting his daughter in Berlin and in accordance with his will, he was cremated.

Lukas was mildly irritated that his father had asked him to scatter his ashes into the River Spree from the bridge at Michaelbrücke. And so for the second time that month, Lukas found himself back in Berlin, standing at a point where East and West had once been divided.

He shook the urn over the parapet and the bitter, northerly wind danced with his father's remains. Lukas Stolz sighed in relief. He felt no compunction to cry. It was over.

He threw the empty ceramic pot into a bin and turned east.

Behind him, a few flakes of ash settled on the embankment, where twenty-two years before, an East German soldier, looking for the body of the woman he'd shot, found only a pool of her blood.

Guardia di Finanza Headquarters, Milan, Italy

Conza returned from the Castello Hotel just after eleven. *'Still two more hours until Kadin's call.'*

He knocked on the colonel's door.

"Sir, I'm sorry to bother you, but I've just interviewed the sister of Lukas Stolz and I need your advice."

...

Conza left the colonel's office an hour later.

He found it difficult to concentrate but read the updated case file anyway. Stolz's bank cards had been used at the airport to withdraw 500 euros, in the Hotel Napoli to pay his bill, in a restaurant on Saturday evening and three times at a café near the Skyguard offices.

The forensics report on Sami Ricci stated he was dead before he entered the river and had been killed between twenty-four and thirty-six hours before his body had been discovered. The report included a map showing tidal flows and time of death. An arc had been drawn fifty kilometres upstream from the barge bridge. It was calculated that from somewhere inside that arc, Ricci had been dumped into the water. Starting at the bridge, Conza traced his finger along the river up to the curved line, but it was hopeless. There were just too many places the river could be accessed via an adjacent road, path or track. He gave up and picked up a report drafted by Sergeant Moretti. Conza shook his head when he read that Mazaa and Nyala Abebe had been aboard the 21:10 flight from Malpensa Airport to Birmingham, England. But he smiled when a triangulation of her mobile phone showed its signal ceased just after the call she'd made to him. Either she switched it off or dumped it.

"Clever girl."

Sergeant Moretti returned from the safe house at half past twelve. He provided Conza with a summary of his conversation with Jamila Bennani.

"Overall, seems like a nice family," said Moretti when he'd finished. "Pretty frightened, of course, but otherwise just normal."

"What about the father?"

"Oh yes, I didn't tell you about him; Issam Bennani. Sounds a bit of a deadbeat. Drinks too much. Crippled from a work-related accident some years ago. Jamila wasn't comfortable talking about her husband, that was obvious."

"We should check to see if he's got a criminal record. It took Mrs Bennani a week to report her husband missing. That may tell us something."

"Already put in a request," said Sergeant Moretti without a flicker of satisfaction. "They'll send it over in the next hour."

"You don't miss much, do you, Georgio?"

"Says you," said Moretti in feigned defence.

Conza walked over to the board and replaced the '????' with the name 'Kadin Bennani'. In the 'Nyala' column he added 'Mazaa Abebe' and 'Birmingham, UK'.

"Sorry, Raffy," said Moretti, but Conza didn't respond.

"She dumped her phone," Conza said as he returned to his desk.

"So I see, that's pretty streetwise don't you think?"

"She's not a criminal, Georgio. I know I'm right about her."

"I know, Raffy, 'she's just a good girl'."

Moretti braced himself, but Conza suddenly laughed.

"You bastard, Georgio."

"Changing the subject while I still can, how did you get on at the Castello?"

"Well, that ended up being a bit of an eye-opener, in truth."

Conza summarised his meeting with Katherine Harper and the threat made by Josef Schuman.

"Bloody hell, Raffy. That's pretty explosive stuff."

"I went to the colonel with it. I had to. I've no idea what to do with information like that."

"No, you're right, Raffy. May even be above his pay-grade."

"Funnily enough, that's more or less what he said. He's going to speak with somebody in Germany. Told me to keep it to myself for now, so don't mention it to anyone."

"Do you think Schuman's threat to kill Stolz was serious?"

"No, not really. Ex-vice-chancellors don't go round bumping off people to settle old scores, do they?"

"Who knows? But if true, it would cast doubt on the mistaken identity theory."

"Not yet. That's still my best guess at what happened. The Schuman thing was probably just an idle threat. It was almost thirty years ago. He was angry. We've all said things we don't mean."

Moretti looked at his watch.

"Fifteen minutes until the witching hour, Raffy. Do you still think Kadin will call?"

"Shut up, Georgio."

In the five minutes before the planned time, Conza and Moretti sat in total silence, checking their watches and idly leafing through documents from Conza's desk. They both knew but wouldn't speak about the consequences of the phone not ringing.

The call from Kadin Bennani came at one o'clock, exactly as Nyala said it would. Conza couldn't resist a smug grin.

He had rigged up a splitter plug so they could both listen in. When his mobile vibrated, Moretti grabbed the earpiece and Conza waited until his partner gave him a 'thumbs up' before answering.

"Lieutenant Conza, Finance."

"Lieutenant Conza, my name is Kadin Bennani, Nyala's friend."

"Hello, Kadin."

"She told me she trusts you. I hope she's right."

"She is right."

"So this call isn't being traced?"

"No Kadin, it isn't. I've taken a big risk for you. I hope I can trust you too?"

"Is my family safe?"

"Yes Kadin, they are in a secure location, although your mother is worried sick about you."

"But she's safe. Where are they?"

"Kadin, you have my word they will come to no harm. Only one trusted colleague knows where they are. Absolutely no one else. They're being guarded by two skilled professionals. Nobody can get to them."

Conza thought he could hear the youth crying, so he waited.

"Thank you," Kadin said eventually.

"Tell me what happened."

"It would take too long," said Kadin, making Conza look up at Moretti in alarm. "You need to come here – to see for yourself.

Afterwards, I will go with you. I know what I've done is very bad. I understand, but I won't run anymore."

Of all the things Conza thought he would hear; this wasn't one of them. He tried to think of why he should not trust this young man, but his instinct wouldn't let him try too hard. Moretti looked shocked but nodded furiously.

"Fine Kadin, I'll come to you but I'm going to bring a colleague. Just me and him."

"Can't you come alone?"

"Kadin, you need to understand I've already broken a hundred rules by speaking to you like this. I must have my colleague with me. I would trust him with my life."

"It's not your life that's on the line, Mr Conza," Kadin said sadly. "But I realise I have no choice; you can bring your friend."

They agreed to meet in Genoa at six o'clock.

Before hanging up, Conza asked, "Kadin, your father wasn't with your family. Do you know where he is?"

Conza heard Kadin take a deep breath.

"He's dead, Lieutenant. He died to save me."

When the call ended, Moretti removed the earpiece.

"Wow, that was a shock. He didn't take much persuading."

"No, Georgio, he didn't. Clearly, he wants to come in. So, for the time being, we do things his way."

Moretti called up train times on the computer.

"There's one in forty minutes, they run every half-hour to Genoa during the week. Fancy getting there early?"

"I'm just going down the corridor to let the colonel know what's happening. In the meantime, chase up the criminal record check on his father. We'll head off once we've squared everything here." Conza was already halfway out the office.

...

By the time he returned, Moretti was reading a copy of Issam Bennani's criminal record.

171

"Captain Brocelli called, he didn't seem very happy and wasn't overjoyed to hear me answer your phone. Accused me of disloyalty!" Moretti said with a wry smile. "It would appear that he'd like you to contact him when convenient."

"Were those his words?"

"More or less."

"Well, well. Mr Bennani has been busy," said Conza, reading the report over Moretti's shoulder.

"Handling stolen goods, selling counterfeit merchandise. He also escaped a count of breaking and entering."

"All pretty minor stuff, though. Never served time. He's hardly Capone, Raffy."

"Al Capone was only ever convicted of tax evasion. Come on, let's go meet the son."

Conza grabbed his jacket and a new notepad from the drawer and they set off for the station.

Valbona Valley, Albania

Alexander Kurti was born in Albania in the 1960s, the third son of a butcher. He was an oversized baby and by the time he was fourteen years of age, he towered over the rest of his family. In later life he was told he'd been born with profound dyslexia, but such diagnoses were rare in the 1960s, especially in a small village nestled in the Valbona Valley, on the border of what is now Macedonia.

His mother died when he was eight and Alex found himself without a protector when his school friends mocked and taunted him because he couldn't read, write or count. Alex's father stopped sending him to school, so he spent his days wandering the foothills with his father's old twelve-bore, picking off rabbits and shooting ducks as they fed from the streams that ran into the River Drin.

At fourteen he began helping local shepherds round up the goats that roamed as far as the grey, flint slopes of Zla Kolata. Alex was fit and very strong, but the shepherds were nervous of his temper, which would flare without warning if he perceived he was being mocked or ridiculed.

His short career as a goatherd ended the day he was told to bring a family of goats down from a steep-sided rocky outcrop. The goats were nimble and surefooted, and Alex became increasingly frustrated at his inability to catch them. The shepherds gathered at the foot of the scree, whooping and laughing at his desperate efforts. Higher and higher the goats climbed, leaping between slender ledges and scrambling up shifting stone in their effort to escape. Alex bounded after them, balancing on his toes, grasping at rocks with bleeding fingers and jamming his skinless knuckles into jagged splits. The higher Alex climbed, the more the shepherds cheered, until at last on a narrow plateau, he cornered the leader of the flock, a large male ram. It was panting and pawing at the rockface, bleating pitifully in fear and exhaustion.

Alex kicked it to death and threw the carcass over the edge of the escarpment. The corpse tumbled and rolled down the hillside until it came to a stop just a few metres from the feet of the now silent herders.

Thereafter, Alex Kurti was shunned by the local villagers, so he made his way on foot, east to Pristina. He was close to starvation by the time he made his mark on the papers that made him a soldier in the Yugoslav People's Army, aged just fifteen. After basic training, he served in the elite Mountain Brigade and in 1982, was sent to Monchegorsk near the Finnish-Russian border, on an exchange tour with the Soviet infantry. Army life suited Alexander Kurti; he was fed, given a warm bed and enough money to get drunk and pay for a prostitute at weekends. He'd found a new home and his violent temper and significant physical strength earned him respect rather than disdain.

Kurti didn't return to Yugoslavia after the exchange tour and a year later, travelled with his new-found Russian comrades to Afghanistan. He quickly earned a reputation for being a fierce and cruel fighter. He was always the first to pick up a weapon, even a shovel or fence post, and would not stop killing until the last of his enemies lay broken and bleeding from his brutal and unrelenting onslaughts.

The brigadier soon identified that Corporal Kurti's lack of emotion made him an ideal candidate to carry out interrogations, and the mujahideen guerrillas soon spoke of a giant who would cut off the hands and feet of his captives if they refused to talk. Almost overnight, Alexander Kurti became the 'Afghan Hound'.

He left the army just in time to witness the collapse of the Berlin Wall. He took jobs acting as a bodyguard to various politicians, the famous and the rich, but more than once he was seen on television beating up a reporter who'd stepped too close to his charge or unwisely pushed a camera into his face. His brutality and short-temper had made him unemployable – at least overtly.

Since then, he'd remained in the shadowy fringe between organised crime and various state-sanctioned 'black ops'.

Whilst he remained an efficient executioner, in recent years, he'd spent most of his time getting people to do things that they didn't want to do. He operated under a plethora of perfectly documented identities and was a consummate torturer. He knew people, knew how to hurt people, and he got things done on behalf of those who were willing to pay and were important enough to protect him from the attention of the law.

...

Just as Conza and Moretti stepped off the train in Genoa, fifty kilometres down the coast, Alex Kurti was sitting on the balcony of his sparsely furnished apartment, drinking coarse red wine from a copper tankard. The sun over the Ligurian Sea was still warm, and he turned his acne-scarred face to the sky.

The phone in the lounge rang and after the third iteration, he swore, got up and went inside.

"Yes."

"Alex, you're losing your touch."

Kurti said nothing.

"I ordered a hit. Clean, simple and definitely without fuss."

"And?"

"And? You ask *and*? I will give you some 'ands'. How about the shooter going missing? *And* the chauffeur being tortured *and* killed? *And* the father of the only other witness getting shot while his daughter runs off to God knows where. *And* the gun used not being where the tip-off said it would be. *And* just about everything else about this so-called clean, simple hit is screaming that it was anything but. Need I go on?"

Kurti thought of fat, bald Marco and his fidgety hands. Kurti gripped the phone, his scarred knuckles white with fury.

"No, I get the picture."

"Good, then punish them Alex. And Alex, clean this mess up or sadly, I will get someone else to clean it up for me."

The phone went dead and Kurti returned to the balcony to finish his wine and contemplate that for the first time since he was fourteen, someone had just threatened to kill him.

58

Genoa, Italy

He was sitting on one of the marble blocks at the base of the great white Columbus statue when they stepped out of the station. They weren't in uniform, but he knew they were policemen. They looked nervous, their eyes darting around looking for potential traps or ambushes.

"He once cut off the ears and nose of a man who'd stolen some corn," Kadin said, looking up at the marble figure as they approached.

"I think we're a little more forgiving these days," said Conza. "Are you Kadin Bennani?"

"Yes. Is my family still safe?"

The two policemen could not avoid noticing the tired eyes and pallid complexion. He hadn't slept much recently, they concluded, independently and without comment.

"They're safe, Kadin. I saw them this morning. Youssef and Soraya miss you," Sergeant Moretti responded.

"And my mother?"

"She's worried sick. We've told her very little about all this. Thought it best until we'd heard your story."

"We need to take a taxi."

"We're right behind you, Kadin," replied Conza, taking up position close to his shoulder while Moretti took Kadin's other flank.

"Are you carrying a weapon?" Conza asked when they'd moved away from the crowds.

"No, I was told to dump the gun in a garage in Milan. As far as I know, it's still there."

"We received a tip-off about that this morning, the garage was empty, no gun."

"That's because they were looking in the wrong place, they need to search the garage next door. But all of this will become clear back at the apartment."

...

In the foyer of Villa Nuova, Sergeant Moretti took the key from Kadin so that, revolver in hand, he could go ahead to check out the building. A few minutes later, he shouted down the stairwell, and Conza followed Kadin up the steps to the top floor. The policemen sat on the sofa and Kadin pulled up a chair.

"First, I'm going to tell you about my father's disappearance last Tuesday and my abduction. Then I'll show you a film and I'll tell you what happened at the Hotel Napoli and my escape here to Genoa. After that, you can ask me questions, I know you will have many. And then my life is in your hands."

The policemen nodded simultaneously.

"We're ready," said Conza taking out a new notepad.

"Before we start, just one more thing," said Kadin, his face pained, torment in his eyes. "I killed a man, in cold blood. My action was evil, and I could have chosen not to pull the trigger. I didn't make that choice and I've regretted it ever since. Whatever happens to me, a man I didn't know has died, and his family will never see him again. I will have to live with that for the rest of my life. What I'm about to tell you does not seek to excuse what I did, but I hope it will at least explain why I did it."

Conza and Moretti stared at him. Kadin's will had been broken and his heart torn apart, of that they had no doubt.

59

Birmingham Airport, England

Ephrem was Nyala's uncle on her mother's side; she recognised the same eyes from her father's photographs. He was brash, loud and happy and found a reason to laugh at just about everything. His two children, aged eight and six, ran around the concourse in their excitement and Ephrem only encouraged them.

In any other circumstance, Nyala would have cherished this moment. But she could not rid herself of the memory of her father, fighting for his life, alone. Nevertheless, for a few brief minutes, Ephrem's laughter and the children's happiness carried her away, and she discovered a sense of relief and comfort that she hadn't believed possible.

Suzie, Ephrem's wife was beautiful. Slender and petite with a bob of chestnut hair and freckles that ran from the bridge of her nose to the corners of her dark brown eyes. She pushed Nyala away, holding her by her shoulders.

"You are as gorgeous as your mother, Nyala, and look at the size of you. I haven't seen you for fifteen years. You were a baby."

Nyala blushed and pulled Suzie towards her.

"Thank you, Aunty, and thank you for coming to meet us. We're so grateful."

"No thanks needed," said Ephrem laughing loudly once more. "You're family."

With that he grabbed Mazaa and hugged her until she begged him to put her down. Suzie stepped in when Ephrem launched a barrage of questions about his brother-in-law. Nyala was avoiding answering and Suzie sensed she was shielding something, something grim and dark. She quickly changed the subject and herded them all towards the car park.

At the house, they had drinks and snacks, while Nyala was shown around the house by her enthusiastic cousins. Mazaa seized the opportunity to take Suzie and Ephrem into the garden.

With trembling lips, she told them that Amadi had been shot as a result of Nyala being caught up in a terrible event. She also explained they needed to stay away from Milan for a while, and it was really important they didn't ask too many questions.

"Nyala has gone through enough over the past few days, she needs to feel safe. She's very scared. We have a plan, but we need your help."

"Whatever it takes," said Suzie with concern.

"Anything!" added Ephrem.

"First, we have almost no money, so I would be grateful if you could let us have a little, just to help us get by."

"Easy," said Ephrem opening his wallet. "How much do you need, Mazaa?"

"Just enough to get a few clothes, toiletries that sort of thing."

Suzie pulled five £20 notes from Ephrem's wallet.

"Here, take this. I can give Nyala some clothes and what doesn't fit, we can buy in town. We have spare toiletries; I will make up washbags for you both."

"Is that enough?" said Ephrem, pulling out another £40.

"I'm sure this will be more than enough. Thank you, Ephrem. Also, Nyala needs to buy a new mobile phone. We lost ours," Mazaa said with a wry smile.

"I have a spare," said Ephrem darting off into the kitchen. "I will go online and buy some credits."

"Thank you, Ephrem. Tomorrow, Nyala needs to call a policeman in Milan. Can you help? She's nervous about speaking to the authorities."

Suzie and Ephrem looked at each other.

"We'll be there, Mazaa, don't worry." Ephrem exclaimed.

Suzie's lips tightened, and she gently wiped a stray hair from her husband's forehead.

"I will sit with Nyala when she makes the call, my love, you need to work tomorrow. You get frustrated with the police. You know you do."

Ephrem started to speak but laughed instead.

"You see what I have to put up with, Mazaa? Ordered around in my own home!"

"I think she's wonderful."

"Then it's all settled. I will call the hospital tomorrow to see if my lazy brother-in-law has dragged his backside out of that bed."

Suzie rolled her eyes, but Mazaa was already hugging Ephrem and they were laughing together.

60

Apartment 3, Villa Nuova, Genoa, Italy

It was nearly one in the morning when Conza finally sat back and closed his notebook. He was physically and emotionally spent. At times, they'd asked Kadin to rewind the film so they could make notes and ask questions. Conza used his mobile to take photos of the men calling themselves Alex and Marco as well as Max and the two other unnamed bodyguards. Finally, they believed they'd seen and heard enough to understand.

When they watched Issam Bennani climb the steps with a rope and turn off the camera, Conza sat with Kadin as he wept. For the first time since meeting him, he saw Kadin as a child. A heartbroken and frightened child.

Sergeant Moretti watched Kadin sobbing into Conza's chest and went for a walk along the marina. When he returned he brought beers and raised his bottle as he spoke Issam's name, simply because he didn't know what else to do.

Conza told Kadin to get some sleep and sat with Moretti in the lounge.

"I've never seen anything like it," admitted Conza, "it's like watching an autopsy for the first time – compelling but innately quite disturbing."

"It made my flesh creep. It will take a long time for him to recover. I think Kadin will have nightmares for the rest of his life."

"I think you're right, but I'll be damned if he has them behind bars."

They finished their beers and Conza fetched some blankets from the cupboard. They decided to get a few hours' rest before returning to Milan. They sat on the sofa and reflected.

"We need to get a techie down here, get a trace on where the barn is located," said Moretti after a while.

"I agree, but right now, I'm trying to work out what to do with Kadin. I can't take him back; they'll throw him in a cell. He could be locked up for weeks while the legal arguments go round and round the court system. It will turn political. These things always do."

"I don't think we have much choice. We can't cover this up. A man's been murdered, and we have his killer. The investigation must be completed, and Kadin will have to tell his story to a judge. It won't be us deciding what happens to him after that."

They sat in silence for a few minutes, then Conza went to the bathroom. When he returned, he switched on the desk lamp.

"House arrest," he exclaimed.

Moretti sat up and shielded his eyes against the sudden brightness.

"We place him under house arrest, pending further enquiries. God knows we have enough evidence to suggest there's a leak at the station and we have a duty to keep Kadin safe, especially as he's a minor."

"We could move him in with his family," added Moretti, excited by Conza's suggestion. "It's where he should be right now. He needs to be with his mother."

"And if he's near the station, it would make it easier to take his statement, that's going to take a day or two."

"But Raffy, Brocelli will have a fit. I can't see him letting us hide a confessed murderer in a location he's not even allowed to know the address of."

"I agree, but I could get the colonel to grant jurisdiction of the case to Finanza, that would take Brocelli out of the picture."

"And place it all in your lap. Is that wise?"

"Problem is, I've never run a case as complex as this," confessed Conza biting his cheek. "The colonel would never let me do it. Especially if Brocelli or the commissioner kick up a stink."

They both contemplated the problems that were about to arise.

"Maybe that's one for the morning, Georgio. I'll head back to the city first thing to kick-start the search for Alex, Marco and the others. I'll send a tech team down here. You stay with Kadin until I clear the way with the colonel."

"Sounds like a plan, Raffy," Moretti replied, trying to sound cheerful.

61

Camogli, Italy

After the phone call, Alex Kurti finished his wine and got behind the wheel of his immaculately clean, American Oldsmobile. He needed to find Marco Fanucci and had little doubt that he would have to kill him. On the way, he called ahead to arrange a meeting, but Fanucci wasn't answering his phone.

"Little shit," muttered Alex, speeding up.

As he reached the bridge over the Torrente Borbera, north of Precipiano, his mobile rang. He answered without speaking.

"Alex, I got your message and I know you're pissed off right now, but you need to listen to me."

"Speak."

"Things have happened that I can't explain. It's a mess and I know you're after my blood. I'm not stupid and I'm not brave. I can't say I blame you, but before you decide to blow a hole in my head, you need to answer one question."

"What?" said Kurti impatiently. He'd heard many men, women and children beg for their lives, but none had ever managed to change his mind.

"Did we take out the right guy?"

"What the fuck do you mean?"

"Alex, what I mean is, did we hit the guy we should have hit? I know you think I'm crazy, but did we hit the right target?"

Kurti wondered if things may actually be worse than he'd imagined.

"You'd better not be fucking with me, Marco. Stay by your phone, I'll call you back."

He turned off the *autostrade* at the next junction and parked in a lay-by just outside Serravalle.

He tried to think. Hitting the wrong mark had not been in the list of failures so eloquently recited to him a few hours ago. Surely, if the wrong guy had been hit, that would have been top of the *'fuck-up'* list. But clearly, Fanucci believed the wrong man was dead. Kurti called him back.

"Why do you think it was the wrong target? And you'd better stay straight with me, Marco, because right now all I want to do is rip your fat, sweaty head from your shoulders."

"There's a guy been trying to find me, name of Zeffirelli. I know him, he's low-life. Ran Czech guns through Austria over the mountains into Italy in the nineties. He's not connected to anyone important but has occasionally run errands for a couple of families. Sees himself as a player."

"Go on," said Kurti remembering how much he hated Marco's tendency to talk around any given subject, "get to the point."

"Well, this Zeffirelli character tracked me down. He began by asking me about Issam Bennani, the techie whose son we used for the hit. I told him to fuck off, but he got wild. Started screaming down the phone that I'd tried to take down his brother-in-law."

"Sounds like a nutcase. Why does he think you've got a contract out on his brother-in-law?"

"He knew the name of Bennani's son. Knew he was the shooter. Tells me his brother-in-law is the spitting image of our target and he was staying in the Hotel Napoli on Sunday."

Kurti stayed silent. A picture was forming, but it was difficult to focus while Marco was still bleating.

"You didn't give me a name, Alex. You said I didn't need it. You just gave me a photograph. The grey-haired man and the black Mercedes, that's all I had."

"Fanucci, shut the fuck up and let me think."

Marco stopped rambling.

"What's the name of the brother-in-law?"

"Salterton. Peter Salterton. He's English. But if we'd hit the wrong guy, you'd know that. So we didn't screw up?"

Confusingly to Fanucci, when Kurti spoke, his tone was softer, more conspiratorial.

"It looks like we did hit the wrong guy, Marco, I just checked. They didn't give me a name either. But it should have been

Salterton. I can see what happened, but we've got to clean this mess up you and I."

"Oh shit, Alex. He's going to string us up by the balls. He doesn't accept failure, you told me that a hundred times."

"Marco, I get it, it's not down to you, I see that. But I need you to get hold of this Zeffirelli character and tell him to call me. Do you understand?"

"I've got it. Alex, this is a shitstorm, but you can see it wasn't my fault. You can see that, can't you?"

"I will sort things out, Marco. It's 11:15 now, get him to call me on this number before midnight, got it? Tell him the contract on Salterton was down to me. Be sure to give him my name. You need to make it clear; he has to call me before midnight, right?"

"I got it Alex, before midnight."

"Now listen, Marco, I will save your backside, but you've got to do what I tell you. Do you hear?"

The crying had stopped.

"Anything Alex, you know I will put things right."

"Good, then meet me at the barn in the morning at seven. Got that, Marco? We've got to finish the job. We'll come up with a plan, OK?"

"OK, I'll be there Alex. I'm so sorry."

62

Germany – Post-Reunification

There was no reason to remain in Potsdam. He knew no one, his father was dead, and he needed to find work. Lukas Stolz had suddenly found his own version of 'liberation' but wasn't sure how to exploit it.

He briefly considered moving to Russia but had to admit there were parts of his new life he'd got used to and didn't feel inclined to surrender. In particular, he enjoyed being able to move around without restriction, amazed that his new passport let him wander around Western Europe as he pleased; as far as Britain to the west and Greece and Italy to the south.

He found the west both fascinating and disturbing. Whilst he was forced to admit that life had become less 'grey' and 'serious', that did not necessarily make him feel comfortable. He found 'choice' more difficult than he could have imagined, but he needed a job.

For two terms, he taught maths in a secondary school just outside Cologne but hated it. The students were shallow, fickle and lacked self-discipline. They'd been provided with too many choices and insufficient resolve to make the most of them.

He yearned for university life, to research and to innovate. He considered applying for his old teaching job in Leipzig, but the memory of his final days in that city still pained him, and he dreaded being recognised by those who had assailed him because he'd rejected their particular brand of 'freedom'.

He found a job writing code for a small software company in Frankfurt, but his duties were repetitive and boring. In Hamburg, he worked for a company developing cloud-based solutions for the military. It was there that he was introduced to the complexities of data links and knew immediately that he'd found his calling.

He soon started giving lectures on data coding. He gained fame amongst a select group of mathematicians and scientists for his innovative ideas and ability to bend numbers to meet his aims.

Within three years, the name Stolz became synonymous with high-level, military-grade encryption. He was headhunted by Skyguard in 1994 and knew straight away that he would never work for anyone else again.

Skyguard revered his mind, and he was given the freedom to develop encryption systems. In particular, he was encouraged to take a central role in creating the data link code behind the Skyguard II missile system.

During vetting, he admitted he'd been an active member of the Communist Party in Leipzig, but his assessors didn't see that as a barrier. More than half of all East German academics had been members of the same organisation and things were different now. In any case, no sane person could harbour loyalty for a doctrine soundly rejected by the overwhelming majority of ex-Soviet citizenry. Wasn't 'freedom' and 'democracy' the salvation of the failed communist states? Lukas Stolz was a clever man, they concluded. He would never contemplate biting the hand that was now so graciously feeding him.

When talking about himself, Stolz quickly learned what to say, and what to omit. He didn't see it as lying, it was pragmatism. *'In any case,'* he told himself, *'I've changed. I no longer feel so bitter towards the west.'*

63

Service Station on the SR10, Tortona, Italy

At eleven-forty-five, he pulled off the A7 motorway and parked under the trees in the forecourt of a run-down service station on the outskirts of Tortona. '*He'll call,*' Kurti told himself without a shred of doubt.

Just before midnight, the phone vibrated.

"You're Zeffirelli, I hear you spoke to Marco Fanucci earlier?"

"And he told me you took out a contract on my brother-in-law. Is that right?"

"I've been caught up in the middle of this. I asked you to ring me so I could set things straight."

"Why should I believe you?"

"Because if you don't, you'll end up dead. You've had enough time to ask around about me. Am I right?"

"Yeah, I spoke to a couple of people. They know you. So, what the hell is going on?"

"You don't need to hear the details. You only need to know I've arranged for Fanucci to meet me in a barn out in the sticks in seven hours. Except I won't be there, you will."

"Why?"

"Because you've been tearing up the city trying to find out who wants to put a bullet in Salterton. Am I right?"

"Maybe."

"Well, I'm giving you Fanucci. He was behind the hit. He took out the contract on your brother-in-law."

"Why did he want Pete dead?"

"Because Fanucci's a frigging idiot, that's why. He gets touchy if he thinks someone is trying to muscle in on his rackets."

"But we didn't know Fanucci was in on the smuggling game!"

"Neither did I. That's the point. He's been acting without authority, do you understand?"

"But he told me it was you who took out the contract. Why would he say that?"

"I told him to say that you prick. I knew it would be the only way to get you to call me."

"Why are you telling me this? Why sell Fanucci out?"

Kurti slammed his hand on the dashboard.

"Because I need you to put the shit you've been spreading all over Milan back in its box, so that we can all go home and sleep with both our eyes closed."

"How do I know you aren't setting me up?"

"You don't. But right now, I'm a little pissed off because you've caused me a whole pile of problems. I don't like problems. So this is going to end. You're going to kill the man who tried to drop your brother-in-law and as a bonus, you get to walk away from this in one piece. But only if you do as you're told. Now get a pen, I will give you the address. Talking's over."

64

Thursday

Guardia di Finanza Headquarters, Milan, Italy

Conza couldn't sleep and took the first train back to Milan. On the kitchen table, he left Sergeant Moretti written instructions to keep Kadin in the apartment until reinforcements arrived. He also told him not to touch Issam's electronic equipment in case he inadvertently deleted the recording.

Back in Milan, Conza stopped off at his apartment and felt a little more alert after a shower and change of clothes. At the Finanza offices, he knocked on the colonel's door.

"Come in, Raffy. I'm looking forward to hearing all about your meeting in Genoa. But before we start, are you available tomorrow morning?"

Conza knew it wasn't really a question.

"I can be free then, sir."

"Excellent, our flight leaves at ten."

"Where are we going? If you don't mind me asking."

"Berlin. We have an appointment with the German Federal Intelligence Service. I will tell you all about it later. For now, tell me about Kadin Bennani."

...

An hour and a half later, two technicians, two forensic examiners and two Finanza junior officers were on their way to Genoa by van.

The colonel invited Captain Brocelli and the State Police commissioner to an urgent meeting in his office. While they waited, the colonel asked to see the photographs from Conza's phone, which he ordered his secretary to have enlarged and printed. The colonel asked Conza to leave the room while he made some phone calls.

...

The meeting with Brocelli and the head of the State Police in Milan started promptly at eleven. The colonel spoke first and provided a short summary of events in Genoa. Brocelli and the commissioner listened intently. The colonel concluded with news that technicians and forensics had already been dispatched to Genoa.

The commissioner responded first.

"Thank you, Colonel, quite a tale. But before we get into what happens next, may I ask a question?"

"Of course Commissioner," the colonel replied, his green eyes sparkling with warmth and amiability.

"Why did you choose to hold this meeting in Finanza? You said on the phone it was important that we met here?"

Captain Brocelli smirked.

"Commissioner, I have reason to believe certain information about this case has been leaked. It's a matter that I was due to discuss with you today, but as it happens, I needed to update you on the Bennani case. It seemed apt to deal with both matters here."

Conza knew the colonel was careful to state "I" not "we". He was taking personal responsibility, and any subsequent culpability, for Conza's story. It should have made Conza feel better, but it didn't.

Captain Brocelli bristled and sat forward in his chair, but the commissioner raised a hand.

"That is a very serious accusation Colonel, and one that I think we should discuss in private. Do you agree?"

The colonel nodded. The commissioner was far from stupid. *'A political animal,'* Conza thought, and not one willing to discuss his department's potential shortcomings in front of juniors. Matters moved on.

Politely, the commissioner asked, "So, can I take it the Bennani boy will be brought into custody today?"

The colonel turned to Brocelli.

"Captain, firstly, as head of this investigation, I wanted to thank you for the diligence and patience shown by your team. Lieutenant Conza has to some extent been working alone, but I know that as an experienced officer you will understand his reasons for doing so."

Brocelli fidgeted but could only offer a quiet "Thank you, sir," in half-muted response.

"Secondly, I am sure, like me, the commissioner would seek your advice as to where we should go from here? If you will forgive me, but I think the position is this. We now have under our control a minor who has admitted killing Lukas Stolz. It appears he was coerced into carrying out the act. We have unknown felons trying to find him. We, as state officials, owe the child a duty of care. I know you will agree that prison is not a safe place for him to be held. His father is dead, and the rest of his family are in hiding. He gave himself up and is therefore not a flight risk. What are your thoughts?"

The commissioner's jaw twitched, but Conza felt like clapping. Captain Brocelli flushed and started to fiddle with his tie.

"Well, sir, it would appear it might be best to place Bennani in some sort of protective custody. After all, he is a minor."

"Right, I see. With his family?"

"That would seem best, I think sir."

"And Captain, would you recommend an arraignment via video link?"

"Yes, sir. A video arraignment is what I would recommend." Brocelli unfastened the button of his collar.

"Excellent, Captain Brocelli. Thank you for your recommendations. In the circumstances, I wholly endorse your position."

"Indeed," said the commissioner tersely.

Conza bit the inside of his cheek. The colonel sat forward, clasping his hands together.

"That would seem to be settled. I have to say, I'm glad Captain Brocelli will continue to head this investigation. It needs the leadership of a seasoned professional. Lieutenant Conza will continue in support and now that Kadin Bennani is out in the open, only the address of the safe house needs to remain a secret."

"Colonel, there is absolutely no reason why the head of this investigation should not be told the location of the safe house. Indeed, I insist on it," the commissioner said sternly.

The colonel raised his hands and sat back in his chair. He looked small again.

"You're right, of course. Captain Brocelli must be told Commissioner. The list of people who know where the Bennani's are being held is very short. One more name won't make any difference."

He turned to Brocelli and leaned forward.

"My apologies, Captain, I sometimes have to be reminded that we at Finanza don't have a monopoly on discretion."

65

Apartment 3, Villa Nuova, Genoa, Italy

Sergeant Moretti woke just before six, Conza had already left. Kadin was in the kitchen and the smell of coffee drifted in from the hallway. Their 'good mornings' were sober and awkward. Kadin was counting the euros and separating them from the sterling.

"This is what Mr Stolz gave me," he explained, handing over a stack of notes. "I expect you'll want it for evidence. I'm sorry, I just put it together with the money my father left in the garage."

"That's OK," said Moretti, "but what do you mean 'gave you'?"

"He thought I was trying to rob him," Kadin replied, closing his eyes and clutching the edge of the table. "It was horrible, I keep seeing his face."

"So he offered you the money?"

"Yes, he just took it out of his wallet and gave it to me."

"You didn't mention this last night, Kadin. Why not?"

"I'm sorry, I felt so ashamed. I think he actually felt pity for me. Before I knew what was happening, he'd pushed the cash into my hand. It all happened so quickly."

"And you took it?"

"It shocked me. I was panicking. I wasn't thinking straight, I'm so sorry." He began to cry.

"It's OK Kadin, I can't imagine what you've been put through. But at least it explains why Stolz's wallet was empty. That really threw us for a while. But you're right, we'll have to bag it up when forensics arrive."

They took their coffees into the lounge.

"Do you know much about him, Lukas Stolz, I mean? I didn't even know his name. They never told me."

"Not much. He was a bit of a loner I think. A bachelor, no family of his own," he added, looking at Kadin to make sure he'd heard. "Maths professor. Worked in England for a defence company."

"There was a picture of a woman and two children."

"His sister's family, not his. It was an old photo, taken in the nineties. The children are grown-ups now."

"He had a dog though."

"Really? How do you know that?"

Kadin went to the kitchen and returned with the photograph.

"It was in amongst his notes."

Moretti turned the picture over as Kadin asked, "Strange name for a dog isn't it?"

"It's an old Italian name. Not one you come across very often."

Moretti went to the kitchen to put the photograph with Stolz's money and when he returned, scribbled 'Stolz's dog – Fideccio' in his notebook.

The TV was showing the live stream from the barn. A large American saloon swung into the yard. It was Alex. They watched him climb the ladder towards the camera. Shortly afterwards, the quadrant went black. The remaining two quadrants went blank shortly afterwards.

"He's turned the cameras off or disconnected them. I wish we knew where he was, we could get a team out there."

"Sorry, I was taken to the barn in the boot of a BMW."

"It's OK, we'll know soon enough."

66

'The Manor House', Hatchmere, Cheshire, England

The shrill ring of his mobile disturbed the dark vision of an unknown hand covering his face with a sheet in a Milanese street.

"Salt, it's Giuli. Everything's been sorted. It's over."

"What time is it?"

"It's just after eight. It's over Salt."

"Tell me," said Salterton, pulling on his dressing gown.

"You were right, the contract was taken out on you. It was Fanucci."

"And that's supposed to make me happy!" Salterton yelled, as he stepped on to the landing.

"Salt, calm down. It was Marco Fanucci. He went off-piste. Embarrassed some dangerous people over here. Seems he thought you and I were muscling in on his turf."

"And were we?"

"No, it was all a big fuck-up. Fanucci was working alone. No one knew what he was up to."

Salterton told his brother-in-law to wait while he made his way downstairs. He poured himself a Scotch and sat down in the conservatory, just as a well-built man in jeans, anorak and trainers strolled by the window. He was carrying a black Mossberg pump-action shotgun. Salterton raised his hand in acknowledgment, but the man didn't respond. Salterton shook his head.

"So, it's sorted then, completely? You're absolutely certain?" he asked, as the mercenary crouched down before disappearing into a clump of rose bushes.

"Completely. I'm certain. Mr Fanucci will not be setting his own agenda again, and I've received a blessing on our trade. The techie topped himself and it won't be long before they find his kid. Everything's been tidied up. It's over."

"Thank fuck for that, Giuli. Shame you didn't get to the shooter though. I can't say I'm happy that someone with my name on his list is still breathing, but I'll have to live with that. These marines give me the creeps and I can't sleep. They have the floodlights on all night. It's been like Blackpool illuminations over here. They've been paid up to Saturday, I'll get rid of them then."

67

Poole Magistrates' Court, Dorset, England

Harry Chase skipped along the wide glass-walled vestry of the building housing Poole Magistrates' Court. He was holding his long, pleated black gown with one hand and pressing his horsehair wig to his head with the other. He was between cases and had just fifteen minutes before he would have to bow to the magistrates in Court 2.

He swiftly gathered a file from the clerk's office and made his way back down the corridor, picking a route between clusters of nervous court attendees.

The door to Consulting Room 4 was open and inside sat Jack Stephens; nineteen years old, bored, thin, angular, and awkward in the tie that his ever-hopeful mother made him wear on such occasions.

"Just for luck, Mr Chase, everyone needs a bit of luck."

Jack Stephens would certainly benefit from a bit of luck, mused Chase, *'that or just a modicum of self-discipline,'* he thought to himself.

Mrs Stephens rose, her red-raw hands clutching a tear-stained handkerchief, her eyes, dark pools of red, water and trepidation.

"Mrs Stephens." Chase acknowledged her before turning to her wayward son, who barely raised his eyes at the arrival of the man who would represent him in court.

"What is it this time, Jack?" Chase asked as he flicked open the case file.

"Drink driving, speeding, dangerous driving, failing to stop, no insurance, no tax, no MOT."

Jack shrugged his shoulders, but his hands remained buried in his oversized denims.

"What's the story then, Jack? Anything I need to know? Says here your blood alcohol level was more than twice the limit. Does that seem about right to you, Jack?"

Jack Stephens shrugged again and stared at his spotless and garishly pink designer trainers.

"Tell him, Jack love," implored his mother as she rested a trembling hand on her son's knee.

Jack shifted, jerking his leg away from her touch.

"Yes, come on Jack, tell me."

After a pause, only interrupted by the whimpering of his mother, Jack sat up a little and glared at the barrister.

"Fucking coppers, Mr Chase, they've always had it in for me."

"Have they done something to you, Jack? What's the problem?"

The boy refused to elaborate and resumed staring at his trainers.

"They're always picking on him, Mr Chase. Got it in for him on account of his dad."

Chase ignored her.

"Look, Jack, in about ten minutes, two policemen are going to tell the magistrates they clocked you racing along the A338 at over 100mph in a car that was uninsured, untaxed and barely roadworthy. They're going to swear that when they eventually got you to stop after chasing you around Ringwood for twenty minutes, you were so pissed you couldn't stand up. The magistrates on hearing this are going to take one look at your long and not so distinguished criminal record and will not hesitate to send you to Crown Court, where, if your tie works, you'll be sent down for two years. Do you understand me, Jack?"

Jack began tapping his foot on the floor impatiently as his mother started crying again.

"So, if you can tell me something that may be of assistance when I'm trying to save your backside, now would be a good time to do so!"

...

Ten minutes later, three magistrates listened wearily to Harry Chase LLB (Hons) as he passionately set out the tragedy that was Jack's life: criminal father, haphazard education, economic hardship, unsuitable influences, long-suffering mother. Chase could recount the story without notes. He was well-practised at it.

Jack Stephens was released on bail to appear at Bournemouth Crown Court on a date to be set. Throughout the short hearing, his hands never left his pockets and when he stood up, the waistband of his denims barely remained in loose proximity to the base of the narrow and shapeless cheeks of his backside. Chase watched Mrs Stephens and her sulking son shuffle across the Sandbanks Road towards the bus stop in front of the park gates.

Chase had come to the law relatively late in life. After serving in the Royal Air Force for sixteen years, he'd only started studying law because it was difficult. He craved the challenge.

He was forty by the time he was awarded a first-class honours degree and a year later, he qualified as a barrister. It had been five years since he'd been called to the Bar and taken a solemn oath in front of an oversized painting of Charles I at the Middle Temple in London.

But now, as he watched the futureless young man waiting for a bus, he wondered if he'd known then what he knew now, would he have just said, "Thanks Charlie, but what's the point?" and walked quietly off into the sunset.

68

Handsworth Wood, Birmingham, England

Suzie squeezed Nyala's hand and tapped in the number. The man who answered spoke Italian very quickly and she wasn't sure she'd reached the right person.

"Good afternoon, is that Lieutenant Conza?"

"It is, speaking."

"Ah, good, you speak English," she heard herself saying, much too slowly.

"Yes, I do, my mother was born in Hampshire. So yes, but I'm a little rusty."

"That will make things much easier, for me at least. My name is Suzie Tadesse, I am Nyala's aunt. Nyala Abebe, do you recognise that name?"

"Nyala, yes, of course. Is she OK? Can I speak to her?"

Suzie covered the phone's mouthpiece and asked Nyala if she wanted to speak to him. Nyala looked unsure.

"Shall I put him on speaker? Would that be OK, Nyala?"

Suzie laid the phone on the table.

"Lieutenant Conza, you're on speaker. It's probably easier for everyone if we converse in English. Nyala can translate for Mazaa if needed."

For the next twenty minutes, Suzie listened while the lieutenant updated Nyala on everything that had happened since they'd last spoken. Her father's condition remained critical, but stable. Conza gave Nyala the details of the hospital so she could speak directly to his nursing team.

The Italian police had interviewed Nyala's friend, and amazingly, seen a film of his captivity and the planning of a murder. Conza told Nyala that Issam Bennani was dead but didn't offer any details. Suzie guessed he'd taken his own life.

"What will happen to Kadin now?" Nyala asked when Conza had finished.

Suzie sensed the vagueness in Conza's response.

"Nyala, he's saying the police will make recommendations as to what happens to Kadin. He's still a child and that will make a great deal of difference, but Lieutenant Conza is trying to tell you he simply doesn't know."

Nyala slowly shook her head as Suzie picked up her phone.

"You are off speaker now, Lieutenant, thank you for looking after Amadi. He's a good father and son."

"He is under close protection, Mrs Tadesse. He's strong, like Nyala, it will make a difference."

"Let's hope so. It's clear Kadin needs a good lawyer; I take it the state will provide one?"

"A lawyer has already been assigned."

They exchanged goodbyes and a promise to stay in touch.

...

Suzie placed a hand on her niece's arm.

"You heard what the lieutenant had to say. As soon as the police announce Kadin has been arrested, you will no longer be in danger. But I agree with him, it might be wise for you to stay with us for a while, just to let the dust settle. What do you think?"

Nyala wasn't sure about the dust, but she understood enough to know that her stay in Birmingham was about to be extended. She spoke in Italian with her grandmother before turning back to Suzie.

"We'll stay here for a couple of weeks, Aunty, but we must return home soon to look after my father."

"I understand, but there's no point rushing back, Amadi's in good hands and there really is nothing you can do for him until he's been released from hospital. In the meantime, I'll stay in touch with Lieutenant Conza and keep you updated with any news, Is that OK?"

"Thanks, Aunty. I think I was right to trust Lieutenant Conza, he'll fight for Kadin."

"I believe you're right, Nyala" Suzie replied. "He sounds like a good man."

69

Chambers of Harry Chase, Bournemouth, England

Harry Chase sat in the small office overlooking the lower town gardens and from his first-floor window, watched a family of holidaymakers sitting on a low wall next to the stream. They removed the wrappers from their ice creams before discarding them in the water. The ducks raced over to the paper in a rush of wings, but there was nothing for them to peck at, so they went back to dipping their heads in search of food.

The scene made Chase feel old and he imagined himself berating the family for their selfish act, knowing it would have no effect. He checked the clock on the mantlepiece and picked up the phone.

"Raphael? It's me, Harry. How the devil are you? I got your message."

"Harry, great to hear your voice, thanks for calling back. Things are a bit hectic over here, how about you and the family?"

"You know, Raffy, same old, same old. Helen's great, puts up with me, so things can't be too bad. Kids are doing well, they're off school this week. Dreaded family holiday is drawing near."

"Stop the miserable old git routine, Harry, you know you love them."

"My kids or family holidays?"

"Both! Now listen, you've been on my mind the past couple of days. It's a case I'm working on, wondered if I could pick your brains?"

"Pick away Raffy, sounds intriguing."

"OK, first of all, if someone is forced to commit murder, do they have a defence?"

"You mean duress? Can you be coerced into committing murder?"

The family in the park laughed as the youngest child chased a distraught duck around the lawn. Chase pulled down the blind.

"I'm not conversant with Italian criminal law, but since the Nuremberg trials, most countries generally don't allow duress as a defence for murder. I strongly suspect that Italy's in that category."

"What if the killer is only seventeen?"

"Age has a bearing, clearly. The problem remains that a court is likely to say that one life is never more valuable than another. Duress, even for a minor isn't a valid defence, I'm afraid."

"Well there isn't much I can do about it for now. The kid will appear before a judge in the morning and I'm guessing he'll plead not guilty. After that, it will take months to come back to court."

"It would help if you could put the people who coerced him behind bars. At least then the media will have their pound of flesh. It won't get him off, but it may stop the dogs barking."

"We're hoping to make some arrests tomorrow, if not this evening."

"Sounds a difficult case."

"You could say that. A murder planned live on television. A phantom robbery. A guy with a body double. A kid coerced into killing the wrong man. Suicide. Tortured witnesses. It's been crazy, but it's coming to a head now."

"Sad to confess, Raffy, but I'm envious. But you said that was the first thing, what's next?"

"Oh yes, the murder victim's name was Lukas Stolz."

As Conza spelt out his name, he thought of Katherine and her brother's betrayal.

"He worked for Skyguard in the Midlands. I'm guessing you know Skyguard from your time in the air force?"

"Let me tell you something, Raffy. When you hang up your flying boots and leave the RAF, you go two ways; civil airlines, or Skyguard. I know half a dozen guys who were headhunted by them when they left the cockpit."

"Sounds like you missed out there, Harry. You got to wear a wig instead."

"I'll thank you not to disparage my working uniform, Lieutenant. Anyway, you said his name was Lukas Stolz – sounds German."

"East German, actually. I'm researching his background. I've already spoken to his sister, and I've put out requests to police in Warwick. But I thought it wouldn't hurt to hear about Stolz from a work colleague. In truth, I don't think Stolz is relevant to the case, I think he was killed by accident. But I have to cross the t's."

"No problem, I'll talk to a pal of mine, Jimmy Appleton. He knows everybody at Skyguard. By way of payment for my magnanimous services, you can tell me a little about the investigation. You know how nosy I am."

They laughed.

Conza gave Chase a brief summary of Lukas Stolz's murder, Kadin's escape and the subsequent inquiries.

"That's one hell of a story. So Stolz wasn't the intended target? They were really after this chap Salterton?"

"It's the only explanation that fits. All except for the evidence going missing, of course."

"Really? Tell me about it."

"You sound like Georgio – Sergeant Moretti. He's always looking for problems."

"So, come on. Tell me about this missing evidence."

"I really don't think it's important. Stolz wasn't the right man. It's just that his belongings went missing from the station the night he was killed."

"That's odd. Was the Bennani kid supposed to take anything from him after he'd been shot?"

"Only his mobile phone. He did take the guy's cash, but it turned out the victim gave it to him voluntarily. Thought he was being robbed. That confused us for a while. Anyway, Kadin was told to drop the phone into a bin near the station, which he did."

"So the organisers needed the real target's mobile phone. I'm assuming it was collected by them."

"Correct again. We have CCTV footage of the man they call Max picking it up the same day."

"So they wanted something stored on the phone. But assuming it wasn't password-protected, they would have quickly realised they'd shot the wrong man."

"I thought about that, Harry, but it doesn't make sense. Salterton is a career criminal. Can you imagine him storing anything incriminating on his mobile phone? In any case, he'd have locked it with a password. You know as well as I do, criminality breeds paranoia. No, I don't think they wanted his phone at all, they just needed Kadin's getaway to be masked. I don't think it's any more complicated than that."

"But you said it was in a suppressing sleeve. They'd already ensured Kadin wasn't tracked. Why go to the trouble of retrieving a phone they didn't need?"

"Harry, I hate you. You know that."

"Don't shoot me; if you pardon the expression. I'm just trying to help. Maybe they were looking for something in his phone case? That would make more sense."

"Sadly, Kadin said it wasn't in a case."

"All right, go back to Stolz for a second. What did he have with him?"

"He'd just checked out of the hotel. He had an overnight bag and an attaché case. His wallet and phone were in his jacket."

"And everything was taken from the police station?"

"That's right. I didn't get a chance to look in his overnight bag, but I did list everything in the briefcase. He had a calculator, an old newspaper, a magazine, his notepad and some keys."

"Which newspaper?"

"*The Times* dated...hold on...fifteenth July last year. The magazine was a *Jane's Defence Weekly* from last month."

"Anything interesting in the notepad?"

Conza told Chase about the conversation he'd had at Skyguard about 'FC-Auto' as well as the string of characters and numbers that Brocelli had found in Stolz's wallet.

"Do you want me to read them out?"

There was hesitation in Chase's reply.

"Listen, Raffy, I'm sure you've got better things to do than feed my curious, but sadly underused brain. Just tell me to bugger off if I'm trying your patience. I would understand. Really."

"You have me all wrong, Harry. There are a thousand things that bother me about this case, but it's usually poor old Georgio that has to put up with my theorising. Whether you believe me or not, it's me who should be apologising. Right now I'm getting a fresh pair of eyes on this case and I'm not even paying for it."

"Not yet, but there's still time. Go on then, read it out."

Conza read out the series of numbers and letters.

"Actually there was something else in Stolz's case. His keys. They were on a key ring which doubled as a USB stick."

"Now that's more like it. What was on it?"

"We have no idea. I didn't have an excuse to look at it at the time. And anyway, it's too late now, the attaché case has gone, with the stick inside, so I guess we'll never know."

"Pity. Oh well, I'll have to go back to pleas in mitigation for a living. Sorry again for being such a nosy bugger. I'll report back once I've spoken to Jimmy."

They promised to speak again at the weekend.

'Unusual case,' thought Harry as he poured himself another mug of tea. *'Lucky sod!'*

Apartment 3, Villa Nuova, Genoa, Italy

Sergeant Moretti and one of the new lieutenants escorted Kadin back to Milan for processing before driving him to the safe house.

In Genoa, the technicians quickly and expertly set up their equipment on the floor next to the television.

They identified the location of the signal transmitting from the barn just before six on Thursday evening.

They called Captain Brocelli.

Manchester Airport, England

At the taxi rank outside Terminal 1 of Manchester Airport, Max opened the door of a Lexus and handed a piece of paper to the driver. Despite efforts to engage him in small talk, the passenger didn't utter a single word during the journey. The driver looked at him a few times in his rear-view mirror and decided he wasn't the sort of guy he would fancy messing with.

Max didn't notice. He was thinking about the job. Fanucci had made all the arrangements. He was good at that.

When they reached the pizza and kebab takeaway in the Northern Quarter, he would be able to collect the weapons. The hotel in Manchester city centre was paid for, as was the rental car that would be delivered to him in the morning.

Marco Fanucci was good at organising things. He gave him that. But on the Hotel Napoli job, he'd used an outsider, an amateur, and the kid had taken out the wrong target. Now he'd been told to do the job properly. Fanucci had been terrified, desperate to get the job done. Must've been that gorilla Alex who scared him. Alex was a very bad man, if his driver's stories were to be believed.

Max had never seen Fanucci scared before, not that he cared. He shook his head in disgust. He would never say it, but if Fanucci had given him the Hotel Napoli job in the first place, they'd have all been paid by now and Fanucci wouldn't be shitting his pants.

Max tried to call him, but Fanucci's phone went straight to voicemail. He didn't leave a message. He didn't need to. He knew what he had to do.

San Carlo, 60 km East of Milan, Italy

It was dusk and the barn cast long shadows over the oil drum and sandbag in the yard. A silver BMW sat on the forecourt.

Squatting low behind the car's rear bumper, Brocelli turned his head to the side and listened. *'Silence.'*

The barn door was propped open, but the interior of the building was unlit. He peered into the darkness. *'No movement.'*

Crawling slowly around to the front of the car, Brocelli felt the bonnet. *'Cold.'*

He cocked his weapon and gave the signal.

The barn was hit by two teams of four from the south and west. The assault was efficient and well-executed, but as it turned out, unnecessary.

The tripod light didn't work. *'Battery's flat,'* thought Brocelli as his eyes adjusted to the dim surroundings.

Two bodies. The first, a bald-headed man. He'd been shot at least three times in the face and neck. Two white teeth protruded through the grotesque mask of dark red, pink and grey. Next to him, a tall, ponytailed man holding a pistol, his chest riddled with automatic gunfire, his jacket a loose collection of thin jagged ribbons, his shirt a blotting-pad of red blooms.

Flies danced nervously above the exposed flesh and sucked at the thick rivers of blood that had congealed between the corpses. Brocelli lifted the man's pistol with his foot. *'Safety's still on. He didn't have time to react.'*

Behind the pallets, he discovered a scattering of 9mm shell cases. *'They were ambushed,'* he thought without sympathy.

The bodies were cold. Brocelli estimated they'd been dead for at least twelve hours.

He called it in but while he was describing the scene, he noticed something grey and white poking out from under the corner of a wooden pallet. Using a set of plastic tweezers, he picked up a creased and torn photograph of a well-dressed, grey-haired man crossing the road in front of the Hotel Napoli.

73

Friday

Flight AL-2394 to Berlin

Five days had passed since the killing of Lukas Stolz. Conza was sitting in first class. When the 'fasten seat belts' sign extinguished, the colonel pulled out a wad of photos from an envelope, laying them out on the pull-down table. The first few Conza recognised as enlargements of the pictures he'd taken in Genoa.

The colonel looked worried.

"Did you speak to Captain Brocelli this morning?"

"No sir, I went straight to the airport. I was going to catch up with him when we get back."

"He'll tell you this man is Marco Fanucci. Brocelli found him in the barn last night, along with one of his henchmen, Stefan Puz. They'd been shot."

"Right. I see."

"Puz was just a mercenary, but Fanucci was a middle-ranking player. Blackmail, corruption of politicians and others in powerful positions. Been known to work for high-end criminal gangs. Specialised in filming his victims in compromising positions."

Conza could guess who would've carried out the technical work but didn't interrupt.

The colonel pointed at another photograph and surprisingly, ordered Conza to stop writing.

"This chap, on the other hand, is a long way up the dark and sinister league table. Alexander Kurti, the 'Afghan Hound'. We have a file on him as thick as the phone book, as do the secret service. You won't ever get to see their file, so I'll tell you what I know. First and foremost, Alexander Kurti does not get involved in assassinations on pond-dwellers like Salterton. He rubs shoulders with those who run state-funded operations. He's dangerous, Raphael, very dangerous."

Conza suddenly felt insignificant and oddly vulnerable.

"Do you remember the killing of Kirillov last year?" the colonel asked him.

Conza did. The head of an ex-Soviet state's secret police was on trial for a catalogue of child sex offences. Astonishingly, while giving testimony, he went off script and confessed that for years, he'd been passing secrets to the west. He'd believed his very public statements would force the hand of either the CIA or MI6. Clearly, he was hoping they would have felt compelled to ride in and save his skin. Two days later, he was found strapped to a dentist's chair in a parking lot. His hands had been amputated and he'd been forced to drink nitric acid.

"Kirillov was Kurti's work. When you showed me the photos yesterday, I recognised him immediately. He's not difficult to spot in a crowd. I called a colleague who knows all about him. He confirmed my suspicion that Kurti would never get embroiled in the killing of Salterton, it's way below him."

"So we need to find Kurti, as a priority?"

"Actually, no. Leave Kurti to me. As soon as I flagged up his name, the jungle drums started beating and I was left in no doubt that I had to back off."

"He's being shielded. Why?"

"I don't know yet, but this isn't good news, Raffy. If I told you from how high up the order came, you would understand why I'm having to tread carefully."

"And I'm guessing you're not going to tell me?"

"Correct. And before you start thinking about ranks closing and old boys' networks, you need to understand that I'm only trying to protect you. When the time is right, I will tell you everything I know, but I've got to be damned sure I'm standing on solid ground before I move in that direction."

Conza knew it was pointless to press further.

"For now, Raffy, have faith. Captain Brocelli has also been told, Kurti is not to be pursued."

"Do you trust Brocelli, sir?"

"Trust? In what way?"

"I don't know, but there's an awful lot of stuff that's happened on his watch. Media being tipped off. Evidence going missing. Zeffirelli finding out about Nyala and Sami Ricci." Conza had an image of Brocelli typing on his laptop. "And he's not good at following rules."

"And you have evidence to support your misgivings, Lieutenant?"

"No sir. I haven't. But I just thought–"

"Don't ever come to me with half-baked conspiracy theories without proof, Lieutenant Conza. Especially when you're levelling accusations against a serving officer. Do you understand?"

Conza didn't need to say anything.

The colonel squeezed past him to use the bathroom. Despite thinking the colonel's defence of the Captain was unjust, Conza pulled out a notepad and wrote '*Brocelli – laptop?*'

When the colonel returned, he looked at Conza with a weak smile.

"He's not what you think, what everyone thinks. He doesn't help himself, I know, but we all have a story to tell, Raffy, and Brocelli's is more tragic than most. You would do well to talk to him, get past his defences. There's a bloody good police officer in there. At least, there used to be."

The matter was closed.

The colonel picked up another photograph from the pile. It was torn along one edge and smudged with grease.

"Brocelli discovered this in the barn. It hasn't been properly analysed yet. The commissioner brought it straight to me."

Conza picked it up.

"That's Stolz."

"Why are you so sure it's not Salterton?"

"For one thing, he's holding a German newspaper." Conza pointed at a small rectangle of white poking out from under the man's arm. "Don't they look like the letters *'Zei'*?"

The colonel brought the photo close to his face.

214

"Maybe. It's difficult to be certain."

"Stolz ordered a *Frankfurter Allgemeine Zeitung* last Friday."

"Keep going."

"The Hotel Napoli sign is in the background and Stolz is wearing the same suit he was wearing when he was shot, even the tie is the same. I'm certain. This is a photograph of Lukas Stolz taken forty-eight hours before he was killed."

Conza opened his notebook.

"There's another thing. In the picture, he's carrying a black attaché case, the same as the one I saw in the incident truck. We know Salterton left his luggage at the hotel and we have a photo of him boarding a train in Milan. His hands are empty, so we know he didn't bring a briefcase with him."

"All right, I think we can agree that the man in this picture is Stolz, and as it was found in the barn, we can assume it was used to brief the Bennani boy on his target. There's just one problem."

Conza braced himself.

"What if the person taking this photograph *thinks* they are taking a photograph of Salterton?"

Conza swore under his breath.

"Sir, I think we have to assume *something*. Otherwise we're in danger of going round in circles. If you permit me, I'll tell you what I think we're dealing with."

Conza took a deep breath and gathered the photographs together.

"One, this is a picture of Lukas Stolz. Two, if what you believe is correct, Kurti doesn't involve himself with contracts taken out on people like Salterton, which means Stolz must have been the intended target. Three, Salterton believed the contract was taken out on him and ever since, Zeffirelli has been trying to find the killer, and the person who hired him. Four, Fanucci was either killed by Kurti because he screwed up, or Kurti was covering his tracks, or... we should leave 'four' for the moment."

The colonel didn't blink.

"Five, Kurti and Fanucci arranged Stolz's murder on behalf of a high-paying client. Those are what I think are the facts."

215

The colonel put his fingertips together as if in prayer and rested them on his lips.

"Let's go back to 'four'. Is it possible Zeffirelli killed Fanucci because he found out he was the person who arranged the killing?"

"Maybe, but I'm struggling with that one. Wouldn't Fanucci have just told Zeffirelli to stop being paranoid? That Kadin killed the man Fanucci had told him to. That Salterton was never the target."

"Captain Brocelli described the scene at the barn as an ambush. Perhaps Zeffirelli didn't give Fanucci a chance to explain. But you're right, until forensics come up with something from the barn, there's nothing to tie Zeffirelli to Fanucci's death."

"Colonel, now we believe Stolz was the real target, we should look again at the theft of his belongings. It may be important."

"You're right, but the commissioner's already on it."

"So that just leaves Katherine Harper's statement."

"Which is why we're heading to Berlin."

Conza tidied the photographs into a neat pile.

"Raffy, how much do you know about Josef Schuman, and his family for that matter?"

"Not much. Only what Katherine told me. Although when I was a child, my father hosted a party attended by Josef Schuman. My father didn't take to him."

"I'll tell you what I know. The man we're going to meet in Berlin will hopefully fill us in on the rest."

Conza started a new page.

"Before escaping East Berlin, Felix Schuman was a very wealthy man. He owned an armaments factory, which made a fortune during the war. At the time, Schuman Defence was a world leader in advanced weapon technology."

"I didn't know. Katherine mentioned a factory in Mitte. I wonder if she was talking about Schuman's place?"

"Maybe. Their head office was in Mitte, I believe."

"She said the Russians took all the machinery."

"That sounds like the Schuman factory. It's exactly what happened. Felix was made bankrupt overnight, although he walked into a job in the defence ministry. There wasn't much he didn't know about guns and missiles."

"So he started spying for the British out of revenge. Anger at the Soviets for destroying his business?"

"No, no. It was much more than anger. The British promised to build him a new factory, machines and all, if he spied for them."

"And did they? Build him a new factory, I mean?"

Conza was staring at the colonel who just smiled in return.

"Bloody hell! Skyguard."

"Well, it wasn't called Skyguard back then, but yes, they fulfilled their promise. He got his factory."

"In England?"

"Yes, but he opened a facility in Cologne quite soon after. The West Germans were keen to lure him back home, so they made a deal with the British. They funded half the project. Schuman Defence became the most successful post-war, Anglo-German company."

"Which Felix ran from the head office in Warwick."

"That's right."

"How did the Italians get involved?"

"The West Germans wanted the Italians in on the deal. They saw it as an important step in post-war reconciliation. It made sense."

"But Josef Schuman went into politics?"

"Yes. He was on a very different mission to his father. After Frankfurt University, he returned to West Berlin. Got himself a seat at the high table on the council in no time. He must have been spotted as a high-flyer very early. He was instrumental in helping East Germans escape to the west. Then in the nineties, he gained fame for arranging for the wall to be dismantled. Became a poster-boy for the newly liberated East Berliners."

"So he wasn't interested in joining the family firm?"

"No, he had nothing to do with it until his father died in 1982. He didn't have much choice then. His father left the whole thing to him."

"That must have been quite a challenge. What was he? Thirty?"

"Twenty-nine. He left them to it. Appointed a board to run it all and went back to politics. He had little to do with the company for a long time. But his shareholding made him a sizeable fortune."

Conza took a coffee from the passing trolley. The colonel declined.

"He moved through the political ranks really quickly," Conza offered after making some calculations. "He attended the reception at our house in '96."

"The year he was made vice-chancellor," the colonel replied. "He was kicked out of the party and his post in '99."

"Why?"

"No one knows, or rather no one's telling. It's one of the questions I hope to get an answer to today. The news at the time said it was just a normal cabinet reshuffle, and he was retiring from politics to spend more time with his family. Which would be more believable if he actually had one. Both his parents were dead, he was an only child and he never married. On top of which, it's pretty unusual for a vice-chancellor to lose his job."

"Did he return to Skyguard?"

"Yes. The company was floated on the German stock market in 2001 and took the name Skyguard Defence Industries. Josef Schuman became even richer. Until fairly recently, he was a major shareholder, but continues to act as chairman to the board."

"Do you think he knew Stolz worked for Skyguard?"

"I think it would have been impossible for him not to know. Lukas Stolz was a big player at Skyguard. Known all over the world. I think we can assume Josef knew."

"And do you think Stolz knew Schuman was the head of Skyguard?"

"He must have done. There's a two-metre-high portrait of Felix Schuman in the reception of Skyguard's headquarters. Stolz would have seen it every day. In Potsdam, Lukas and Josef knew each other well enough for Josef to tell Lukas about his father's spying. It wouldn't have taken Stolz long to work out the head of the company was his old schoolfriend."

"But I guess Stolz thought he was safe as long as Josef Schuman never found out he'd told the Stasi about his father's spying," Conza concluded, almost to himself.

"You're missing the point, Raffy. In 1990, Schuman was angry enough to threaten to murder Stolz, but in 1994, Stolz started working for Skyguard. By then, Josef Schuman had known for four years that Stolz had betrayed his father."

"Surely that exonerates him doesn't it? He told Katherine he was going to kill Lukas almost thirty years ago. He never followed through with his threat. He even let Stolz work for his company."

"So it would appear. Even if he didn't know Stolz was hired in '94, he would have found out soon after. But he didn't get Stolz sacked or expose his Stasi dealings to the press or anyone else for that matter. Don't you find that odd?"

"I agree, it's strange. From what Katherine told me, Josef Schuman doesn't sound like the forgive-and-forget type. You'd expect him to be vindictive, at least angry. He certainly wouldn't let Stolz anywhere near Skyguard. And in truth, who could blame him? Stolz destroyed the Schumans' life, the whole family could have been executed."

"But he did nothing. He allowed a man who he knew had betrayed the Schuman family to join his company. It doesn't add up. Which is why we're going to Berlin. We need answers, Raffy."

Hatchmere Woods, Cheshire, England

The house was built into the side of a shallow valley. Clumps of trees littered the banks, and the yellow brickwork of the main building was designed to blend in with the clover covered grass that ran up to the three-metre-high walls that encircled it.

Max found a vantage point near the top of the hill just off a bridleway that cut across the valley at an oblique angle. The fields were used mainly for grazing, and the fences were dotted with stiles and kissing gates.

For much of Friday, he skirted the perimeter, never closer than two hundred metres from the high stone wall. He counted his paces and made notes at regular intervals.

He came across a lean-to stable that backed onto woodland about three-quarters of the way up the valley side. When he lay on the roof, he had an unobscured view of the estate. The backdrop of trees also meant he wasn't sky-lined and couldn't be seen from further down the valley.

He climbed down and counted the steps back to the main bridleway. Using a small magnetic compass, he memorised the directions and practised finding the stable from a fence post on which he fixed some lime-green tape.

Max had found his observation post.

San Carlo, 60 km East of Milan, Italy

Alexander Kurti packed his few belongings and locked the door. Within an hour, the apartment would be cleaned, sanitised and every trace of his brief occupation would have been removed. The Oldsmobile was already back in storage. He'd been in Camogli for just three months. Never longer than three months; anywhere. He was sick of moving around and looked forward to spending his time away from everyone and the phone. He would get to drink his wine in relative peace.

After arranging for Zeffirelli to meet Fanucci, he'd driven out to the barn in San Carlo to disconnect the cameras. Fanucci had said they were switched off, but he didn't trust Fanucci, and he hated cameras.

He parked the car on the far side of the village and walked across fields of scrub until he reached a position from where he could watch the barn.

Zeffirelli was cautious. Two cars drove past the barn a number of times, before a lone figure was deposited at the gates. *'Reconnaissance,'* thought Kurti.

Eventually, six men were dropped off in the yard and the cars emptied of guns and ammunition.

Fanucci arrived with Stefan Puz just before seven. *'No Max,'* thought Kurti. It irritated him but wasn't fatal.

The six-second ripple of automatic gunfire scattered a brace of plover from the gorse. The sound reminded Kurti of cave clearing in Afghanistan. Two more shots. *'Finishers,'* thought Kurti with satisfaction, *'job done.'*

When it was over, he watched six men climb back into their cars and drive off in opposite directions.

The shit was back in its box. Time to leave Italy.

Chambers of Harry Chase, Bournemouth, England

Chase went for a walk through the ornamental gardens that ran down towards the sea. Holidaymakers thronged the beach, and the promenade was busy, so he sat on a wall to eat his ice cream.

Not for the first time, he wondered why he'd entered the thankless world of criminal law. He despised the system, which he saw as paying lip service to justice. No one ever tried to stop bad things happening, it was all about dealing with the misery afterwards. *'Litter-picking.'* The establishment's futile effort to hold back the rising tide of petty criminality, anti-social behaviour, and general short-sighted hubris.

He didn't make a difference anymore. He wondered if he ever had. He couldn't. Most of the time, he was paid a pittance to spend a few minutes trying to establish excuses or explain away whatever crime had been committed. Innocence was a luxury he no longer wasted his time on.

Qualifying as a barrister had meant something – then. He was convinced Britain without law would descend into anarchy. He'd joined a system that upheld that belief. But he'd stopped believing. Anarchy was already here, not in the absence of law, but despite it. Too many people had withdrawn their consent to be ruled under it. *'Vox populi,'* and the voice was growing louder.

But the call with Raphael Conza had awakened something. Maybe because the Stolz case wasn't petty, it was new and exciting and complex. He'd started to think of the law again like he used to – as a solid and unshakeable structure around which everyday life revolved and evolved.

Raphael Conza. Now there's someone who still cared, still trying to make a difference, hadn't had his spirit crushed. It made Chase feel guilty, ashamed of himself and the cynic he'd become.

He returned to the office and looked up the number of his friend Jimmy Appleton.

"Bloody hell, Harry. Good to hear from you."

Jimmy was a cheerful soul, well-liked, funny and ridiculously clever. He also possessed the uncanny knack of making people feel special. The product of an expensive public school and Oxbridge, Jimmy exuded confidence. He was a half-decent rugby player too. When he was out drinking, he kept his front teeth in a pocket so he wouldn't lose them. The dentures being the result of a particularly feisty match against the Royal Navy. His blond curly hair, red cheeks and toothless grin always reminded Harry of a very happy and carefree scarecrow.

They hadn't spoken for a couple of years, but as is the way with ex-forces people, they talked as if they had seen each other yesterday. They reminisced for a while, chatting about scrapes they'd been in together and people they'd known. The conversation followed a familiar pattern. They'd engaged this way many times before.

But Jimmy had never been naïve.

"Come on then, Hatch, you've never done anything in your life without a reason and as much I dearly cherish talking to my old mate, I've a feeling you didn't pick up the phone because you missed me!"

"Never could fool you Jimmy, and by the way, it's strange being called Hatch again. Brings back memories."

"What's it all about? Something exciting I expect."

"I won't spin you a line, Jimmy, it's a personal favour."

"Oh, OK. That sounds ominous. I don't have the number of that air trafficker from Gütersloh any more you know."

"Bloody hell, I'd forgotten about her. No, it concerns a chap who works for Skyguard, Lukas Stolz. Do you know him?"

"The guy who was killed in Milan. Yes, his murder's been a hot topic here all week. Caused quite a stir. I only met him once. Bit of a stiff fish, God rest his whatsits and so on."

"What do you know about him?"

"Very high up. Worked with numbers. Hush-hush. Designed the encryption code for our data link system. Weird sort of chap, loner. Can't say I know much more than that. Why the interest? Is it a case you're working on?"

"Sort of, but unofficially. In truth, I'm trying to help a friend. Do you happen to know why Stolz was in Milan?"

"No, I didn't know he was over there, but I wouldn't. Different department. He works out of our head office in Warwick. I could probably find out though."

"Thanks Jimmy, but I don't want the world crashing down on your head."

"Don't be daft, Harry, he's the dish of the day at the moment, half the company is asking questions about him. I'll interrogate a few trusted friends, discreetly. No one will know. Everyone loves Jimmy, you know that. If you're asking, it must be important. Leave it with me."

"There's one more thing, Jimmy. May I read out something found in Stolz's notebook, my friend is trying to work out what it means, if anything."

"Go ahead Harry, ready to receive."

"OK, it's DLR-EAC1–"

Jimmy interrupted him.

"DLR. That's easy Harry. Stands for Data Link Remote. It's the system we use to update software in our black boxes. 'EAC1' will be the line number. Read the rest out to me."

"4D, 9C and 555."

"Give me a second, Harry."

Chase suddenly became nervous and when his friend returned, stopped him.

"Jimmy, wait. Isn't this stuff secret? Are we talking about confidential information here?"

"No, not really. I grant you, you wouldn't find this stuff on the internet, but the line of data you just gave me is just one of millions. Stolz was a stickler for security, kept most of the really important stuff very close to his chest. The fact he had this in his notebook must mean it's not of vital national importance."

"OK, as long as you're sure this conversation isn't going to get you in trouble."

"We're fine Harry, they won't shoot me, I promise. Everyone loves Jimmy! Now, what you read out to me is just hex."

"What the hell is hex? Is it computer code?"

"Nothing as complex as that. All computers work in binary, they must have taught that in the crumbling comprehensive you went to?"

"Yes Jimmy, noughts and ones. And it was a grammar school, so sod off!"

"Hexadecimal. It's just a different way of counting. It's used to represent lines of binary digits. Everyone uses it, standard practice. Decimal is nought to nine and hex, nought to fifteen. Ten to fifteen uses the letters A to F instead of digits."

"So in hex, you count 0,1,2,3,4,5,6,7,8,9,A,B,C,D,E,F – is that right?"

"Spot on. Fifteen is F and sixteen is one, zero. Hold on a tick."

Chase heard Jimmy tapping on a keyboard.

"You could do it yourself on any scientific calculator. The line number translates to 60097 and the groups 77, 156 and 1365. No secrets divulged. All I did was convert hex into decimal."

"But what are they used for?"

"Now that is nearing the dark side. However, I can tell you those numbers are commands to bits of kit in the system."

"Without telling me anything they can arrest you for, explain that in terms a simple comprehensive schoolboy would understand."

"OK, but you can watch a film about this on our website. The Skyguard II system uses two distinct data links. Just clever radios really. One is the 'DLO', 'Data Link Operational'. That distributes sensor data gathered from all the platforms on the link."

"Ground radars, airborne radars, that sort of thing?"

"You've got it, plus a whole load more. The idea is that everyone on the same datalink can help build and see the same air and ground picture."

"And I'm guessing the data is encrypted, the stuff Stolz designed?"

"Right again. But the hex strings you just gave me refer to the 'DLR', the 'Data Link Remote'. It's a sort of admin feed. All platforms on the same network are signed on to it whenever they power up."

"So what's it for?"

"We use it to synchronise the platforms. In effect, making sure all the radars, tanks and aircraft use the same time frame. Time is critical in a data link system."

"It acts like a speaking clock."

"Yes, something like that, but it's also used to record missile firings and update system software. If we need to make a software change, we distribute it via the DLR."

"OK, I get it, so Stolz's numbers are commands to the system on the DLR."

"That's right. Think about your car radio. You can switch it on or off with a knob. The function of the knob is set by the manufacturers. If you wanted to turn the on-off switch into a tuning knob, you would have to remove the radio, open it up and reconfigure the electronics. In essence, we can do the same thing without leaving the office. We send reconfiguration instructions to the address of the on-off switch. The groups of numbers you gave me relate to particular functions of the system."

"Very clever. But isn't that kind of dangerous? It means you could really screw things up with just a bit of code."

"Welcome to my world, Harry. But functionality changes require two hundred signatures and months of testing. Stolz is the only person who can give final sign-off authority and he's a stickler for protocol. There have been one or two screw-ups over the years, but nothing significant, Stolz wouldn't allow it."

"What sort of screw-ups?"

"I'm not part of the inner circle, so much of what I hear is just rumour and gossip, but there was an almighty flap around this time last year. A goodwill deployment of Skyguard II to Latvia, hugely political. NATO showing the Russians they're ready to repel borders on behalf of the Baltic states."

"And something went wrong?"

"Truthfully, I don't know. There was a tale going around that a missile had been fired by accident. Personally, I think the Russians were trying to stir up trouble. The story appeared in the papers at the time, but it died as quickly as it started. The Russians stopped bleating and the British media didn't do a follow-up, which should tell you something. It all went away."

"What do you think happened, Jimmy?"

"I'd put my house on the accidental firing stuff being a load of bollocks. As soon as the Russians made their complaint public, the bigwigs flew out to Riga, but nothing happened. No one was put on the carpet, no internal investigation and nothing was ever said."

"What was the Russian story?"

"They said a civilian aircraft flying from Moscow to Stockholm was intercepted by a NATO missile fired from Latvia. The aircraft took some minor damage and turned back. There were photos in the Russian papers showing an engine casing with a small hole in it, but you know the mess a missile causes. This hole was tiny. My guess is the damage was caused by a piece of debris from the runway, and the Russians created a fairy tale around it."

"But they dropped the accusation?"

"Like a stone, almost as soon as it was released. No retraction of course. The story just died."

"So nothing to do with Skyguard in Latvia then."

"No, but something did happen out there, I just don't know what. Maybe the British Army cocked something up and Skyguard was told to keep quiet. The army had only been operating the system for a few months and it would have been a disaster for the MOD, and NATO, if it transpired ordinary soldiers were incapable of operating a sophisticated system like Skyguard II."

"So you don't think some overly keen corporal pulled the trigger when he shouldn't have?"

"Definitely not. Skyguard II isn't like firing a rifle. Missiles only launch if the target meets certain parameters. It's fail-safe, designed to prevent trigger-happy corporals from shooting something down they're not supposed to."

"What parameters?"

"Skyguard II analyses every contact on the network. It looks for friendly and hostile criteria. If a radar contact pops up doing three hundred knots, it receives a high points score. If it's a fast-moving, low-level contact coming from the direction of the enemy, it loses a load of points. If it's travelling on a known civil air route, it gets a zillion points. Basically, the missile can't launch unless the points score falls below a pre-set threshold."

"That's really clever."

"And that's why I think the accidental firing stuff is rubbish. The system just wouldn't allow a missile to suddenly run up the rails. Too many things have to happen first."

"But something did happen in Riga?"

"Tilza actually, it's a small town near the border. No one's allowed to mention Tilza round here. Dirty word and guaranteed to result in your marching orders. But yes, something happened, but it wasn't a missile firing at an airliner, of that I'm certain."

"Jimmy, you're a star. I really do owe you one."

"My pleasure, Harry. I'll ask around about Stolz for you. But do me a favour, keep the Tilza thing under your hat. Don't want to poke the tigers."

Chase regretted calling his friend as soon as he put the phone down. *'This is stupid and none of my business,'* he chided himself. But he opened up his computer and found a copy of *The Times* dated fifteenth of July last year, all the same.

77

Temporary Office of the
Bundesnachrichtendienst (BND),
Habersaathstrasse, Berlin, Germany

Construction of the enormous sand-coloured building in Chausseestrasse was nearing completion, but the offices were not yet occupied by members of the German Federal Intelligence Service, so they were taken to a nearby, white, three-storey terraced house in Habersaathstrasse.

After security checks, and the surrender of their mobile phones, they passed through two different scanners before being asked to wait in a small, unadorned reception area, complete with the obligatory CCTV. They were not offered a drink.

Ten minutes later, they followed a uniformed policeman down a corridor on the first floor. He flashed a card across a metal plate and the door buzzed as it popped open. The meeting room was windowless, with walls of white, grainy tiles. Where the tiles met the door frame, Conza noticed the lining of dense, grey foam. *'Soundproofed,'* he concluded.

The square room contained a long, narrow table surrounded by six chrome and leather armchairs. A screen took up almost the entire wall at the far end. A single speaker sat in the middle of the table, its cable disappearing through a hole in the floor.

They sat down and waited again.

The door buzzed loudly, and the man who entered, spoke in fluent English.

"Good morning, Colonel Scutari, Lieutenant Conza. Welcome to Berlin. You may call me Ralf. Please sit down."

He avoided eye contact and his hand was warm and soft. His handshake was languid and weak. *'Fingers of a pianist.'*

By the time the colonel spoke, Ralf was already seated and browsing a pink file he'd brought with him.

"Thank you for agreeing to meet us, Ralf…"

He raised a hand but didn't look up.

"Just one moment, Colonel. I've been instructed to wait for someone else."

'...and I don't think you appreciated that instruction,' Conza considered.

Conza watched Ralf as he read. He was around thirty years of age, slim, pale, almost translucent skin, wavy brown hair. Neatly dressed. Ribbed, red tie, white shirt, blue linen jacket and grey woollen trousers. *'Casual enough to feel at home, smart enough to appear efficient,'* thought Conza.

The door buzzed once more.

The newcomer wore a black, pinstripe, three-piece suit. His tie was dark blue with small, winged dagger motifs running in diagonals. His hair, which hadn't seen a comb for a while, was a tangle of black-grey waves. Broad shoulders, wine-stained cheeks and nose, and deep wrinkles around his quick, blue eyes. *'At least fifty,'* thought Conza as the man breezed towards him, grinning.

"This is Mr Smith, Colonel," said Ralf, without raising his head, the piano player's fingers waving in their general direction. "He's British."

"Charles Babcock, lovely to meet you. MI6 actually. I think the colonel can know that much, Ralf," he exclaimed, grasping the colonel's hand and shaking it vigorously.

"All on the same side now. And you must be Lieutenant Conza. Raphael, isn't it?"

"That's right, everybody calls me Raffy." Babcock's fingers were hard, dry and very strong.

"Then Raffy it is. Come on, take a seat. Ralf informs me you have a story to tell. I'm all ears."

Ralf opened his eyes and closed the folder impatiently.

"Before we begin, I would like to ask the colonel a few questions."

Ralf's back straightened as he leant forward, clasping his hands together neatly. Babcock winked at Conza.

"Colonel, whilst I don't doubt that we're all 'on the same side', I was surprised to receive your request for a meeting with the BND. You work for the finance ministry in Italy, I believe. Berlin is not a part of Italy. Are you not outside of your area of jurisdiction?"

The colonel was unperturbed. And it suddenly occurred to Conza, he never was.

"Firstly, thank you for agreeing to accept my request for a meeting."

Ralf smiled painfully.

"You are of course correct. Guardia di Finanza normally involves itself in internal matters; borders, smuggling, docks, airports, that sort of thing. However, we do have a remit to investigate organised crime, wherever that may lead us."

"But we have no Italian mafia in Berlin, Colonel."

"Plenty of bloody Russians though," chirped Babcock, with a grin.

Conza covered his mouth with the back of his hand.

The colonel responded.

"The mafia is only one of many organised crime organisations operating across Italy, and across the whole of Europe and the United States for that matter, as you are aware. Last Sunday a German businessman was killed in Milan. Italian State Police are investigating his murder. Guardia di Finanza are involved because the assassination has the hallmarks of organised crime. Therefore, whilst Berlin is not within my jurisdiction, the murder of one of your citizens is. As he came from Berlin, I thought you may wish to assist."

Babcock had already taken to the colonel and was nodding encouragingly. But Ralf wasn't going to concede so easily.

"Then the normal procedure is for you to make enquiries with the German police authorities, not the German secret service."

The colonel sat back in his chair.

"And had you not granted my request for this meeting, that is exactly what I would have done. However, you didn't refuse, which tells me you are interested in what we have to say. So why don't we drop the bullshit and try to find out who killed one of your citizens?"

Even Babcock held his breath.

231

Ralf was looking down again. His shoulders rolled back as if he was stretching the muscles in his neck.

"We do have an interest in Herr Stolz, Colonel, you are correct. But I reserve the right to call a halt to this meeting if at any time I believe it conflicts with German national interests."

The colonel sat forward again, ignoring him.

"Mr Babcock, whilst I'm pleased that you're here, your attendance is something of a surprise."

"To be fair to Ralf, that was his idea. We too have a stake in the activities of Lukas Stolz, and Ralf thought it would be a good idea if I came along."

"In which case, thank you Ralf."

"It was a logical step," Ralf muttered into his chest, before opening his folder again. "Now perhaps, Colonel, you would be good enough to bring us up to date with your enquiries."

The colonel summarised the Stolz investigation, bringing out photographs as he referred to individuals. When the grainy picture of Alexander Kurti was put on the table, Babcock snatched at it. His forehead creased. He wasn't grinning anymore.

"Alexander Kurti. Now there's a bad egg."

Ralf nodded without emotion.

After summarising Conza's conversation with Katherine Harper, the colonel sat down.

"Well, I don't mind kicking off," said Babcock earnestly.

Conza flipped his notepad open.

"The Schuman deal was pretty much as you describe. Felix contacted us in '66, he had a job in Berlin as a weapons adviser to the East Germans. His information was pure gold. The Americans were green as hell. Spying was cloak and dagger back then. Secret drop-offs, secure radios, that sort of thing. Felix Schuman was pretty good at it, by all accounts."

"Until Lukas Stolz told the Stasi about him spying for you in '68," said Conza, determined not to be left out.

They all looked at Ralf.

"Lieutenant, the evidence of Lukas Stolz being a Stasi informer, the documents in the possession of Dieter Stolz that he

232

showed to his daughter. Do you know whether they were originals or copies?"

"Originals. Katherine was certain."

"Did she show them to you?"

"No, he didn't let her keep them. She said her father told her they would be sent to Josef Schuman."

"In the letter, delivered to Schuman in 1990 shortly after Dieter Stolz died?"

"Yes."

"That's a shame."

Ralf was taking his time. Conza couldn't work out if he just enjoyed being the focus of their attention, or he was making sure he didn't divulge anything useful.

"And are you taking seriously Mrs Harper's assertion that Josef Schuman intended to kill Lukas Stolz?"

"No, I don't think we can. Schuman knew Stolz was an informer in 1990, but in 1994, he let him join his company. Since then, Stolz has worked unmolested. Personally, I think Schuman's threat was just said in a moment of anger."

"I see. Have you interviewed Josef Schuman, Lieutenant?"

The colonel interrupted.

"Be assured, that was our next step. Would that cause you a problem?"

"No problem to me, Colonel, but I'm not sure he will cooperate. Mr Schuman is very well protected."

Ralf splayed his hands on the table.

"By an army of lawyers for one. And he still has friends in powerful positions in Berlin."

"Are you saying the German government would shield him from an investigation?" asked the colonel abruptly.

Ralf gave a sickly smile and shrugged his shoulders.

"I didn't say that Colonel. I merely wish to warn you that it will not be easy to interview Herr Schuman. For one thing, you have no jurisdiction in Germany. His lawyers will know that you cannot compel him to talk to you."

"And you won't help us?" asked Conza becoming irritated.

"As I just told your colonel, Lieutenant. There are procedures, channels through which such requests should be made. I'm sure the German police will provide you with every assistance. If they can."

The colonel didn't flinch. His voice remained calm and controlled.

"Do you know why Schuman was sacked as vice-chancellor in '99?"

Ralf's eyes flicked towards Babcock.

"I don't think we have a choice, in the circumstances," the Englishman said with a shrug.

Ralf winced again. Disclosures seemed to cause him physical pain.

"Yes, we know why he left. It is our job to know such things."

Babcock took over.

"He was caught with his trousers down, if you'll excuse the vernacular."

"Really?" said the colonel. "By whom?"

"By us of course," said Ralf, emphatically. "Josef Schuman had a significantly high sex-drive. It was well known that he regularly indulged in sexual practices that may have exposed certain vulnerabilities."

"He was a potential blackmail victim you mean?" offered the colonel.

"He was as randy as an old goat and screwed everything that moved. Bollocks before brain, that was his problem. And he wasn't particular whose wife or daughter he was caught with either. Complaints about him littered the Bundestag."

Ralf closed his eyes.

"The truth is that Schuman's extra-marital affairs were appearing in the Sunday newspapers. He was making a laughingstock of the cabinet and it had to be stopped."

"Did he jump, or was he pushed?" Conza asked.

"Oh, I think it's safe to say that Mr Schuman did not leave voluntarily."

"What's the British interest in all this, Mr Babcock?" asked the colonel.

For the first time since they'd sat down, Babcock looked uncomfortable.

"Skyguard is an important British asset, Colonel."

"Anglo-German asset," interjected Ralf indignantly.

"Actually, it's Anglo-German-Italian," said Conza with a sheepish smile.

Babcock grinned.

"Quite right, Raffy. I forget sometimes. All in this together. But Skyguard is incredibly important to the Brits. It's not just the defence angle, and God knows that's important enough. There's the money. Half the pension schemes in Britain rely on Skyguard shares. It's a mainstay of the economy. Jewel in the crown, so to speak."

"So alarm bells rang when Stolz was killed?"

"Absolutely. We need to know if there was anything sinister behind his death."

"Do you believe there is, Colonel? Anything sinister about his death?" Ralf asked clasping his hands together.

"Not sure about 'sinister'. But there are plenty of unanswered questions. Why, for example did Schuman let Stolz work for Skyguard, when he knew he'd informed on his father?"

Conza caught a smile flicker across Ralf's lips. The colonel had seen it too, but it was Babcock who responded.

"Perhaps he'd just forgiven him. The reunification thing resulted in a lot of wounds in need of healing. Maybe this was just another one. Let bygones be bygones."

"I think that's unlikely in these particular circumstances," replied the colonel, never taking his eyes from the German. "Ralf, may I go back to your earlier question? You asked Lieutenant Conza whether he'd seen the documents showing Stolz had been a Stasi informer. Why did you ask that?"

Ralf's hand movements were as measured as his voice.

"Before the Berlin Wall was demolished, the Stasi destroyed many of their records. But contrary to popular opinion, Germans aren't always as efficient as the world thinks."

'So you are capable of laughing,' thought Conza.

"A significant number of documents remained untouched, or at least capable of restoration. When you contacted us, I personally looked into what remained of the files recovered from the Stasi office in Potsdam. I found no mention of Lukas Stolz in the role of an informer, nor did I find his statement accusing Felix Schuman of spying. Hence my interest."

"But you said yourself, many of the records were destroyed."

"Exactly, which begs the question how did Dieter Reisman, or Dieter Stolz, as he became known, gain possession of original documents purporting to show Lukas Stolz was an informer?"

"Katherine told me Stolz had always known his son worked for the Stasi. Maybe he got hold of the records before they started destroying them?"

"That would be more believable if they were just copies. I'm not a detective, but if the originals had been removed from the Stasi repository before they started destroying them, I think someone may have noticed they'd gone missing."

Conza suddenly felt quite inadequate.

"Again, I don't wish to tell you how to do your job Lieutenant, but it may be worth finding out when Dieter Stolz left his letter and the Stasi file on Stolz with his solicitor. If it was from before East Germany began to disintegrate…"

"They can't have been originals. They must have been copies. Or forgeries!" Conza erupted, still angry with himself.

Ralf started writing on a sheet of paper.

"This is the address of someone you may wish to speak to. He was a major in the Stasi in Potsdam. He served in the Brandenburg Police Force after reunification, as did many ex-Stasi. He's quite old now, but a bottle of Asbach should help his memory."

The colonel took the paper from Ralf's slender fingers.

"You don't believe it do you? You don't think Lukas Stolz was a Stasi informer?"

Ralf considered the question for a few seconds.

"Truthfully, Colonel, I have no idea whether he was or he wasn't."

The colonel leant forward and fixed Ralf with a stare.

"But I can guess who was."

"Who?" said Conza, with far too much excitement.

"Josef Schuman."

"This meeting is over gentlemen. I will arrange for someone to show you out."

78

Café Roma, Milan, Italy

At ten o'clock on Friday morning, Giuliani received a text message from his contact Troy. It read simply '*Coffee 13:00*'. He looked at his clock and rolled over to go back to sleep. He'd been up all night.

'Fat fucking queer. What does he want now?'

...

The policeman was already sitting in the café when Zeffirelli joined him and ordered coffee. It was twenty-past-one.

"What you got?"

'He's nervous,' thought Zeffirelli, noticing the beads of sweat clinging to grey stubble on the policeman's top lip. *'Maybe he's still pissed off at being outed in front of the museum queue.'*

"Things are really bad at the station; the commissioner is on the warpath again. He's running another inquisition."

"So fucking what? Sounds like a personal problem to me. What have you dragged me down here for?"

"Forensics have put your boys Leo and Paolo at the bakery. The old man is still in a coma, but the girl will testify. She'll hang them."

The policeman was pale, his hands trembling as he put the cup to his lips.

"They got sloppy. I've sent them away for a while, no sweat. Is that it? She'll never testify. We'll sort her out when we need to. If we need to."

The policeman leant forward, his voice barely a whisper.

"I know where they're holding the Bennani boy."

"I don't need him anymore. I've sorted things out."

"OK, that's your call. I'm sorry I wasted your time." He got up to leave.

"Tell me anyway," Zeffirelli said, grabbing the policeman's arm and pulling him back down into his seat.

He passed a piece of paper across the table, which Zeffirelli read and pushed into his breast pocket.

"The whole family's under police protection. Isn't that right? I couldn't get near him if I wanted to."

"That could be sorted."

"How?"

"That's my problem. But it would cost you."

"Why would you do this?"

"I need the money. I'm leaving Milan. Away from you, away from the police force, away from the shit I have to put up with every day. It's my ticket out of here."

"No one ever truly gets away. The shit always catches up with you in the end."

"Not for me. Now, do you want me to make the arrangements or not?"

"How much?"

"A hundred thousand. Upfront, and that isn't negotiable."

"Go screw yourself. A hundred thousand. Everything's negotiable."

"Not this time it isn't," the policeman said, rising once more.

"Sit down, you faggot – we're still talking here."

Something had changed. Zeffirelli wasn't sure and the policeman knew it. He also knew Zeffirelli well enough to know he wouldn't resist buying what he had to sell.

79

Habersaathstrasse, Berlin, Germany

Babcock held open the door of his claret-coloured Daimler. "It's no trouble, really. Come on, hop in. I'll take you to the airport, and on the way we can drop in on Major Fischer."

"How did you know? About Josef being a Stasi informer?" asked Conza, turning to the colonel.

"I wasn't sure. Bit of a stab in the dark, really. It may not be true of course."

Babcock interjected.

"I think Ralf's reaction spoke a thousand words, don't you?"

"You may be right. But if Ralf wasn't

willing to tell us, why would he point us at the ex-Stasi major? I strongly suspect he'll give us a definitive answer, one way or the other."

"Because the truth won't be coming out of his mouth, that's why Colonel. He personally told us nothing."

"In which case, there's division inside the BND."

"How do you know that?" said Conza trying to keep up.

"Because he wanted to tell us something he'd been told not to," Babcock replied.

"So we've got an ally?"

"I wouldn't go that far, Raffy. But at least we know Ralf won't place obstacles in our way. He was trying to tell us as much, I'm sure."

"Mr Babcock, do you know this Major Fischer?" asked Conza as they joined the traffic at the end of the road.

"No, never met the chap, but Ralf says he likes Asbach, so he's all right in my book. We'll have to pick up a bottle at the supermarket. Lovely stuff, German brandy, made with grape skins."

The colonel sat forward.

"And you also want to hear what he has to say. Am I right?"

Babcock looked hard at the colonel's reflection in the rear-view mirror.

"There's much that I can't tell you, Colonel. You know how it works. Suffice to say that Stolz and Schuman are very large blips on MI6's radar right now."

"And you want to know if there's been any sort of security breach. Am I right?"

"Let's just say, I need to know who was behind Stolz's murder and just as importantly, why he was killed."

"We know it was arranged by Alexander Kurti," offered Conza.

"So I understand. I'm ashamed to say we've used Kurti in the past. Only once mind. But he did take the Queen's shilling for a job."

"Can you tell me about it?" asked the colonel.

Conza suddenly felt invisible.

"It was after the massacres in Bosnia. We were hunting down some of the senior perpetrators. They escaped south, into the hills. We used Kurti. He knew the territory, had a lot of contacts in Yugoslavia."

"Did it work? Did you get them?"

"Every single one. All dead, of course. He's a killing machine. They call him the Afghan Hound, you know."

"What other countries has he worked for?"

"Russia, obviously. One or two other ex-Soviets. And Uncle Sam."

"What did he do for the United States? Ah, of course. Afghanistan again," the colonel said, quickly.

"He still does the odd job for them over there."

Conza heard himself say, "Jesus."

"It's a screwed-up world, Raffy. Your colonel knows. Sometimes we can't tell the good guys from the bad guys."

"Who's protecting Kurti? Is it our own government?"

"Colonel, if you don't mind." Babcock pulled over into a supermarket carpark.

"Raffy, don't get wrapped around the axle on this. It's not as simple as you think. The problem is that Kurti's very existence is an embarrassment to a great number of people. Taxpayers have been funding his antics for an awfully long time. That's not something one or two politicians want us to read about on a Sunday morning."

"But who's putting pressure on the Italian Finance Minister this time? Do you know?"

"It's not us, I can tell you that. Using Kurti was a mistake, one our organisation would like to see buried. He's one of the last hangovers from the dark days. Kurti's was the era of the iron curtain, Bay of Pigs, state-sponsored assassinations. Expediency was the watchword back then. Along with expendability."

"So why don't you just kill him? Britain is certainly capable of it," Conza said, glancing at Babcock's tie.

"Everything's changed, Raffy. Britain's not the same. We don't go around killing those we don't like anymore. Accountability and proportionality. That's the new European order. Kurti's protected by the system."

"Then put the bastard on trial. We've got enough evidence to try him five times over. Make him face the system."

"You think the politicians who once paid him to do their dirty work, want him standing in the dock, spilling the beans?"

'They know every trick in the book,' Conza heard Harry Chase say. He felt empty.

"Cheer up, Raffy. Kurti and his type, they're running out of allies. All his protectors are dying of old age."

"So we let Kurti die of old age with them. Is that it?"

The colonel intervened.

"You said MI6 wants him buried?"

"It would be nice. We're just biding our time. Waiting for the right moment. When his shields abandon him."

Conza was incensed.

"But that's madness. I watched that bastard plot the death of not only Lukas Stolz, but a child and his father. He has no humanity. He's evil and I will not watch him walk away as if nothing happened. He destroys lives."

Conza pushed the car door open and got out. He was sitting on a bench when he felt the colonel's hand on his shoulder.

"Don't blame Babcock. He doesn't like it any more than we do. I think he's trying to help."

The colonel pushed an envelope onto Conza's knees.

"He gave this to me. Says the Germans would have a fit if they knew. Take a look."

Conza pulled out a black and white photograph. Five people in evening suits, walking down broad steps. In the centre of shot, a short, stocky man was pointing and laughing.

"Is that Josef Schuman? And that's Kurti right behind him. My God, Colonel, they know each other."

Conza turned the photograph over. "When was this taken?"

"Babcock says two years ago. He wants to help us. As much as he can, anyway."

"But our own government has told you to back off. What the hell do we do?"

The colonel was staring past Conza, remembering something painful.

"I was always going to pursue him, Raffy, I just didn't want to take you down with me. I still don't."

The memory faded and he held Conza's gaze.

"You're at the start of your career, Raffy. This will be the end of mine."

Conza leant forward and managed a smile.

"Careers are overrated, Colonel. Brocelli told me."

"If you follow me down that road, there will be repercussions. You really understand that don't you?"

"I'll teach history. I hear they're crying out for good teachers in prison."

"Getting locked up would be one of the better outcomes, Raffy. You know what I'm saying?"

"No one lives for ever, Colonel."

"That's easy to say sitting on a bench in the sun. But so be it. I'll talk to Babcock. You and I will come up with a plan when we return to Milan. Now come on, I saw him with a bottle of Asbach. Let's go meet the Stasi major."

80

Central Police Headquarters, Milan, Italy

The flight from Berlin didn't land until early evening, so Conza was surprised to see Brocelli still at his desk, reading the sports section of a local newspaper. He barely raised an eyebrow when Conza knocked on his door, and without being invited, sat down.

'There's a bloody good police officer in there.'

"Good result out at the barn last night. The colonel told me."

'He's not what you think. What everyone thinks.'

"You found Fanucci, I hear?"

'You'd do well to talk to him someday. Get past his defences.'

"Only one of his henchmen though."

Brocelli turned the page.

"You really don't like me do you, Captain?"

Slowly, his eyes lifted.

"You're wrong again, Lieutenant. I actually couldn't give a toss about you, one way or the other."

Conza smiled and wondered at what point in his life Brocelli had decided to be an asshole.

"OK, well let's assume you don't like me. What I'm about to say is not going to change that. In fact, I think it's going to make it worse."

Brocelli grunted, but Conza caught a flicker of a grin.

"The point is, you're not good at following rules are you?"

Brocelli slammed his fist onto the desk, making the newspaper rise at the corner.

"I have no idea what you are talking about, Lieutenant, but I don't answer to you. If you've got a problem, take it to the commissioner."

Conza had jumped when Brocelli's hand crashed into the desk.

"You misunderstand me, Captain Brocelli. I'm actually counting on the fact that you don't follow the rules. I need you to have not followed the rules."

Brocelli stood up, chest puffed out, cheeks reddening. He hitched his trousers above the bulge of his ample waist. Dots of white spittle illuminating the corners of his mouth.

"Before you blow your top, just hear me out. You don't use the police computer system. You use your own laptop. I get it, and quite frankly, I don't care. It's not my problem. But you had access to Stolz's USB stick, and I'm guessing you couldn't resist taking a peek at what was on it. I wish I had. Am I right?"

Brocelli sat down again and picked up his paper.

"Fuck off, Conza."

Sighing heavily, Conza got up to leave. *'I tried.'*

"Do you know why you think people like me don't like you?"

"No, tell me."

"Because you want them not to like you. It makes you feel less guilty about not liking them."

Conza was stunned, but Brocelli hadn't finished.

"We're not so different you and I, just ten more kilos around your waist and twenty-five more years of pushing shit uphill and before you know it, you too will stop following the rules."

The damning synopsis irritated Conza far more than he thought possible. Brocelli reached into his desk and unceremoniously tossed him Stolz's key fob.

"It won't do you any good, it's password-protected."

"Jesus, Brocelli. You kept it. You've had it all along."

"Never got the chance to put it back."

Conza stood there, not sure what to say or whether to thank him. He settled on exoneration.

"You're a star, Captain Brocelli. Rest assured; I will take full responsibility for this. If anyone asks, tell them I took it and if there's any comeback, it's on my head, I promise you."

"There you go again, Conza. You still don't get it do you? Despite all your brains and university education. You've missed the point; I really couldn't give a shit."

81

Saturday

'The Manor House', Hatchmere, Cheshire, England

On Saturday morning, Max arrived in the dark and quickly retraced the path to the stable. He wanted to focus on the estate's activities in the period two hours either side of dawn. As the sun rose above the valley side, he made notes and took a few pictures. He made a sketch showing the gatehouse, main building, cameras, and floodlights. He also noted the position of a large oak tree overhanging the wall running down the side of the house.

The guards operated from a makeshift control room in the garage adjoined to the side of the main building. They hadn't set up in the gatehouse; too far removed from the asset they were paid to protect. They knew what they were doing. *'Professional British soldiers, maybe paras, marines or SAS,'* Max concluded.

He identified three men, at least one of whom was always on patrol in the grounds. Changeover times were imprecise, but roughly equated to four hours on, eight hours off. For the first time since he'd left Milan, he wished Puz was with him.

He concluded there would be no ground sensors; patrol routes were irregular, and it would have been too difficult to keep switching them on and off as a soldier passed through a particular area. The floodlights remained on until sunrise at around five-thirty, and he decided it would be almost impossible to move around the grounds unseen while they were working.

He decided he would enter the grounds just before six. Half an hour after daybreak on Sunday morning.

He returned to the hotel, ate breakfast and went back to his room, making sure that the *'Do Not Disturb'* tag was securely fixed to the door handle.

He stripped and cleaned the Heckler & Koch Mk 23 semi-automatic pistol and fitted the silencer. He filled each of four magazines with ten rounds and laid out his clothes on the armchair. He loaded the pistol and placed the remaining three magazines in a pouch on his utility belt. He checked his torch was working and tugged at the sheath. Finally, he returned the small compass to the recess in the handle of his commando knife, which he sharpened on a sheet of wet sandpaper before placing it under his pillow.

He was ready. Max could sleep.

82

Guardia di Finanza Headquarters, Milan, Italy

Conza was at his desk before six. He'd already confirmed Brocelli's proclamation that Stolz's fob was password-protected. But for the third time, he slid it into a USB port. The now familiar invitation to enter the password popped up, along with the words that continued to depress him: 'WARNING – ONLY TWO ATTEMPTS REMAINING'.

"Damn Brocelli."

"Sorry about that. Stupid really."

The voice caught Conza by surprise.

"Captain Brocelli. What are you doing at Finanza?"

"I called Moretti, he told me you'd be here."

Conza looked at his watch.

"I bet that cheered him up."

Brocelli seemed different. His voice was less angry, and he was out of uniform. Conza couldn't believe the difference the change of clothes made. He suddenly appeared *'more normal'*.

Brocelli placed a folder on Conza's desk; a Europol criminal record file. Without thinking, Conza began reading it.

"We recovered Fanucci and Puz's bodies from the barn. Unfortunately, this guy wasn't with them. His name is Maksim Yahontov, known as Max. Ex-Russian special forces, trained sniper and small arms instructor. Highly skilled with a knife – wrote the book on killing silently. Kicked out of the army for a reason that isn't recorded. Rumours are he slit the throat of a high-ranking officer at a party."

Conza took a new notepad from the box.

"Often goes by the name of Milo Berentov, but he's used other identities. Known to the police in Ravenna, where he was charged but not convicted of kidnapping a child. Although the ransom was paid, the girl's remains were discovered three weeks later. She'd starved to death."

Brocelli was staring at Yahontov's profile.

"We know he was in Russia last May, but probably returned to Italy under a different name. We're going back through immigration records to see what passport he used this time."

"Kadin said he was evil. I mean, not just bad, evil," Conza said, still thinking of the little girl.

Brocelli suddenly looked very old and tired. He spoke as if trying to capture a thought that was evading him.

"Kadin is right. I've met this animal. A more cruel and evil man has never walked this earth."

'We all have a story to tell and his is more tragic than most.'

"How do you know him?"

"I was on the kidnap investigation team. We arrested him quite soon after Violetta Donnini was snatched. One of Yahontov's gang lost their bottle and turned himself in. Didn't want to be involved in the murder of a child, I guess."

"So she died soon after she was kidnapped?"

"No, they kept her alive to begin with, but Yahontov made it clear that whatever happened, the girl had to be killed. She'd seen their faces, you see."

"How old was she?"

"Eight."

"What happened?"

"This guy turned up at the police station in Ravenna. Confessed to taking her from a park. Gave us the address where Yahontov and his buddy were holding her. His buddy was Stefan Puz, by the way."

"But the girl wasn't there?"

"No, just Puz and Yahontov. They laughed at us. At me. I lost my temper. They loved it."

"What had they done with her?"

"Tied her up and hid her in a storm drain a few kilometres away. Pumped her full of drugs and dumped her as soon as they realised the other gang member had gone missing. They guessed he was going to turn them in."

"But you must found forensics at the farmhouse?"

"Piles. We could prove Violetta had been there. We even found her headband. There was more than enough to charge them."

"What went wrong?"

"They were locked up, but we didn't have a clue where Violetta was. Yahontov told us the girl was underground with a limited air supply and we only had forty-eight hours to find her. He knew we wouldn't."

"They cut a deal didn't they? Agreed to tell you where Violetta was if you released them?"

"I don't think the Ravenna commissioner would have caved in, but he was under enormous pressure from on high. The girl's father was rich and had influence in Rome."

"So you let them go?"

"I watched them walk away. I knew the girl wouldn't be found alive, but they weren't listening to me. The Americans had the technology to track them, but the commissioner wouldn't let me set it up. I was told to be quiet and go away. I followed orders."

"You didn't have a choice, Brocelli."

"Yes I did. Of course I had a choice. I picked blind, stupid obedience over the life of an eight-year-old girl."

"When was this?"

"Twelve years ago."

"Yahontov and Puz ran, I take it?"

"They crossed the border into Switzerland. After that, they just vanished."

"And never told you where she was. But why? They had nothing to lose by then, you already knew they were involved?"

"Because Yahontov would have enjoyed it. The thought of us running around the countryside digging holes would have pleased him. I think he was punishing me – all of us. Evil. Plain and simple."

Both men stared at Yahontov's photograph. The man in the picture was smirking. Conza began to understand.

"Listen, Brocelli. Have you got anything on today? I could do with a chat."

"I don't need your sympathy, Conza."

"I'm not going to give you any. It wouldn't do any good, anyway. No, I need your help. I'm in over my head and could do with some advice."

"As long as it's not about a woman."

"Chance would be a fine thing. Do you know Benito's on Mercato?"

"Yes."

"Can you be there at one? I need to make some calls first."

Brocelli nodded before turning to go.

"Is it anything to do with your trip to Berlin yesterday?" he asked as he reached the door.

"How did you guess?"

83

Central Police Headquarters, Milan, Italy

Conza decided to walk across town to the police station. A niggly headache had started behind his eyes, and he needed fresh air. He stopped off at Gina's and ordered a double espresso. He sat in an alcove at the back of the café, away from the morning sun.

Brocelli's story had thrown him and scared him too. These men he was pursuing, they really were evil. They had no empathy. They didn't understand suffering, other than as a means to an end. They had dealt with Kadin and his father as if they were already dead. They starved small children to death. They reduced everyone to nameless and soulless entities; masters in the art of dehumanisation.

Trying to beat them by following the rules until they were locked away was the '*shit*' that Brocelli could no longer '*push uphill*'. Brocelli was wrong, Conza did get it, Harry Chase had said something similar to him before. He hadn't understood at the time. He did now.

He drank his coffee and called Sergeant Moretti.

"Where are you, Georgio?"

"I've just arrived at the safe house to finish taking Kadin's statement. Twenty-two pages so far. But we're nearly done."

The weariness in Moretti's voice made Conza think of Brocelli.

"I need you in my office at noon. What time can you get away?"

"It's Saturday, Raffy. If I come to your office, I won't get away until Sunday."

Conza waited.

"All right, I'll be there at twelve. I'm not going to ask why you need me, it would spoil the surprise of whatever bomb you are about to lob in my direction."

"You know me so well, Georgio. See you at twelve."

...

Police headquarters was unusually quiet, and no one was in the incident room. Conza read the updated investigation folder and was satisfied to see that there had been a possible sighting of the bakery assailants. He wrote a note on a new page which he called *'Georgio'*.

Pulling out Stolz's USB, Conza called Lanfranco Pisani's mobile.

Pisani wasn't too happy at being called on a Saturday but warmed when given the opportunity to talk about a technical matter.

"They all have a Skyguard-designed password-protection system, Lieutenant. Lukas Stolz invented the encryption algorithm. He called it the Skyguard Encrypted Data Safe, SEDS."

"So, in simple terms, how does SEDS work?"

"Think of it as an information bank."

"Tell me about how to access it, the password system."

"OK, so we all use passwords that act like a key. You put your data in the room and lock the door. If you want to access the data, you need to unlock the door with the correct key."

"So far, so good."

"The problem with that is the data is stored in a readable form. If you bypass the password or break down the door, you can access the information."

"I can see that."

"SEDS is different, you set the password before storing the data. Think of the room now containing trillions of boxes. The password determines which box is used to store each bit of data. As each tiny fragment of information goes through the door, it is sent to a box determined by the password, in other words, the data becomes incoherent; encrypted."

"So even if you break down the door, the data is unreadable?"

"You've got it, but there's more to SEDS than that. It isn't just a data storage device. It's physically secure. Tamper-proof and able to withstand extreme temperatures. It runs off a microprocessor; programmable to meet the needs of the user. For example, it can be set up to prevent copying, or only usable on a particular device. There are lots of options."

"Tell me about the password system."

"You get three goes to input the password correctly. If the third attempt fails, the system scrambles the data. Impossible to read even if you subsequently apply the correct password. It will do the same sort of thing if it senses a threat."

"You make it sound alive."

"It's a good way to think of it, Lieutenant. Whilst it's a clever gimmick to demonstrate Skyguard's attitude to security, in reality, SEDS is a dynamic and highly sensitive storage system."

"How many characters in the password?"

"Ten, always ten. Numbers, symbols, letters, upper or lower case."

"Great, that reduces the chances of cracking it to about a million to one."

"Actually, it's about two billion, billion, billion to one."

"Great. As you've probably guessed, we're trying to get into Stolz's fob. The data may be relevant to his murder. You don't happen to know his password do you?"

"Sorry, no. As I told you, Lukas Stolz rarely talked to any of us, or anyone else for that matter. Not the sort of chap to share secrets."

"Can you suggest anything, Mr Pisani? I'm in a hole."

The phone went quiet briefly.

"About a year ago, Skyguard reconfigured SEDS. People kept forgetting their password and as a result lost their data – permanently. Nothing Skyguard could do to help; there's no backdoor. But even though Stolz didn't like it, the company added a password reminder function."

"How do I access it?"

"It's not obvious. Look for the letters 'PR' in the bottom right-hand corner of the screen, double-click on it and the reminder should appear."

Conza had one final question.

"What's a backdoor?"

"Basically, it's a means by which a program's code writer is able to bypass normal protocols to read the data or alter its parameters. Clearly, they're highly controversial and strictly forbidden in the defence industry."

Conza thanked Pisani and rang off. He logged on to a computer, twisted the fob and inserted it into the USB port. The now familiar pop-up appeared with the Skyguard logo. He hadn't noticed the small shaded 'PR' before. Clicking on it caused a second pop-up to appear entitled 'Password Reminder'. It was a single word: 'Hund'.

Conza closed the program and typed 'Hund' into an internet search engine. The webpage filled with variations on the same theme: 'Hund' was German for dog.

Katherine Harper had a dog. He checked his notebook. 'Lulu.' He compiled a list of ten-character possibilities. 'Katherine.' Only nine letters. Her two children, Felix and Jennifer. Put together, they added up to thirteen characters. 'Lukas Stolz.' *'Too predictable.'* The code he'd copied from Stolz's notebook, 'DLR-EAC1 4D/9C/555', eighteen characters if you include the space.

"Shit. This is futile."

He tore the page from the pad and tossed it in the bin.

84

Guardia di Finanza Headquarters, Milan, Italy

Sergeant Moretti was already waiting at Finanza when Conza returned from the police station. They discussed Kadin's statement.

"Nearly finished, thank goodness. Should have it wrapped up by Monday."

"How's he doing?"

"Kadin? Mentally, he's pretty beaten up. Being with his family has helped, but he's not eating or sleeping much."

"We should tell the doctor."

"Already sorted. He's going out there today."

"Well done, Georgio, and thanks for coming in."

Conza told him about the conversation he'd had with the colonel about Kurti. He didn't mention his trip to Berlin.

"So we're now working on the basis that Stolz was the intended target?"

"Correct. Well I am. You're going to continue feeding the legend that Stolz was killed as a result of mistaken identity."

"Why?"

"Georgio, you're going to have to trust me. The mistaken identity story will buy me the time I need."

"To do what?"

Conza just stared at him.

"OK Raffy, I give up. I won't ask any more questions."

"I want you to lead the hunt for Zeffirelli's men."

"Has Brocelli agreed?"

"He will, I'm meeting him in half an hour. He'll play ball."

"I love your confidence."

"Before I tell you what I need you to do, I want to show you something." He brought out the SEDS fob.

"Where the hell did that come from? Have they found Stolz's stuff?"

"No. Brocelli had it the whole time. Don't ask."

Conza told Moretti about his conversation with Lanfranco Pisani.

"So, does it have a password reminder?"

"Yes, but it doesn't help. It just says '*Hund*', which is German for dog."

"Bloody hell, Raffy," Moretti exploded, standing up to search through his pocketbook.

"Fideccio. That was the name on the picture!"

Conza was deeply confused.

"Here it is. Fideccio. Kadin told me he found a photo of a dog amongst Stolz's money, on the back he'd written 'Fideccio'. I saw it."

"Kadin? When? It doesn't matter, show me."

Conza sighed with disappointment.

"Not enough letters, the password needs to be ten characters long. Pisani told me. Fideccio only has eight."

"There must be a connection. It can't be a coincidence."

Moretti picked up the phone and dialled the number for the Milan Skyguard office.

"Mr Pisani, it's Sergeant Moretti. Yes, I know he's with me now."

…

"I understand, but I won't keep you a minute. Just one more question. Do you happen to know if Stolz owned a dog?"

…

"Damn it. OK. We think he did, by the name of Fideccio. Does that name mean anything to you?"

…

"F I D E C C I O, that's right."

…

"OK thanks anyway, it was a long shot. You too."

Moretti put down the phone and walked to the board.

"Pisani doesn't know if Stolz had a dog and the name didn't mean anything. But I'm not letting go of this."

"Katherine had a dog, named Lulu," Conza said, in resignation.

But Moretti wasn't listening. Under the 'Stolz' column on the whiteboard, he wrote 'FIDECCIO' and 'HUND'.

Conza sauntered over and, picking up a pen, added a large red question mark.

85

'Benito's', Via Mercato, Milan, Italy

Conza had already ordered drinks by the time Brocelli arrived. They sat at the far end of the room in the booth Conza usually shared with Moretti when they needed to talk in private.

"I assumed you'd want a beer."

"Actually, I don't drink."

"Really? I'm sorry, what can I get you instead?"

"Just kidding."

Brocelli took a long draught and put the half-empty glass on the bar. Conza shook his head slowly.

"That's it isn't it? I just don't know you at all, do I?"

"Don't worry about it. Not many do. But that's my fault. Cheers."

Conza ordered Brocelli another beer.

"What you said to me about pushing shit uphill. I get it you know."

"You shouldn't take too much notice of me, Conza. I'm a dinosaur. Cynical and twisted. I'm battle-scarred."

"The colonel is a fan of yours, did you know that?"

"Really? No, I didn't. He's a very clever man. Served with him a while back. You'd go a long way to find someone better to follow."

"You still would then? Follow him, I mean."

"He's a frosty sod, but a damn good officer. Yes, I'd follow him. But I'm guessing you didn't ask me here for career advice."

"You're right." Conza took a sip of beer. "But before I tell you, I'm going to have to ask you to swear something."

"Why on earth would you believe any promise I made, Conza? It's not like we're best buddies."

"Because the colonel trusts you and that's good enough for me. All I want is your word that if you don't buy into what I'm about to tell you, this meeting never happened."

"Bloody hell, Conza. Have you buggered the commissioner or something?"

Conza's expression didn't change.

"All right. I swear. You've got me interested and I didn't think you were capable of that. So, come on. What's all this about?"

Conza told Brocelli about the meeting at the BND and his discussions with the colonel. He also summarised the meeting with Major Fischer. Brocelli listened with neither comment nor question.

"That's some story." He met Conza's gaze. "You're going after them aren't you?"

"The colonel is and I'm not letting him do it on his own."

"What do you want me to do? That's why I'm here, presumably?"

"I want to tell the colonel you're in. We can't do it alone and to be honest, I need your experience. I'm out of my depth."

"Where's your buddy, Moretti? Why hasn't he got your back?"

"I've sent him up north to chase down Zeffirelli's boys. I needed him as far away from me as possible."

"To protect him?"

"He's newly married, with a kid on the way. He can make something of his life."

"Whereas I'm old, have no career and my wife left me years ago. Thanks."

"I'm sorry…"

"Shut up, Raffy. I'm only joking. Half-joking anyway. But what about you? Your future? I always thought you were a high-flyer?"

"I can't let them walk away from this, Brocelli. Someone told me once, about putting justice above obedience."

"You should be more careful who you take coaching from, son."

"Too late, I'm afraid."

260

Brocelli slapped Conza on the shoulder.

"OK, I'm in. Do you have a plan?"

Conza felt his mobile vibrate and he listened to a voicemail from Harry Chase. He emptied his glass and threw twenty euros on the table.

"I've got to call a friend but I'm meeting the colonel tomorrow. I'll phone you afterwards. The three of us need to get together."

Brocelli waved an arm in response.

"And you lied to me, Brocelli?"

"How so, Lieutenant?"

"You do give a shit. See you later."

86

Guardia di Finanza Headquarters, Milan, Italy

Conza walked slowly back to the office. There was so much to think about, and he wasn't sure he was making the right choices. He dropped by the colonel's office on the off-chance, but his office was empty.

He called Harry Chase and tried to sound cheerful.

"Thanks for calling back, Raffy. I have news. I called Jimmy, asked him about Stolz, why he was in Milan and so forth. Seems Stolz had been acting strangely for some time. He'd always been a bit cold, but lately, he'd become quite reclusive as well. My friend thinks he may have been affected by something that happened last year in a place called Tilza in Latvia."

"Stolz travelled to Latvia last year, it was in his passport."

Conza shuffled through a notepad.

"Here you go, entered via Riga Airport on the thirteenth of July. He was there for three days. He was also there for two days from the twenty-seventh."

"That matches. Jimmy said something went wrong with the Skyguard system around the thirteenth of July. Significant enough for half the board to fly out to Latvia."

"Does Jimmy know what the problem was?"

"No. But he did tell me the Russians were peddling a tale about NATO shooting at an airliner."

"Bloody hell, Harry."

"You know the newspaper Conza had in his bag? The story was on page three. I've sent it to you in an email."

Conza could hear excitement in Harry's voice, but there was something else. He was nervous.

"Those numbers you gave me from Stolz's wallet. Turns out they were software instructions for the Skyguard data link. Written in hexadecimal. Do you know hex?"

Conza didn't.

"It's a number system, like decimal but it runs up to fifteen instead of nine. It's all in my email."

"So Stolz was carrying secrets around with him?"

"Jimmy says not. They're just numbers. Meaningless without a context. But I do think they were important. To cut a long story short, Jimmy did some poking around. Checked the data at work."

"What did he find?"

"That's the strange thing. He called me this morning, quite agitated. Said the numbers led him to discover something."

"What?"

"He wouldn't say. But I got the impression he was really concerned, scared even. I've known Jimmy for twenty years, and I've never known him to be frightened, but he was today."

"That's worrying, Harry."

"I agree. I hope I haven't dropped him in it. The road to hell is paved with good intentions, Raffy."

"I don't believe that, and nor do you. What's he going to do about it?"

"He's called an emergency meeting tomorrow with the Skyguard board of directors. He's taken it pretty seriously."

"Let's hope whatever he found, isn't as bad as he thinks. Sorry to drag you and Jimmy into all this, Harry."

"I wasn't dragged into anything, Raffy, I jumped. How's it going over there anyway?"

"Don't ask. But we found Stolz's USB. We can't access it though, it's password-protected."

"But at least it counts as progress."

"Not really. We don't have the password and the reminder just says 'dog' in German. We think Stolz had a dog called Fideccio, but it doesn't help. The password needs to be ten characters long."

Conza heard Chase murmuring to himself.

"Spell it for me."

"F I D E C C I O."

"Give me a minute, Raffy. I'll call you straight back."

Conza sat at his desk staring at the red question mark on the whiteboard. When the phone rang, he snatched at the receiver.

"Raffy, probably barking up the wrong tree, but Fideccio translates to '4 0 5 7 9 1 0 2 8 8'. That's ten digits."

"How?"

"Hex. Well almost. If 'I' is one and 'O' is zero. Don't thank me, thank Jimmy, he put me onto it. Let me know how you get on."

Conza thought he could hear the dull thud of his heart in his ear as he inserted the SEDS fob into his computer.

'WARNING – ONLY TWO ATTEMPTS REMAINING.'

Slowly and carefully, he typed in the digits.

The pop-up disappeared as the computer's hard drive whirred into life. A new window opened showing two icons: 'Event Log 1307/Op/LAT/01' and 'Diary'.

Conza sat back, hands on head and offered a silent blessing to an English barrister and his Skyguard friend. When he double-clicked on 'Event Log', a new window opened, which rapidly filled with rows of four-character groups. *'There must be ten thousand,'* he thought in amazement. The word 'event' struck a chord, and he scrambled to find the notes of his conversation with Pisani in Skyguard's Milan office. 'Missile firing = event.'

Clicking on the 'Diary' icon brought up yet another window, in which appeared Lukas Stolz, sitting behind a desk, staring straight into the camera. Grey hair immaculately swept to one side, narrow jaw and cheeks etched in fine lines. Behind the thick-rimmed glasses, sad and tired eyes. *'Bloody hell, he made a video.'* Conza pressed play. Stolz began talking, his voice deep and serious; in German. Conza tried to pick up the sense of what he was saying but couldn't understand. However, every so often Stolz uttered something recognisable; 'Leipzig', 'Berlin', 'Potsdam', 'Skyguard', 'Milan'.

Conza fast forwarded the film and when it restarted, he thought Stolz said, "Tilza". He rewound the film and played it again. There was no doubt, Stolz had referred to the Latvian town.

Conza tried making notes but had to guess too often. He was about to press stop in frustration when Stolz, now looking angry, slammed his hand onto the desk.

"Backdoor," he said, in the middle of a German tirade. Twice, he said it.

"Backdoor," repeated Conza.

He thought of Chase, Jimmy and his emergency meeting at Skyguard. He jotted down the time Stolz uttered the phrase and opened Harry's email. He read the story from *The Times*. It was entitled '*Russians allege NATO missile firing*'. He read it again.

"Shit," he said, as he hit the print button.

Conza phoned Pisani who was clearly irritated by the policeman's request.

"I'm at a family party, Lieutenant. Can't this wait until Monday?"

They compromised and Pisani agreed to meet him at the Skyguard office in the morning. Conza checked his watch and called Harry Chase.

"Harry, you were right about the password. It worked."

"That's brilliant, Raffy. What have you found?"

"That's why I am calling. I'm really sorry, but I need your help again. Feel free to tell me to bugger off. I really wouldn't blame you. But you served in Germany for quite a while, didn't you?"

"That's right, at Wildenrath and then Laarbruch. I was there for six years, on and off."

"I thought so. How's your German?"

87

Sunday

'The Manor House', Hatchmere, Cheshire, England

Max Yahontov slid into position at five o'clock on Sunday morning and immediately knew his plan would have to change. The floodlights had already been switched off and other than the dim light cast by a lamp above the garage door, the house was shrouded in darkness.

He checked his watch and waited. For an hour he stared at the house, but the sentries didn't appear. Nothing stirred and even the chill breeze relented.

He lay on top of the stable and tried to figure out what might have happened. Fanucci told him the target's name was Salterton. A career criminal. '*A hard man*'. He'd known many hard men, but none of them had survived a bullet to the head. Maybe Salterton had run? Found somewhere safe to hide out. Did Salterton know he was coming? Maybe someone had warned him. It wasn't likely, but possible. Maybe it was a trap?

He decided to move closer. If it were a trap, they would have to be very good to catch him unawares. He cocked the pistol and turned off the safety. With barely a sound, he slid off the roof and crept towards the high wall sitting as a black square against the grey morning sky. A bird flew low overhead in a flash of white, swooping to take its prey from the grassy shadows. Using a branch of the overhanging oak, he deftly pulled himself up and over the wall. A few seconds after he landed on the damp earth, a light in an upstairs window spilt a narrow, yellow band across the gravel. He froze. A minute later, the light went out.

He edged forwards, staying low and using the cover afforded by bushes and trees until he was at the edge of the wide sweeping lawn that encircled the house, drive and outbuildings. In the early morning light, the grass was grey and silver with damp. He calculated it would take him less than three seconds to cross the open ground. He took a deep breath and broke cover. *'No turning back now,'* he thought. *'If you're here, come and get me.'*

Reaching the rear wall of the garage, he pressed against the brickwork and stood still. No sound, no lights. After a couple of minutes he crept around to the window, which he'd seen being opened and closed by the soldiers. It was secured by a simple drop-catch, which he swiftly opened with his knife. He quickly and silently clambered into the shadows.

His torch revealed two empty camp beds, a large crate, a table and three armchairs. The radio was switched off and cold to the touch. *'They've left,'* he concluded in surprise.

The door leading to the kitchen was unlocked, and he made his way along the hallway to the foot of a wide, sweeping staircase that split at its mid-point, arcing in two directions up to the landing.

He switched off the torch and stowed it in his belt. The heavy drapes in the hallway held back the morning light and he was wrapped in darkness once again. With both hands holding the machine pistol, he slowly started to mount the stairs. As he neared the top flight, he halted. Slightly above him and to the right, he thought he saw a shadow sway, just a few inches, almost imperceptibly.

The light that suddenly filled the hallway startled him, just as he was bringing his gun to bear on the moving figure. Now, he could see that the swaying shape was a man's head; a grey-haired man's head. Yahontov found himself blinking and squinting down the barrel of a black, pump-action shotgun.

Their eyes met for an instant before the barrel exploded in a blue and orange flame. Maksim Yahontov's chest felt the force of a thousand hammers propelling him upward and backwards against the wall.

He felt no pain even though his mouth was a fountain of warm salty liquid and his eyes were struggling to focus. But he could still make out the shape of his pistol balanced on the edge of the top stair. He knew instinctively that he was only a few seconds from death. He knew death.

And then, Salterton was standing over him, screaming and cursing and spitting. Max sensed the warmth of the gun's muzzle on his cheek. Salterton saw him smile, and then felt the searing pain of the eight-inch blade slicing through his thigh and into his groin. The shotgun went off again and the right side of the Russian's face disintegrated in a shower of blood, teeth and flesh. Max's final conscious thought was that warm liquid was cascading over his fingers and down his arm.

He took his final breath three seconds later, but on what was left of his mouth, a smile persisted.

Maksim Yahontov had completed his mission.

88

Skyguard's Regional Office, Milan, Italy

A s Conza ambled past the shuttered shopfronts on Via Torino, he thought about Kadin and the man he'd been forced to kill. Even when Conza had discovered Lukas Stolz's message, his inability to understand German had denied him the ability to comprehend what lay behind the contract. The frustration was overwhelming. He thought of Harry. He would be the first to know why Kadin had been forced to kill Lukas Stolz.

Instinctively, he knew the film was about to change everything. The case was about to reach a whole new level, and others would decide how the story would be concluded. And Conza knew, that in the fallout from his discoveries, Kurti may be allowed to walk away. The colonel would console him, of course. *'Next time, Raffy. We'll get him next time.'* The realisation was depressing.

...

Lanfranco Pisani was waiting in reception when he arrived and despite Conza's apologies, it was clear the manager was going to sulk.

"Mr Pisani, I need your help. When we met before, you told me this office is responsible for the analysis of all Skyguard missile firings; events. Did I understand you correctly?"

"Yes, that's right."

"Can you please check your records and tell me if you analysed an event that occurred on the thirteenth of July last year?"

"Lieutenant Conza, this is a very sensitive area, and I must insist on receiving Ministry instructions in terms of what I can and cannot discuss with you. I'm sorry, but I'm bound by the law in this respect."

"I understand, and I'm sorry if my request places you in a difficult position, but I wouldn't ask if it wasn't vital to my investigation into the murder of your colleague."

"I'm not in a difficult position, Lieutenant. You are. Either come back with a duly issued warrant or speak to my superior tomorrow morning. I cannot and will not be compromised like this."

Conza had no choice. He only had one card to play.

"Mr Pisani, please look at this."

He handed over a printed copy of the event log. Pisani's eyes widened and he stuttered an expletive.

"Where the hell did you get this? It's highly classified. This is crazy."

"Stolz had it on his SEDS. I need to know when this event occurred. I promise you everything will be handed over to the proper authorities as soon as I've finished here. But I need to know when this event happened."

Pisani was in turmoil, but seeing Conza's expression, he turned away in disgust and logged on to his computer. He tapped at the keyboard and squinted at the screen.

"Lieutenant, this event did not occur, the log is a fake. No missile firings have ever been associated with this log number."

Conza looked at him and thought for a moment.

"OK, I accept it's a fake, but can you tell me the time and date it says the event took place?"

"It's here in the second line of data."

Pisani picked up a calculator and started tapping.

"08:40:14 GMT, thirteenth of July last year."

"Were there any events recorded around that time?"

"No. There were no missile firings within two months of that date."

"Did Lukas Stolz visit this office on or after that date?"

"Around the thirteenth of July?" asked Pisani scrolling through another spreadsheet.

"No, he couldn't have. The office was closed for two days. We had a computer virus on the thirteenth. We were ordered to shut down and vacate the office. A technical team came in to clear it. Skyguard are utterly paranoid about viruses."

"When were you given the instruction to vacate – exactly?"

"We were told to leave immediately. I cannot tell you when that happened, exactly. But I do know I was the last one out of the office at 10:22."

"Taking into account time differences, that's just one hour after the event," Conza said to himself.

"OK Mr Pisani, you have been extremely helpful, and I'm sorry that this has been so stressful. One final question. Who issued the order for you to vacate the office?"

"That I don't mind telling you, Lieutenant. It was Professor Stolz. I insisted the order was sent to me in writing. One has to be so careful in this line of work."

89

Hotel Napoli, Milan, Italy

While Conza was walking back to the office, the magnitude of what he'd discovered started to sink in. By the time he passed the statue of Vittorio Emanuele II, his initial rush of excitement had been replaced by dread.

This wasn't police business. It was espionage, sabotage, spying, maybe even treason. He'd entered a world he knew almost nothing about. He suddenly felt childish, naïve, and ignorant. Babcock had talked about the effects on the British economy for Christ's sake. This wasn't a mob shooting of some hoodlum, with a smoking gun and a corpse in an alley. There were international repercussions to what he knew, and he didn't know everything. He wasn't sure he should be trying to find out the rest.

His mobile rang.

"Lieutenant Conza?"

"Yes, Colonel."

"Meet me in an hour, Hotel Napoli."

The phone went dead. Something was very wrong. He walked up to the piazza on Via Cordusio and took a taxi.

The hotel bar wasn't yet open so Conza asked for a coffee at reception and took a table at the rear of the large lounge, from where he could view the street. His coffee cup was cold long before they were due to meet.

The colonel wasn't in uniform and when he waved through the window, Conza noticed that there was stubble on his chin, and he looked tired. There was concern in his eyes and his cheeks were pale and stretched. He sat down wearily and Conza waited.

"It's over, Raffy. I was suspended this morning. I'm not allowed back in the office and have to fly to Rome this evening."

"Why? What's happened?"

The colonel clasped his hands together and stared at the table.

"They found out about the meeting in Berlin. I seem to have annoyed some powerful people."

"The meeting with the BND? Why?"

"I have been accused of acting outside my authority, and let's face it, I was."

"But you were just following up my investigation. Doing your job."

"They're not that naïve, Raffy, and nor are you. In any case, I can't approach the intelligence agents of a foreign power without permission. I knew it wouldn't be granted, which is why I didn't ask."

"What will happen to you?"

"I think much of that will depend on where this case takes us, how many feathers I've ruffled. But you'll be OK, I've made it clear you were acting on my orders."

"I'm not worried about me, Colonel."

"You should be worried, Raffy. I had no right to expose you to such a risk. I was foolish and I'm sorry. But if it ends here, today, I think they'll leave you alone."

"I'm a grown-up, Colonel. I wasn't dragged to Berlin kicking and screaming. But this isn't about you breaking protocol, is it? This is about the powerful people Ralf mentioned, protecting themselves."

"Almost certainly. And I made the mistake of underestimating their reach."

Conza looked out of the window.

"Things have happened that you don't know about. I was going to hand everything over to you this afternoon."

The colonel sat up.

"I've got a lot to tell you, but you need a coffee and so do I."

Conza went to reception. When he returned, the colonel had shifted along the bench and was peering through the window.

"That's where Stolz was shot, I take it?"

Conza laid the event log on the table.

"It is. And I know why. Well at least, I think I do. I'm waiting for a friend to get back to me."

For the next forty minutes, Conza told the story of Stolz's SEDS, his conversations with Pisani, the Russian report about the missile firing, Tilza and the event log.

"You think the Skyguard system was altered in some way, causing a missile to fire?" the colonel asked when Conza had finished.

"I'm pretty certain of it."

"Who by?"

"Stolz. He was the only person with unfettered access to the code. Probably the only person who would know how to do it too."

"So why did the Russians drop the story? They could have made a meal out of it – for a very long time."

"Maybe because the plan failed. The airliner only received minor damage. They were embarrassed because nothing could be proved. The story would just look like fake news."

"But Skyguard knew a missile fired when it shouldn't have. It wouldn't have taken them long to work out it must have been Stolz who sabotaged the system."

"Josef Schuman. I think he protected Stolz. Probably concocted a story about software glitches or something like that. NATO and the British defence ministry would have been desperate to believe him. There's too much money tied up in it for it to fail."

"But why would Schuman shield Stolz? That goes against everything the Stasi major told us."

It was Conza's turn to wait. The colonel's eyes suddenly flashed in understanding.

"My God, Raffy. You're absolutely right. But who's this friend you're waiting for?"

"A lawyer in England. He's translating Stolz's video for me. I just hope it confirms my theory."

The colonel leaned forward.

"I'm sure I don't need to tell you, what you've discovered changes everything. We've got to hand it all over to the security services. There are repercussions for more than just Italy. The fallout is going to shake much of the world, one way or another."

"And in the turmoil, Kurti gets away, again."

"I'm sorry, Raffy. That's likely to be true."

"They can't afford to let any of this out can they? The public can never know. The whole thing will be swept under a very thick carpet."

"You're probably right. But they've got to deal with it somehow, and that won't be easy."

"So who do we give it to? Who will make sure all of these people face the music?"

"Babcock would be my choice. Certainly not Rome or Berlin."

"He's my choice too."

Conza took a deep breath as he steeled himself.

"Colonel, are you sure that there's nothing we can do, on our own?"

"On our own? Don't go crazy on me, Raffy. I'm suspended and whilst you're a first-class detective, you haven't got the experience or knowledge to deal with this sort of thing yourself. We're talking about national security matters. I wouldn't allow it."

"I'm not alone," Conza responded defensively. "Captain Brocelli said he would help us."

"Brocelli. How much does he know about all this?"

"He knows the SEDS exists, but not what's on it. But he's agreed to help us track down Kurti."

"Stop. Just stop. You can't be serious. A junior officer and a man on the edge of retirement. It's over, Lieutenant."

90

Guardia di Finanza Headquarters, Milan, Italy

Utterly deflated, he decided he would call Babcock from home but changed his mind as he climbed into the taxi and asked the driver to drop him at his office instead.

At the end of the corridor, the colonel's office door was half-open. Conza peered in.

"Who the devil are you?" asked the senior officer curtly, eyeing him over half-moon spectacles balanced on the end of his long nose. *'Shit. Brigadier de Falco.'*

"Lieutenant Conza, sir."

"Colonel Scutari is not here. He's been reassigned. You'd better come in, Lieutenant. I wanted to talk to you."

Conza's temples suddenly throbbed and his legs felt weak.

"You smell of beer, Lieutenant."

Conza stared at the Finanza crest on the wall behind the brigadier: *'Nec recisa recedit'* – *'Does not retreat, even if broken.'*

"You went to Berlin with Colonel Scutari yesterday. Is that right?"

"Yes. It was part of the investigation into the murder of Lukas Stolz."

The brigadier stared at him with contempt and waited.

"Sir," Conza added, eventually.

"You had no authority to consult the intelligence agency of a foreign power. However, I don't hold you responsible. Scutari should've known better. What did you find out?"

'Careful, Raffy.'

"I'm afraid I don't remember too much, sir. All a bit over my head. May I suggest you refer to the colonel's report?"

The brigadier bit down. Conza could see the muscles in his jaw flex and tighten.

"Don't come the smartarse with me, Lieutenant. There isn't a report, which is why I'm asking you. The only reason you haven't been suspended is that you were in the company of a senior officer. Anyway, I thought Herr Stolz was killed during a robbery? We've apprehended the killer. Why hasn't this case been closed?"

"I did locate and arrest Kadin Bennani for the murder of Lukas Stolz, but I needed some background."

"Background?"

'He still has friends in powerful positions.'

"We were investigating possible links between Lukas Stolz and people he knew in Potsdam, sir."

"Potsdam? The man was living in England, wasn't he?"

"Just background, sir. It's standard procedure in a murder case."

"Don't tell me what standard procedure looks like, you smug little shit."

'He's not angry. He's scared.'

"Unfortunately, sir, it was a waste of time. We didn't discover anything of assistance."

The brigadier pulled his jacket down by the lapels and twisted his neck to release the collar from his blotchy skin.

"Did you discuss a man called Josef Schuman?"

"I'm sorry sir, I don't recognise that name. But I could check my notes."

The brigadier closed his eyes for a moment.

"Your sense of loyalty is misguided, Lieutenant. But I won't waste any more time on you."

He looked down at a folder on the desk.

"You're overdue some leave. You will go back to your office and bring me your notebook, after which you will take two weeks' holiday. Those are not requests. I will decide on what your future holds when you return to work."

Conza's mouth was dry.

"I'm sorry, sir. My notebook is at home. I wasn't supposed to be at work today."

"Have it on my desk, first thing tomorrow morning. Then you will disappear, Lieutenant."

"On the colonel's desk, sir. Right."

Conza turned and departed. He didn't salute.

Benito's, Via Mercato Milan, Italy

Conza determined on the way to the bar that he was going to get drunk. Forty minutes later, he'd achieved his objective.

On the phone, Conza was shocked at how calmly Brocelli took the news about the colonel's suspension. He wasn't the least bit surprised, which made Conza even more angry. For a fleeting moment, he wondered if Brocelli had been behind it, but the notion made him feel guilty.

'It's over. The colonel's right,' he told himself as he ordered another beer and bourbon chaser. He'd never drunk bourbon before but had decided it would help.

'They've won. Stolz is dead. Issam's dead. Amadi is being kept alive by a machine. Kadin will go to jail for the rest of his life. Kurti will be free to kill and destroy, and Schuman...don't talk to me about Schuman.'

But no one was talking about Schuman and they never would. That was the problem. This is what Harry meant. Brocelli too. *'I'm such a mug.'*

Conza's bladder ached, but he knew he would fall over if he tried to stand.

"Bastards. Well, that's it. I'm finished. I'm not joining your club. I wash my hands of the whole damn lot of you."

The barman chuckled to himself. He was used to watching policemen disintegrate after a bad day at work.

13th July Last Year

Tilza, Latvia

Captain Shaun Griffiths was glad to escape the summer heat as he stepped into the air-conditioned cabin. He'd chosen to walk the two kilometres to the command vehicle, and whilst he'd enjoyed the relative quiet of his wooded surroundings, the trees made the air heavy and breathless and turned his shirt into a patchwork of tan and dark brown.

He signed in on the console and took a handover brief. All was quiet. The next VIP visit was not until tomorrow. He could look forward to a quiet shift.

He checked the monitor and, using the fixed roller-ball mouse, clicked on the five missile-shaped icons that formed an imperfect 200-kilometre-long oval around the central square. Each missile reported itself operational, so he poured himself a mug of tea from the pot and leaned back in his chair.

Summarised Transcript of Event No. 1307/Op/LAT/01

08:39:11 Zulu. Skyguard was tracking forty-seven airborne contacts. Their flightpaths, speed, height and other characteristics were subject to update by various ground and airborne radars, including a NATO Boeing E3 AEW flying over the Baltic Sea.

08:39:32 Zulu. Track No. 16 was identified as a civilian airliner operated by Baltair out of Moscow heading north-west. It was at flight level 270 over Lake Peipus on the border between Estonia and Russia. Track No.16 was designated as 'civilian' and associated with a four-digit number the Finnish pilot had entered into his transponder on instruction from air traffic. Control of the aircraft was handed between 'Moscow West' and 'Estonia Central'. The Skyguard Threat Assessment Figure of Track No.16 showed +25,231 points.

08:39:43 Zulu. A 'DL Tracking' warning appeared on the main console.

For the next 28 seconds, it was subsequently established that Captain Griffiths carried out the actions in response to a 'DL Tracking' failure in accordance with his Operator Manual.

08:40:11 Zulu. The Event Log recorded that the Fire Control switch was changed from 'FC-MAN' to 'FC-AUTO'; the final step in response to a 'DL Tracking' failure.

08:40:12 Zulu. The Skyguard Threat Assessment Figure of Track No.16 dropped to -5,020 points. The Skyguard system commanded missiles 23/04, 23/05 and 23/07 to power up.

08:40:13 Zulu. The Skyguard system calculated that missile number 23/04 was in the optimum position to intercept Track No.16. The flight time of missile 23/04 was calculated as 26.712 seconds.

08:40:14 Zulu. Missile number 23/04 launched autonomously. The event was recorded and given the descriptor 1307/Op/LAT/01.

08:40:15 Zulu. Missile 23/04 reported positive acquisition of Track No.16 and entered 'Armed Mode'.

08:40:16 Zulu. Missile 23/04 reported an altitude of 14,191 feet on a heading of 013.68 degrees. The flight time of missile 23/04 from launch to impact was recalculated as 27.234 seconds.

08:40:38 Zulu. A self-destruct command to missile 23/04 was initiated on the command console.

08:40:40 Zulu. Missile 23/04 reported 'Loss of Tracking Data' and the Skyguard system initiated a 'Missile Failure' warning on the command console.

08:40:49 Zulu. A valid 'Command Override Key' was entered on the command console. The Skyguard system powered down.

08:41:03 Zulu. Event Log ceased recording.

93

Monday

Raphael Conza's Apartment, Milan, Italy

The nightmare didn't end when he woke at six-fifteen. He suspected that the bones of his skull were about to unknit, and his brain would ooze out. His mouth was dry, but he could still taste bourbon. The brown stain on his bed emitted an odour of stale beer and cheese. *'I'm never drinking again.'*

After a shower, he still felt sick, just cleaner. His head had stopped pounding, but he felt giddy as his eyes and ears battled for supremacy.

The call from Brocelli came at seven.

"How are you feeling?"

"Like shit. I called you last night, didn't I?"

"You did. You were pretty angry. So they got to the colonel. No great surprise, he knew he was taking a risk talking to the BND."

"You want to meet up later?"

"Can't. I'm working tonight. I'm going back to bed in a minute."

"What the hell do I do, Brocelli?"

"You go on holiday. Forget the case. Forget Kurti. Give yourself a break. You can't fix the world. I know, I've tried and look what it did to me."

Conza decided not to tell Brocelli about the Stolz recording or Tilza. It wasn't paranoia, he just wanted to keep the number of people involved in this mess to an absolute minimum.

"They've won haven't they?"

"They always win, son. It's just the way it is. If you fight them, they still win, it just takes a little longer."

"I'm going to resign, Brocelli. I can't live in their world. I won't be part of it."

"That's your call, Conza. But if all the good guys go, where does that leave the rest of us?"

'What did Babcock say? 'Sometimes, we can't tell the good guys from the bad guys.'

"What did you call for anyway?"

"Thought you'd like to know. Salterton's dead. Along with Max Yahontov."

The news made Conza sit up in bed.

"How? What happened?"

"Manchester police were called by a neighbour who'd heard gunshots coming from Salterton's place. They arrived to find both men dead on the stairs. Most of Yahontov's head had been blown away and Salterton died with a commando knife embedded in his groin. His femoral artery had been sliced open. He bled to death before reaching the bottom step."

"That's crazy. Salterton was never the target – how the hell did this happen? Why?"

"Beats me. This case is full of surprises. But as luck would have it," Brocelli said without irony, "he'd only just got rid of his protection. Up until Saturday, Salterton had three ex-marines guarding him."

Despite his headache returning, Conza understood the sadness in Brocelli's voice.

"How do you feel now that he's dead? Yahontov, I mean?"

"It's strange, Raffy. I always imagined killing him myself. I've thought about it a hundred times. I still wish I had. But I didn't and, as a result, a little girl died in the most horrible way. I dream about her sometimes. I should've sent him back to hell when I had the chance."

"She may have died anyway, Brocelli, you know that."

"Or maybe she wouldn't."

Conza knew he had to let it go.

"I know you want to pack it all in, Raffy. But if you ever get the same chance, don't do what I did. People like Yahontov only live to kill again because of our doubts."

Brocelli hung up. Conza went to the bathroom and spoke to the pale face in the mirror.

'You've got to leave this job, Raphael. You'll just end up like Brocelli. Broken, bitter and haunted by those you can't stop. That's the truth isn't it?'

He turned away. He didn't like the question and the answer only made his stomach twist with pain.

Village of Brenner, Italy

Brenner is a pretty, two-road village in the valley straddling the border between Italy and Austria. Many of the houses are built in the style of the Tyrol, and most have white, high-sided walls and long wood-beamed roofs. The eastern side of the village is dominated by the rail depot, servicing the trains that carry goods and passengers through the pass of the same name.

Sergeant Moretti parked his car next to the sidings and watched a goods train gathering wagons. The sun was shining, and the air smelt of pine. The tree-covered mountains stretched into the distance in both directions and not for the first time, Moretti considered leaving the choked streets of Milan.

Brenner police station stands on the southern intersection of the loop that runs around the village. Moretti sighed, crossed the narrow road and pressed the intercom button on the iron gate. He was met by a tanned, fit and cheerful middle-aged lieutenant. Moretti knew he had to get out of Milan.

They went inside and passed more contented-looking policemen.

"We've kept them under observation since Saturday, Sergeant, as requested," he said handing over a photograph.

"Thank you, sir. That's definitely the guys we're after. Who spotted them?"

The lieutenant pointed through the glass wall of his office.

"Corporal Lombardi. He's only been with us for a year. He came to us from Milan, actually." Moretti grimaced. "He's one of the few officers around here who puts effort into reading the bulletins you guys send out. Nothing much happens up here."

"He's done well. Where are they now?"

The lieutenant looked at his watch.

"In about half an hour they'll be sitting in 'Vesuvio's'. It's what they do every lunchtime. It's a local bar, but popular with backpackers."

"Do you think there'll be many people in there today?"

"Hopefully not. But once the targets are inside, I will put a man at each end of the street to stop anyone else entering."

"That'll be fine. I'll decide if it's a 'go' once I see who's in there. I'd prefer to get them when they're on their backsides, if possible. But if it's too busy, we'll grab them as they come out."

"Are you expecting trouble, Sergeant?"

"No, I don't think so. They're almost certainly armed, but I plan to render them harmless before they know what's happening."

"How many men would you like in support?"

"Four should be enough, a policewoman would be good. And can Corporal Lombardi come along? He should see the fruits of his labour."

"Good idea, and Sergeant Bosco is female. I'll come along too. As I said, we don't have too much excitement in Brenner. Mostly border issues."

"Can everyone get changed into civvies please, sir?"

Sergeant Moretti toured the village before briefing his team. They were attentive, keen and respectful. *'I'm definitely moving up here,'* he said to himself as they left the station in pairs.

Vesuvio's was a small bar with a pastel-coloured fresco of a volcano painted on the wall behind the counter. Just eight tables, each flanked by three-seater vinyl-covered benches.

They were not difficult to spot; a man with a bandaged head and the other wearing a plaster cast on his arm. Three tables were occupied; Paolo de Costa and Leo Calpresi on one, a couple trying to look casual on another, and on the third, a lone young man drinking Coke. The lieutenant entered through the kitchen at the rear of the building and was moving towards Moretti as he entered through the front door.

As Moretti drew alongside their table, he grabbed de Costa's arm, yanking him violently upward and sideways onto the floor. Corporal Lombardi launched himself over the back of the bench, landing heavily on de Costa's narrow back.

Simultaneously, the couple on the opposite side of the aisle flung themselves sideways, pinning Leo Calpresi to the table. He tried to fight back, but the lieutenant grabbed him from behind, and was too strong. He forced Calpresi's good arm up behind his shoulder blade, making him yelp in pain. Until they were sure all was safe, the police didn't utter a sound.

Moretti slammed cuffs on de Costa making him shout in protest, and he swore when Corporal Lombardi removed the blade he had hidden up his sleeve. Sergeant Bosco held up Calpresi's pistol like she'd won it at a fairground side-show.

From the moment Moretti entered the bar, the entire operation had taken less than six seconds.

Raphael Conza's Apartment, Milan, Italy

His hangover was beginning to subside by noon when the phone rang. It was Harry Chase.

"Raffy, you need to read the translation I've just emailed you. I'm not going to say anything now. Just call me when you're done."

...

Forty minutes later, Conza called him back.

"I'm so sorry I involved you in all of this, Harry. It's worse than I thought. I won't mention you when it blows up. Thank you for doing it though. I can never repay you."

"Raffy, what you have there, is dynamite. I don't have to spell out the ramifications, do I? What on earth are you going to do with it?"

"The colonel said it should go to MI6. I don't have any better ideas."

"Do what your colonel tells you, Raffy. You need to get this off your hands as soon as you can."

"Right. I know."

"Stay safe, my friend. Let me know when it's all over. We should talk."

From his wallet, Conza retrieved a simple white card. The initials CB were printed on one side. He rang the number shown on the reverse. A man's voice answered.

"Hello?"

"Mr Babcock, it's Raphael Conza. We need to talk."

Village of Bussero, about 20 km East of Milan, Italy

Like most Italian villages around midnight on a Monday, it was sleeping.

They drove past the small stone church for the third time. Nothing stirred and none of the windows were lit in any of the buildings that hugged the narrow, winding lane.

The safe house was at the end of a mud-lined track. No lights, no movement. An SUV was parked in the carport and he could see the outline of the single-storey house against the cloudless canvas of stars. On the roof, a three-metre-long whip-aerial swayed in the gentle breeze.

When they'd driven past the house for the fourth time, he ordered the driver to pull over as he picked up the Webley sub-machine pistol. He turned off the courtesy light, cocked the gun and opened the door. Leaning over the driver's shoulder, he whispered, "Go up there and turn around at the junction. Kill your lights and drive back until you reach this point. Then wait until I signal." He held up the pocket torch.

"When I flash, park at the end of the track, but leave your engine running – I won't be long."

He gently pushed the door closed until he heard it click shut. He crouched behind the hedge while the car moved off. Staying low, he shuffled forward until he heard the car drawing up behind him. From the rear of the houses came the mournful baying of a fox and in the hedgerow, something small scuttled through the dried twigs and parched leaves.

He moved forward again until the hedge fell back, and he could see the silhouette of the house. Cupping his hand over the torch, he flicked at the switch and for an instant, his fingers glowed pink. He heard the gentle crunch of car tyres rolling towards him.

Crossing the track, he stepped over a low fence marking the boundary of an orchard. Slowly and silently, he felt his way forward between the trees, until just a few metres of broken asphalt stood between him and the front door.

He pictured the layout as it had been described. The front door will be unlocked. In the hall, the first two doors on the right are bedrooms, the second one is where the boy sleeps. He brought the pistol up to his chest.

He stepped out of the trees and a great number of things seemed to happen all at once. The fizz of electricity as a circuit closed and the entire area was flooded in bright white light. The field that ran down the far side of the house spawned at least ten black-clad, helmeted figures holding rifles. A loudspeaker ordered him to "stand still" and "drop your weapon". And behind him, two police cars, red and blue lights flashing, screeched to a halt either side of the maroon Alfa Romeo.

"Shit," was all he could muster, as he let the gun slip from his fingers.

In silent resignation, he raised his arms. A few seconds later, he felt himself being pulled down from behind. Captain Brocelli drove a knee into the small of his back and snapped heavy cuffs onto his wrists.

"Giuliani Zeffirelli, you are under arrest for murder and conspiracy to …"

Zeffirelli spat on the captain's shiny black boots and grinned. Brocelli grabbed his hair and yanked his head forward until their noses almost touched.

"By the way, you homophobic prick, Troy sends his love. He fucked you really good though, didn't he?"

97

Tuesday

Central Police Headquarters, Milan, Italy

He hadn't slept well, and his stomach was still gurgling when Captain Brocelli called him just after ten.

"Conza, where are you?"

"Just on my way to Finanza to comply with an order – a day late, you'll be proud to hear. Why?"

"When you're done there, come round to the station. I need to show you something."

"I'm out, Brocelli. I'm on holiday and don't want to know anymore."

"When you've finished feeling sorry for yourself, get your arse down here. If it's the last thing you do, you need to see what I've found."

Conza was only at Finanza for a few minutes. In the colonel's office, he placed a single, sparsely filled notebook on the desk along with a letter addressed to 'Whoever It May Concern'. Next to it, he left his service revolver, badge and identity card.

...

At the station, Brocelli was sitting in his office looking agitated.

"I hear you arrested Zeffirelli?"

"Screw him. Come with me."

Brocelli led Conza down the corridor to a side office he had to unlock. The room was equipped with a television and playback facilities for films and CCTV. Brocelli pushed Conza in and locked the door.

"All Bennani's equipment was brought back from Genoa last week."

"Yes, I know. I ordered its recovery."

"One of my techies was playing around with one of his boxes this morning and found something."

"What?"

"The film of the barn wasn't the only recording Issam Bennani left for us."

"Show me."

98

Holding Cell #2, Central Police Headquarters, Milan, Italy

Zeffirelli was lying on the plastic-covered mattress when Brocelli entered, pulling the cell door closed behind him.

"What the fuck d'you want?"

Brocelli tossed a photograph onto his chest.

"Anyone you know?"

The picture was of a man lying head down on a flight of stairs. His face was turned towards the camera, dressing gown ruffed up around his waist. A pool of blood had formed on the two steps below his thigh. Zeffirelli tried to ignore it, but recognition got the better of him.

"What the hell," he exclaimed, sitting up. "Who did this? Shit. You bastard. Who did this?"

"The same person who's going to get you. The same person who set you up to kill Fanucci. You're a talking corpse, Zeffirelli. Kurti always gets his man. Just thought you'd like to know."

Brocelli held his breath. 'I hope Conza's right about this.'

"Kurti wouldn't do this. You're shitting me." *'You're such a smartarse, Raffy.'*

"Why would I lie? We've got enough to lock you up for three of your miserable lives. I've got nothing to gain. I just enjoy watching the chickens coming home to roost."

Zeffirelli walked to the small window near the ceiling and rubbed his forehead.

"This is bullshit. Kurti doesn't want me dead. He didn't kill Salt. You think I'm stupid?"

"Hey, screw your head back on, you ignorant prick. Think. What reason did he give you for killing Fanucci? We're in a cell without your lawyer, anything you say to me isn't worth a crap and you know it. So tell me, I'm curious."

"He didn't want the competition. Fanucci took out a contract on Salt."

Brocelli started to laugh.

"You really are a dumb twat, Zeffirelli. Fanucci's game is blackmail and extortion. He's very particular. He's not a smuggler. Guns or people. It was Kurti who took out the contract. Fanucci and his boys just did some running around for him."

"Why would Kurti want Pete dead?"

"That's the really funny part, Zeffirelli. He didn't. The contract was taken out on the guy who was shot. There was no mistake. It was nothing to do with you or your brother-in-law."

"This is bullshit. I saw him. He looked just like Pete. He was in the same hotel. He was picked up by a black Merc. It all fitted. Pete knew he was the target."

"That's because your brother-in-law is paranoid. You know how Salterton's brother died in '98?"

"A rival gang. There was a turf war. They blew his head off outside a restaurant."

"Are you getting it yet, Zeffirelli?"

"Salterton sent you off to wipe out whoever he thought was trying to kill him. That annoyed Kurti, he's not a man who likes loose ends. Ultimately, I think he wanted all of you dead, but settled for Fanucci in the short term. And you did his dirty work for him."

Brocelli was laughing again.

"You're lying, you bastard."

Zeffirelli lunged forward, fists raised but the policeman was expecting it and sidestepped the blow before bringing his fist down on the back of his neck. Zeffirelli lay on the floor groaning.

"Thing is, you're scared to death right now, because you know it's true. Kurti's going to finish you off. In jail, out of jail, who knows? But I wouldn't give him longer than three weeks to find a way to reach you."

"I want protection. It's the law. You have to give me protection."

Zeffirelli was trying to sit up, but Brocelli placed a foot on his chest.

"Why on earth would I help you, Zeffirelli? You're scum."

"I want my lawyer."

"No worries, I'll send him down here. But he won't be able to help. The families won't get involved with Kurti; we both know that. Take a look at the photograph. Your brother-in-law was wiped out when he was being protected by an army of guards. He must have told you about his pet soldiers?"

Brocelli lifted his foot allowing Zeffirelli to rub his neck.

"What do you want?"

"You get one go, Zeffirelli. If you turn me down or lie to me, I'll make sure your location is leaked to every low-life in Italy. Do you hear me?"

"What the fuck do you want, you bastard?"

"I want to know how to contact Kurti."

Zeffirelli snorted with contempt and shook his head.

"You think it's that simple? To trace someone like Kurti through his mobile. You're the dumb one."

"We don't want to trace him, so tell me anyway."

"You don't call Kurti. A man like him will change his phone every week, maybe every day. You call an answering service. It could be in Outer Mongolia for all I know. If he's expecting your call or wants to talk to you, they connect you. Otherwise you're left holding your dick."

"So, I need the number of his answer service."

"You can have it, my friend, it's worthless. But first, I need it in writing that I get protection."

"I walk in three seconds. Look at the photograph. There won't be a second chance, Zeffirelli. One... Two..."

99

Wednesday

Campione d'Italia, Italy

Conza couldn't remember the last time he'd cried. But he'd never been so sad, or scared before, so he forgave himself. There was no turning back.

"Raphael. What a lovely surprise," his mother said, offering her cheek as she pulled him inside.

"Are you OK? You look tired. Has something happened?"

"Everything's fine, Mama. I just needed a break." *'To see you one last time. To say goodbye.'*

"Come in, I was just making pasta. How's Milan?"

They talked while she cooked. Conza took comfort from the fact she seemed settled. It made him happy. *'She'll be fine,'* he consoled himself as she launched into a tale about her neighbour's dog.

In the afternoon, he took a boat over to Lugano and retraced the steps he'd taken with his friend Harry Chase, the day they sat atop Monte San Salvatore. *'Three years ago. Was it really only three years?'*

Tourists bustled around the small chapel at the top of the hill, so he headed down the footpath signposted Via Ferrata. He reached a point where the brown, scraped earth divided and followed down the less worn path. When the route ended abruptly at the cliff edge, he turned left and scrambled back up the mountain through thickets of juniper bushes, until he reached a white-painted concrete shell of an abandoned building.

He sat on the broken outer wall to catch his breath. On the silver-flecked lake below, water taxis and pleasure boats left trails of white as they darted in and out of inlets and coves. His mobile phone signal showed five bars.

'It's now or never, Raffy.' He tapped in the number.

"Salvador shipping. How may I help you?"

"I need to get a message to Alexander Kurti."

"I'm sorry, sir –"

"Don't bother telling me you've never heard of him. Just give him this message. Are you ready to write?"

Silence.

"Tell him to tell his boss, we've found the backdoor to Tilza. He can reach me on this number at ten, Paris time, tomorrow morning."

"I'm sorry, sir –"

But Conza had already switched the phone off. *'Mobile phones are like beacons,'* Conza heard Issam Bennani say to his son.

...

In her chalet, Mrs Conza went into the bedroom to find her scissors, but something caught her eye. She gasped and clutched at her chest. On the wall above her bed there was a small Goya sketch of three fish, and a note, which read, *'Just to fill a space. X.'*

100

Thursday

Geneva, Switzerland

Conza took a bus from his hotel to the Parc Mon Repos on the Avenue de France. He wandered past a two-storey villa set back from the path. The sign read, 'Academy of International Humanitarian Law and Human Rights'. He turned his back on the building and headed east towards the shore. *'I'm not dealing with people who practise humanity.'*

At one minute before ten, he switched on the phone. Seventy-five seconds later, it lit up.

"Who am I speaking to?" The voice was harsh, with an East European accent.

"My name is Raphael Conza. Since Monday, I'm an ex-policeman. I worked on the Stolz murder."

Conza's heart was racing and his mouth had dried up. His legs felt heavy.

"What do you want, Conza?"

"To speak to Schuman. And please don't insult me by asking 'who?'"

"What for? If I know him, I'll give him a message."

"He has six hours from now to call me. If he fails, his world ends. I know everything and if I don't hear from him, so will everyone else."

"You sure you know what you're dealing with, mister ex-policeman?"

"Five hours, fifty-nine minutes."

Conza disconnected the call, turned off the phone and leant over the railings. Forty minutes until his next train. He felt sick.

Lyon, France

He tried to eat something in a bistro on the Rue d'Aubigny but could only stomach a couple of mouthfuls of salad. He sauntered back to the station at Part-Dieu and rechecked the timetable. His next train would leave in an hour.

He wandered back outside and found a quiet spot at the side of the glass-fronted building. He switched on his mobile.

The voice was confident, relaxed and German.

"You wanted to speak to me?"

"You Schuman?"

"Yes. What do you want?"

"What was your mother's maiden name?"

"Schiller."

"What I want, Mr Schuman, is five million euros."

Conza heard him chuckle.

"Why would I give you five million euros?"

"Tilza. The backdoor. There's a lot riding on that five million. It's small change to you."

"I hear you're a policeman?"

"Ex."

"So what is this, a retirement fund? You're the twenty-nine-year-old son of a dead diplomat. A little early to hang up your boots isn't it?"

Conza was expecting it, but a chill still ran across his scalp.

"Drop the threats, Schuman. They won't work. Kids do homework. You're not so special."

There was a moment's pause. *'Slowly, Raffy. Don't get angry.'*

Schuman spoke again.

"The Tilza thing was a mistake. It's been put to bed. No one's interested in your theories."

"And Stolz. Was that another mistake? I know everything, Schuman."

"Robbed in the street, wasn't he? Very unfortunate."

'Don't let him go.'

'Stolz left a video. A confession. Your face is going to be plastered across every television set in Europe by this time tomorrow."

"You're lying."

"You know I'm not lying. And I'm about to lose my patience. Stolz made a filmed admission. You knew he was about to spill the beans, which is why you had to kill him. I'm right aren't I? It's also why you had his belongings taken from Milan. You were scared of what he might have left behind."

Conza crossed his fingers.

"This is a waste of my time."

'There it is: fear.'

"And you may have got away with it, if Salterton hadn't started bumping people off. He believed the bullet was meant for him and sent his brother-in-law off to find out who was behind it. If Ricci hadn't been tortured to death and the Abebe girl left alone, Stolz's death would have been put down to robbery and his luggage going missing as an administrative cock-up. You were so close Schuman."

"You seem to have it all worked out."

"It took me longer than it should. It confused me why Kadin hadn't been told to take Stolz's belongings when he killed him. But it was Salterton who helped me figure that one out. When Salterton left the hotel, he wanted to move quickly, so he left his luggage behind. Kadin would never have been able to carry all of Stolz's belongings on a Vespa, so you arranged to have them taken from the station instead."

"Your annual report said you're a clever detective."

"Napoleon said something about lucky generals over clever generals didn't he? I just got lucky."

"So where did Lukas leave this so-called confession? It wasn't on his mobile."

"On his key fob. It was stored on his SEDS. I kept it."

Another pause.

"Why five million?"

"It's enough to make me disappear."

"No one ever really disappears, Raphael."

"I'm not stupid, Schuman. It's enough to keep my story from being told. And before you ask, no, you won't have any guarantees. But as you say, no one ever truly disappears, and I don't want to spend the rest of my days looking over my shoulder. My fear; that's something you can rely on."

"So that's what I get for five million? The hope that you don't piss it up against the wall in Benito's and suddenly need another five, and then another five."

Conza had to stifle a gasp with the back of his hand.

"I won't. You'll never hear from me again. But you will get Stolz's tape and the only transcript. No one in Milan has seen either of them, except me."

"So how do you want this to happen?"

Conza breathed heavily. He felt cold, even though the sun was tingling his neck.

"We do a handover in England. I'll give you the details tomorrow."

"You don't need me there. I'll send Kurti."

Conza tried to make his laugh sound convincing. *This is the moment, Raffy. It's make or break.*

"No way, Schuman. I don't deal with scum like Kurti. It's you or nobody."

"That's just not possible, Conza. I'm not in Europe right now."

"You're in Berlin. So don't fuck with me."

Conza heard Schuman's intake of breath. *You're not the only one who can find things out, you bastard.*

"Are you working alone, Conza?"

"Who the fuck wants to work with me? My badge and gun are in the file marked *'Resigned before Fired'*. But I'm not dead yet and I'm not leaving this world without taking a small cut from the guys they won't let me lock up. So yes, I'm on my own, Schuman. For the first time in my life, I'm doing something for me."

Conza thought he could hear him muttering to somebody.

301

"It will take a few days to get the money together."

"You have until Saturday."

"I'll see what I can do."

"You'll do better than that, I just know you will. I'll call your service tomorrow at ten with a new phone number. You'll get five minutes to return my call."

"You have the whole thing worked out don't you? Your colleagues say you're pretty smart."

Conza hung up.

His hands were shaking as he turned the phone off and crushed it under his heel. He deposited the mess of cracked plastic, wire and circuit boards in three separate bins as he made his way back into the station.

102

Friday

St Catherine's Dock, London, England

Conza watched an old barge loaded with waste fighting its way north-east against the Thames' tide, thick black smoke in its trail. He thought of Brocelli and Harry.

Schuman returned his call inside a minute. While they talked, Conza paced up and down the quayside.

"So you've got the address. You have plenty of time to check it out, which I know you will."

"Oh we will, Conza, don't you worry. And if I get the slightest whiff of trouble, you'll never see me, but you can expect others will come calling. Maybe even visit your mother in her new home."

Conza needed every ounce of willpower to let the threat pass.

"What do you mean 'we', Schuman?"

"Kurti will be with me." The German was angry, it wasn't a request.

'You have to fight him, Raffy.'

"No way, Schuman. You come alone. This deal is between the two of us. No Kurti."

"Then it's off. I'm not meeting you in the middle of nowhere without protection. Who the hell do you think you're dealing with?"

'Patience, Raffy. Don't surrender too easily.'

"I'm not happy about this."

Silence.

"You need to keep him on a tight rein."

"He does what he's told."

"In that case, I get to bring my lawyer with me."

"What the fuck do you want a lawyer there for?"

"Insurance. He's going to witness the deal. Put it all in writing. He's the one holding copies of everything. In case I have an accident or something. Or Kurti gets trigger-happy."

"What's this about copies? You said you were going to hand everything over."

"Come on, Schuman. What do you take me for? I'd be dead before I reach the door. So please don't pretend you're shocked. This way, you get the Stolz stuff and I live in peace. We both walk away happy. The lawyer never sends anything to anyone and when I die of old age, he throws it into an incinerator."

Conza heard Kurti's voice raised in objection, but Schuman was ignoring him.

"You'd better not be playing smart, Conza. I don't forget much, and I never forgive. The same goes for my Albanian colleague."

103

Saturday

Old Fruit Store, St Margaret's Bay, Kent, England

It had been almost two weeks since Lukas Stolz was murdered outside the Hotel Napoli. To Raphael Conza it could have been two years. He was exhausted from lack of food and sleep. In the past few days, food seemed to stick in his gut and sleep just invited nightmares. He knew it was only fear and adrenaline standing between him and mental shutdown.

From the upper floor of a derelict byre high up on a hill, he used binoculars to watch Alexander Kurti circling the brown brick storehouse that was once filled with the fruit of Kentish orchards.

Kurti didn't come alone. Conza knew he wouldn't. As his jeep crawled along the narrow lanes, three men, each carrying a long green case, were dropped off. They took up positions overlooking the store, less than half a mile away, to its north, west and south. To the east, white-topped waves dashed against chalk cliffs. No need for back-up on that side.

Conza put down his binoculars and lay on his back.

"It's not too late, you know. We could make a run for it."

"Yes it is. And we wouldn't get far."

...

Josef Schuman was standing in the middle of the stone-slabbed floor when they entered, a brown briefcase at his feet. Kurti was standing behind him, a scowl on his pitted face and one enormous hand covering the area of his crotch. He was talking into a radio handset.

For days Conza had rehearsed what he was going to say when the time came, but in that moment of fear and anxiety, the words he'd practiced, eluded him. So, he waited for Kurti to finish muttering and went on the offensive.

"Why the extra protection? That's who Kurti is talking to, isn't it? The three shooters out there. I thought we understood each other?"

"What extra…" Schuman stopped, deciding not to bother with a denial. "Are we going to do this?"

'He's only a man. Just keep saying it, Raffy.'

"When I'm ready, Schuman. I've sacrificed a great deal to be here and I'm not in a hurry."

"Well, I am, so get on with it. Where's the tape?"

"It's on there." Conza tossed the SEDS to the German.

"And the transcript."

"In a moment. First I have a question."

"Don't play games, Conza. You don't have the pedigree."

Kurti shifted his weight and slipped the radio into his jacket pocket. He wanted his hands to be free.

"It's just to satisfy my curiosity. Indulge me. I believe I've earned it."

"Go on."

"I just wondered. How old were you when you started working for the Stasi?"

"Is that the best you can do? Go screw yourself."

"I reckon you weren't much older than thirteen or fourteen. Major Fischer, or Captain Fischer as he was then, remembers you."

Schuman was trying to look bored, but his eyes kept flicking back to Conza.

"Was it just hatred, Josef? You must have been very angry with your father to inform on him. To tell the Stasi about him spying for the British. But then again, you're a vindictive son of a bitch, aren't you? What happened? Did he tell you off for being out late or not doing your homework? It doesn't take much to rile you, does it?"

"You're barking up the wrong tree, Conza. Lukas Stolz was the informant. He was the one who handed my father over to the Stasi."

"I must admit, you had me believing it once. Katherine certainly believed it. And so did her father. He died believing it."

"Is there a point to all this?"

"Stolz was your pet, even back then wasn't he? He was a blank page, knew everything about numbers, but nothing about people. He wasn't political, until you started feeding it to him. That's right isn't it? Katherine told me he would have believed anything if it met his idea of logic."

Schuman was looking down. His shoulders started shaking. The laughter was coarse and harsh.

"Lukas Stolz was a foolish genius. I made him."

"And destroyed him, at will, whenever it suited you. You must have been really angry when Katherine and her mother got your family out of East Berlin. You were expecting your father to be dragged off and shot. But they helped you escape instead. No wonder you hated Katherine."

"I didn't need saving. It was my father who was a traitor. I made as much noise as I could that night. The guards must have been asleep." The smile was for Conza's benefit.

"But they did wake up, didn't they? Just in time to shoot Katherine's mother."

"So fucking what? She was another traitor."

"All this talk of traitors. I don't buy it, Schuman. You were never motivated by politics. It was always just a means to an end. It was about power, wasn't it? One word from you and the Stasi would drag away whoever pissed you off. You got a kick out of it."

Schuman pushed his hands deep into his coat pockets.

"You and Lukas were friends. You spent quite a bit of time at the Stolz house. You knew that Lukas and his father hardly ever spoke. It became worse after Mrs Stolz was shot. I wonder why? Maybe because you'd managed to turn father against son. Was it easy getting him to believe Lukas was an informer? Just a whisper in Dieter's ear, was that it? Broke it to him gently, that his son was a Stasi puppet."

"You must think you're very clever."

"Not as clever as you, I know that. But you were very young at the time and the irony is that even if your Stasi dealings had been discovered, I doubt anyone would have been too critical of you. You were just a kid."

"I don't leave things to chance. That much, you should have learned about me."

"No, I admit, it took me a while to work that out. When the Berlin Wall started crumbling, you knew your Stasi affiliations would be uncovered and you couldn't risk that affecting your political career. So you got yourself a council job in West Berlin and in the months leading up to reunification, you helped East Berliners escape, among them Stasi officers. They bought their passage to the west with old Stasi records. In particular, documents naming you as their informant. Major Fischer told us you approached him with the same offer, but he turned you down. He wasn't afraid, was he? He didn't think he'd done anything wrong wearing the uniform of a Stasi officer. He still doesn't."

"Fischer was a bleeding heart."

"You doctored the Stasi records, replacing your name with that of your old friend Lukas Stolz. And just for fun, you sent them to Dieter about a year before he died. Much to my shame, I didn't question how he'd managed to get hold of them and neither did Katherine when Dieter showed them to her in Berlin. Your forger was a skilled man."

"Woman actually."

Conza waited.

"You think you know everything don't you? But you seem to have missed the part when Lukas Stolz acted as an informer all on his own, when he was teaching in Leipzig."

"Yes, he mentions that in his video. From what I can make out, it was mostly tittle-tattle. He didn't have a malicious bone in his body. He was playing a part you'd given him as a teenager. He'd been indoctrinated. He believed in you. Believed everything you told him. But you shouldn't congratulate yourself too much. I think Lukas Stolz was a sensitive, naïve, trusting soul who would have believed anything told to him by someone he thought cared for him. Being cared for wasn't something he was used to."

"You can't judge me, you little shit."

"But your control over him didn't end in '68 when you escaped, did it? I've a feeling that you had been watching Stolz ever since he'd started to make a name for himself in the world of data links. You realised he could be useful to you. So you arranged for Skyguard to recruit him in '94. Gave him the keys to the jewel house. Provided him with a new home and a fresh purpose. He must have been so grateful. His old friend from Potsdam looking after him once again."

"He had everything he ever wanted."

"Except his mother, sister and the love of his father. Yes, I'm sure he had everything he ever wanted."

"Don't get sentimental on me. Lukas only ever cared for numbers."

"Yes, he says something similar in the film. But he loved you, once. You were his guiding light, his guardian angel. It must have been easy persuading him to build a backdoor into the Skyguard system. Told him it was necessary in case it was ever turned against NATO, Britain, Germany or Italy. That part of his confession is particularly revealing."

"There's no evidence the backdoor ever existed. He's spent the past year undoing it all."

"Ever since he was reunited with his sister."

"Yes. That was unfortunate. I thought I'd stoked up Dieter Stolz enough to put her off seeing Lukas for life."

"It nearly worked. They didn't see each other for almost fifty years, but blood is thicker than water, it seems. When she accused Lukas of betraying your father, he was devastated. I think for a while he may even have believed that he had somehow done exactly that. After all, he knew about Felix Schuman's radio – you told him. Maybe he thought he'd let it slip. But eventually, he worked out the truth, didn't he?"

"He came to see me. I thought I'd convinced him that he'd got it all wrong, but apparently not."

"It was Tilza when he really turned against you, though. When he saw you for what you really are and how you had used him. He knew then that he'd been betrayed."

"I don't fail very often. Just a little bad luck."

"It's the only part I'm still a little unsure about. Did you sell the backdoor code to the Russians? Did they set up Skyguard to shoot down the airliner? My colonel was convinced it was. One of their airliners is hit by a British missile, Russia takes the moral high ground, while NATO and Europe look like a bunch of blundering cowboys. It would certainly have put the Baltic states' future in doubt for a generation."

"You're a cynic, Mr Conza. You read too many western newspapers. Not even the Kremlin would fire missiles at their own people. I didn't need them. There are scores of disgruntled ex-Soviets who want to stir it up in the Baltic. It wasn't difficult finding a backer willing to pay."

"So Skyguard was configured to fire when the parameters matched the criteria they'd set. Pretty clever."

"I thought so. It almost worked."

"But for the quick thinking of a British Army officer. And of course, even when the plan failed, you were above suspicion. What possible motive could you have for sabotaging your own missile system?"

"Stolz would have taken the blame. He was an ex-East German informer. It was perfect."

"And had it worked, Kurti would have been ready to assist in his suicide, no doubt."

Schuman's smile was thin, his laughter forced.

"But had the missile blown up that aircraft, Skyguard would have been dead in the water. The company bankrupted; its shares worthless. Which is why you've been slowly offloading them for the past five years. But there's more to it than money, I think. Your motives are more visceral than that."

"Tell me, I'm genuinely intrigued. There's very little I value more than money."

"It wasn't really your company was it? It was your father's. He was the one who had generated the real success. It struck me when I did some digging around. I believe there's a portrait of your father hanging in reception at Skyguard headquarters. That must needle you, seeing the great man's face every time you go to work. A constant reminder the man you loathed was the real brains behind Schuman Industries."

"You know nothing. My father was a tyrant. He hated me and mother."

"I can't imagine why."

Conza was drawing to a close. He could see the bulge of Kurti's pistol in his jacket. He looked back over his shoulder and smiled.

"Which leads us to the murder of Lukas Stolz. In the film, he tells of the argument you two had. His naïve threat to expose you for the shit you are. He even told you he was going to turn you over to MI6. He'd signed his own death warrant from that moment, of course. But I think he knew as much, which is why he made the film."

"As I said, he was a foolish genius."

"But there's something you don't know. It will be of particular interest to the piece of shit behind you."

Schuman turned to look at Kurti.

"Issam Bennani. That name mean anything to you, Kurti?"

He wasn't going to react.

"OK, I'll remind you. He was the technician who worked for Marco Fanucci. He's good with cameras. Including the ones you raised your hand to when you first entered the barn a couple of weeks ago. The cameras you said you hated and personally disconnected last week."

For the first time, Conza saw Kurti's jaw tense, his eyes flashing in contempt.

"So you do remember. It's just that Issam rigged them in a way that meant they were always on, always recording. The bit when you're planning to kill Stolz is particularly good quality. There you are with your pal Fanucci, like two old women discussing the weather."

Kurti moved forward but Schuman put out a restraining hand.

"Why are you telling me this? What's your point?"

"We'll discuss that in a minute. But first, you should know that I found other films saved in Bennani's black boxes."

Schuman still had his hand in the air, frozen in trepidation. Kurti was twitching.

"Fanucci productions, I call them. All the time, Issam Bennani was making copies of your blackmail activities; politicians with their hands in the till, senior police officers with a penchant for kids, a judge with a cocaine habit. Even my boss's boss got screwed over by you guys. And there's dozens more. It was a brilliant set-up. Fanucci made money, your victims helped you up the ladders and Kurti could never face trial. Problem was, Bennani recorded everything."

"You bastard, Conza, you have no idea who you're screwing with," yelled Schuman, breathing heavily.

"I think I do. And it certainly explains your meteoric rise in the political world. Your path to vice-chancellorship was on the backs of those you blackmailed. Until someone decided to fight back in '99. That brought an end to your glittering career. Sadly, we don't have films from then, but we have about twelve years' worth."

Kurti edged forward and Conza heard feet shuffling behind him.

"And so finally, we come to Ravenna."

Schuman's head snapped back at Conza, his thick neck reddening.

"I see that's a name you recognise. Problem is, I'm a nosy sod, so when a friend told me about a little girl being kidnapped and then murdered in Ravenna, I felt compelled to look into it."

"That was nothing to do with me," said Schuman, palms upturned.

"Oh, but I think it's everything to do with you. The plan to take her isn't on film, but plenty of conversations afterwards are. I think you'd gone too far even for Issam Bennani. I think it was at that time, he decided to keep copies of your rackets."

"I'm telling you, Conza, that all happened without me knowing."

"Shut up, Schuman. You ordered your pack of dogs to snatch her. Just so you could take revenge on her father. Remind me, what was the argument about? Oh yes, a parking space. Please tell me I'm wrong."

"The kid wasn't supposed to get killed. I just wanted her father to suffer for a few days. I don't kill kids, Conza."

"There were thirty-seven children on that flight from Moscow last year. Please forgive me if I don't believe you."

"Tell him, Kurti. Tell him it wasn't supposed to happen."

The big man shrugged. "Max did what he had to."

From over Conza's shoulder, a metallic click. Kurti's arm arced upwards, but age wasn't on his side and his hand froze in mid-air.

Silence descended over the warehouse.

"Her name was Violetta. She was eight years old. She was left to die in agony – alone," the voice hissed from the back of the room.

Schuman panicked.

"Come on, Conza. It was never meant to happen. It was Yahontov. I told him it was unnecessary. Tell him, Kurti."

But Kurti wasn't listening. He stepped forward; hand still poised by his breast pocket.

"Who the fuck are you? You ain't a lawyer, that's for certain."

"My name is Brocelli. Captain Brocelli. I was the arresting officer on the kidnap."

Two whistle blasts came from the rear of the building and in the distance they heard the crack of gunfire and the sound of vehicles racing towards them up the lane.

"What the hell is going on, Conza?" Schuman yelled.

"It's a fucking set-up you idiot. I warned you," Kurti said through clenched teeth.

Schuman put what little remained of his self-control into one final roll of the dice.

"You're dead, Conza. They won't try me. I know too much. You've screwed yourself. I'll walk and you'll die a slow and painful death. No matter how long it takes, I will kill you and every person who ever knew your name."

Schuman didn't take his eyes off Brocelli's pistol.

"I don't think so, Schuman. Your days of wielding power are over. It's why we're in England. They can try you in secret here, a good friend told me about it. Nothing about Skyguard will ever be aired in public; it's too important to the Brits. But a jury will hear about everything else you've done. Skyguard will be repaired. You'll go to jail for the rest of your days and everything you own will be taken away from you. Everyone you ever blackmailed will either get moved on or locked up. Either way, in two years' time, nobody will remember your name and your father's portrait will still preside over Skyguard. The justice system over here doesn't mess around. Didn't you know? They're stubbornly resisting the new European order on this island. 'Proportionality' may be on the horizon, but 'expediency' isn't quite dead yet."

As the cars skidded to a halt, Kurti's rage was released.

"They'll never put me on the stand, you smug fuck. I've worked for their government. I'll be back on the streets in a day or two and then I'll find you. Both of you. You're going to regret…"

Kurti's face erupted and the back of his head disintegrated in a shower of blood, brain and bone. Schuman screamed and fell to his knees. Kurti staggered back two paces, mouth frozen in surprise as his legs buckled, sending his heavy frame to the floor with a thud that made the floor judder.

"No more doubts," Brocelli whispered with neither joy nor satisfaction. He dropped the pistol and raised his hands as three armed officers burst through the door, followed closely by Charles Babcock. The Englishman stopped to survey the scene.

"Special Branch will take it from here, chaps."

Schuman was on his face, being cuffed as Brocelli lowered his trembling arms. Babcock passed him a hip flask.

"It's what's left of the Asbach, Captain. You look like you need it. Welcome to England. You OK, Raffy?"

"We're fine Charles. We're all fine."

Epilogue

In accordance with his will, Lukas Stolz was buried in Berlin alongside his mother. His sister lays flowers on their grave every year on the anniversary of her brother's death.

At his trial, it took seven minutes to read out the list of charges brought against Josef Schuman. Much of the evidence was heard behind closed doors and has never been made public. He received a whole life sentence for his crimes and now resides in a high-security prison in an undisclosed location.

Alexander Kurti's body was buried in an unmarked grave in the grounds of HMP Maidstone. Nobody attended his funeral.

Giuliani Zeffirelli was jailed for the murders of Marco Fanucci and Stefan Puz. He was also found guilty of the attempted murder of Kadin Bennani. He is still in prison and is not eligible for parole for another twenty-seven years. His request for permanent solitary confinement was denied.

Both Leo Calpresi and Paolo de Costa are serving concurrent life sentences for the torture and murder of Sami Ricci and, in Leo Calpresi's case, the attempted murder of Amadi Abebe. Calpresi's arm never healed properly despite undergoing multiple surgeries to relieve his pain.

Zeffirelli's contact, 'Troy', was dismissed from the State Police. He narrowly escaped a prison sentence but was permitted to enter the witness protection programme in recognition of his role in the capture and subsequent conviction of Giuliani Zeffirelli. His whereabouts today are unknown.

Colonel Scutari decided to take early retirement rather than reinstatement. He now acts as a security consultant to ministries and specialist police units throughout western Europe. Charles Babcock is thinking of joining him.

Captain Angelo Brocelli retired shortly after returning from England. He recently travelled to Ravenna to lay flowers on the grave of a little girl who died aged eight. He owns and runs a small bar in the old fishing village of Camogli, just a few hundred metres from Kurti's temporary home. Brocelli named the bar 'Violetta's'.

Sergeant Georgio Moretti acts as a special liaison officer to families and young people involved in, or who have been the victims of crime. His wife Sanza gave birth to a baby girl just a month ago. The baby took over the spare room.

Lanfranco Pisani continues to run Skyguard's office in Milan and remains adamant that no missile firing ever occurred in Latvia.

Kadin Bennani was never charged with the murder of Lukas Stolz, the Ministry of Justice concluding such a prosecution would not serve the public interest. He never knew that his release was in large part due to the sworn testimonies of Raphael Conza, Georgio Moretti and Angelo Brocelli.

Kadin Bennani and Nyala Abebe were reunited in Milan for a short time, but Kadin never recovered from his ordeal and turned to alcohol. One night just a few weeks ago, Jamila Bennani reported her son missing. Georgio Moretti discovered Kadin's body in an isolated barn in the village of San Carlo; he had hanged himself.

Amadi Abebe was released from hospital after three months. Following Kadin's death, he moved Nyala and Mazaa to England. Nyala attends Winchester University and she recently broke the county 5000 metre record for a junior athlete. She hopes to run in the London Marathon next year. When she's not training, she spends much of her time with her cousins. Her Uncle Ephrem still laughs at everything.

The Hotel Napoli is still open for business, although it is now under new management, the previous manager having quit work to write crime fiction books.

Jimmy Appleton was commended for his work in rewriting parts of the Skyguard DLR encryption code. He was nominated for an OBE in this year's Queen's birthday honours list. During the celebration party that followed, he lost his dentures for the final time. He is due to have implants fitted next week.

Lieutenant Raphael Conza's resignation letter was never opened, and he was promoted to captain. He now has an office in Finanza HQ that he doesn't have to share. He still enjoys a beer with Georgio Moretti on a Friday night, and has been with the same girlfriend for six weeks. He no longer keeps a diary, and his mother thinks of him every night.

Harry Chase continues to work out of his chambers in Bournemouth. In the summer, he can often be seen sitting in the lower gardens eating an ice cream. He has plans to visit his friend Raffy, next summer. His family plan to go with him.

With the help of his barrister, Jack Stephens secured work at a local builder's merchant. The Crown Court accepted his barrister's plea in mitigation; that Stephens was making genuine efforts to turn his life around. He was given a suspended sentence and every day he wears a tie to work.

The End

Dear Reader,

Thank you for reading my debut novel, *'The Milan Contract'*. I sincerely hope you enjoyed it! Feel free to leave a review on Amazon or if you prefer, drop me a line with your thoughts on the story:

stephenfranks@mooncatbooks.com

Thanks again for being part of the journey.

Stephen Franks

Future Novels by Stephen Franks

Subscribe today on our website to receive news about forthcoming titles by Stephen Franks, plus get the chance to win Advanced Reader Copies, FREE signed copies of future books and a whole lot more!

mooncatbooks.com